I0658493

THE
KILLING
Of
GREGORY
NOBLE

THE
KILLING
Of
GREGORY
NOBLE

Niara A. Savage

TAJI PUBLISHING

THE KILLING *Of* GREGORY NOBLE
Published by:
Taji Publishing
Ballwin, Missouri
Niaraalexandra@gmail.com

Niara Savage / Publisher
Yvonne Rose/Quality Press.info, Book Packager

ALL RIGHTS RESERVED
No parts of this book may be reproduced or transmitted in any form or by any means electronic or mechanical, including photocopying, recording or any information storage and retrieved system without the written permission from the authors, except for the inclusion of brief quotations in a review.

This is a work of fiction. Names, characters, businesses, places, events, locales, and incidents are either the products of the author's imagination or used in a fictitious manner. Any resemblance to actual persons, living or dead, or actual events is purely coincidental.

Copyright © 2018 by Niara Savage
Paperback ISBN #: 978-0-6921160-9-8
Library of Congress Control Number: 2018906895

For my parents, my professors,
and everyone who believed

THE END

There's a certain combination of numbness and hyper-awareness that permeates the last moments of life. After all of the bargaining and grieving of the life you once lived, it's calming to know, without a doubt, that you are finally about to die. That surreal sense of peace that inevitably floods the human mind when in the presence of certainty is comforting and gives way to more space for thinking about the things you've never thought of before. That's how it is for me at least. I think it's because there's never another moment in the entire length of a human life when you can be absolutely certain of anything, except for the moment when you know that you are going to die.

And so, now that you know this, and you've accepted it, you have no choice but to be okay with it and embrace it, even if you notice all the bullshit you never even thought about before. Like how utterly perfect a night-time summer breeze really is, especially when it's intertwined with that light scent that tells you it just rained. And the fact that somebody is always dying. While you wake up in the morning, clinging to the warmth of your blankets and dreading having to get up and go about the new day, somebody is dying. When you're frustrated because the YouTube ad happens to be one of the ones you can't skip, somebody is dying. It's always somebody's time to go.

Perhaps if I'd thought about this before this moment, I

would have lived my whole life differently, but I didn't. And now I'm here, realizing how small and temporary I am, and how shallow all of my life endeavors and New Year's resolutions ever were.

Never, in a million years, would I have guessed that I would die this way, at midnight, in the middle of a dark Walmart parking lot with a kid holding a gun to my forehead. I'd imagined that God would at least do me the small favor of giving me a semi-cool way of dying to help counter the fact that I'd lived an incredibly boring, pointless, and mediocre 33 years. But no. No, of course not. No sacrificing my own life while taking down a plane that's been hijacked by terrorists heading for the Pentagon. I did not survive on some random Caribbean island for 35 years only to collapse and fall to my death only seconds after being rescued. I won't die in the line of duty, with a badge on my chest, serving my city. Of all the ways to go out, I'm going to die in a fucking Walmart parking lot, of all places, at the hand of a dead Black man.

He cocks the gun and the sound pierces the night air, and I'm thinking, *what's going to be my last thought before I die?* Then I realize that it's probably going to be me thinking about what my last thought before I die is going to be. Tears are streaming down my face. They are not tears of sadness, or desperation, or fear. They are tears of unprecedented serenity, and hint of amusement. They are mixing with the mucus above my top lip, so I sniff and use the sleeve of my coat to wipe it off. At least my face won't be covered in snot when I die.

HUNTER GARRETT

The jelly stain on the carpet gets bigger and smaller as I struggle to push myself up, straighten my arms, then lower my body again, so close to the floor I can see the little shredded strawberry bits in the stain. My fingers dig into the carpet, my back caving, body shaking as the lactic acid eats away at my muscles. Push-ups are the worst punishment. Down, up, ten. Five more to go. Tiny footsteps beat wildly up the stairs and down the hall as one of the boys stops outside the room. Slamming his hands on the outside of the door, he imitates a deep-voiced cop and says, "Open up! I have a warrant for your arrest!" I'm not sure if it's Artie or Emerson, until he gives away his identity when his miniature toes slide underneath the closed door. Artie. I'm regretting not locking it and hoping I can get these last four in before he busts in the room and climbs up on my back to wrestle; when, as if on cue, he says, "Alright I gave you a chance. I'm coming in!" and bursts through the door, leaps across the room and latches onto my back.

"Daddddy lets wessle!" he shrieks in his high-pitched five-year old-voice. The second his weight hits my back, my body caves and my chest is forced against the floor. My heartbeat echoes out into the carpet as he wraps his tiny arms around my neck and leans over until he's so close to my face I can smell his potent strawberry jelly breath, wild blondee hair framing his grinning face. "Got you!" he says through his missing-a-tooth-or-two smile.

More thankful than I'd like to admit for a valid excuse not to have to do those last four push-ups, I turn sideways, knocking my son gently onto the floor beside me, scoop him up and toss him into the air. He giggles and screams in midair before landing on the king-size bed in the middle of the room, reaching for a pillow upon landing.

"I thought you had me!" I tease, smirking and shrugging my shoulders before pretending to turn and leave the room, when a pillow smacks the back of my head. I fake being surprised and fall to the ground. "Ouch!"

Artie laughs again before all-out leaping into the air, holding a second pillow high above his head and lands on top of me, perfectly timing the landing and the slamming of the pillow against my head like some sort of ninja child.

The sound he makes landing on top of me is surprisingly loud for such a small child and my wife yells up from the bottom of the stairs, "HUNTER!" Artie's eyes go wide, his mouth opens up, and he immediately stops pillow-whipping me, freezing with the pillow still over his head. "Stop all that fighting! One of them is going to get hurt."

"They're not gonna get hurt, Leah." I yell back at her, angling my head towards the open bedroom door. Artie giggles when I roll my eyes as I say it.

She sighs a sigh loud enough for me to hear it all the way up the stairs and says, "Well it's time for them to get dressed for school anyway."

Offering my son a slightly apologetic look, I motion towards the door and Artie pouts in response, before reluctantly dropping the pillow and stomping down the hall to his room.

For some reason, I dare to creep downstairs for something to drink, even though I know Leah's pissed. Before I can say anything, she stops cleaning off the table, throws the rag down to cross her arms and says, "Hunter, you *know* I don't like you fighting with them like that. They're kids; eventually one of them is going to get hurt."

Wordlessly, I brush by her towards the fridge for a beer. Her expression doesn't change as I open it, let the cap clatter to the floor, and tilt my head back to drain half the bottle in a few gulps. I set the rest of it down on the side of the table she had just finished cleaning.

"Leah. You know I'd never hurt the boys." I lazily lift a hand to make it seem like I'm actually trying to cover my mouth when I burp, and she shakes her head before going back to wiping down the table.

I'm thinking about what to say next and wondering why she has to be such a bitch about everything when I hear, "Daddy, why don't you like niggers?" I didn't even hear Emerson and Artie come downstairs to the carpet in front of the TV in the room next to us.

Pause: *don't judge me on this one okay? I know it probably isn't the best idea to have my son using the N-word so freely, but it's not me, you know? I didn't tell him to say it. I mean… he may or may not have heard me say it, but I didn't like, tell him to go around saying it. That's just the culture here. I mean shit, I'm not a racist.*

Artie is sitting there barefoot, in boxers and a T-shirt, (meaning he still hasn't changed for school) eyes gaping open, expectantly waiting for my response. I answer him honestly.

"It's not that I don't like 'em Artie, it's just that sometimes, you know, they forget their place, who built this country, and who it was that brought 'em here in the first place."

Before I can add anything else, my eldest son Emerson, who's two years older, turns around to face me from his position on the carpet to say, "Yeah, some of the niggers in my class don't like to say the pledge of 'legiance in the morning and Ms. Anderson usually sends them to the office. She says she does it so they can learn to respect America," he shouts out proudly from beside his brother.

I can hear Leah chuckle and sigh through her nose as she reaches for the broom. Silently we exchange looks and choose whether or not to condone or condemn what our kid just said. But she's thinking the same thing I am: *It's a gorgeous Wednesday morning and no one has time for discussing euphemisms and political correctness.*

"Artie, please go get dressed," she says, exasperated. The younger boy makes his way towards the steps, taking as long as possible to get there, as Emerson points to his collared shirt and says, "I'm already dressed, see?"

"Yes, I see Em, good job." Leah doesn't look at him as she pulls the dustpan out of the closet with one hand, brushing a few stray strands of dark hair away from her eyes with the other. Her three-week-old purple nail polish is chipped and cracked.

My phone buzzes from the bathroom counter and my heart jumps, partly from excitement and partly from fear. It's adrenaline. It's a taste of who I was meant to be. I make my way across the room, and, flipping my phone over so it's face up, recognize the number right away. It's Ms. Thompson. The old woman lives alone in a home just a couple of houses down from ours. She calls at least once a week worried about one thing or another. Last Tuesday it was a box someone left on the curb in front of her house and the woman was absolutely convinced that there must have been a bomb or a poisonous snake, or the beginning of the end of the world inside of it.

"Damnit... Hey Leah, guess who?" I asked lifting my eyebrows at my wife.

"Thompson," she guesses, without disrupting the swift movements of the broom moving across the floor.

"Hello ma'am." I try my hardest to be polite. In Alabama we still try and respect our elders.

"Hi Hunter." The old woman's voice is so shaky and barely audible, but I hear loud and clear what it is she says next. "Mr. Garrett I'm so sorry to bother you, I know you're busy with you wife and kids and all."

I'm wondering why she's gotta make it a point to call me every week if she's as sympathetic to my hectic life as she says; though I say, "It's just fine ma'am, what can I do for you?"

She continues, "I wanted you to know there's a Black man just wandering around outside my house. He ain't actually caused no trouble yet but he's wearing a hood and just standing, and you know wandering around out there, you know? I'm not sure what he could be doing around here at this time of day. He's a pretty big guy and he's got his hands in his pockets and well, I think he may be selling drugs, and since you're The Watch, I was just wondering if maybe you could just, you know-"

Let me fill you in: Dilson, Alabama is divided into two parts. The East side is inundated by subsidized apartment buildings, and high rise public housing crowds the already minimal space.

Factories pump filth into the warm southern air, and you can't walk outside at night without running into pimps and drug dealers, and gunshots and sirens are the soundtrack of the city. The East side is of course, mostly Black, and full of poor people rotting in their own criminal filth.

The Black part of Dilson has half the geographic space, yet twice the population density as over here on the North side where we live. Good schools, public parks, middle class families and the vast majority White. Originally, these two regions were actually two separate towns. The White part was always Dilson, but the poor Black area was called Lawden. In 1968 following the death of Martin Luther King Jr, the two towns came together as one in some sort of false show of unity. But if you're from here, you know it was a facade. Even though both my family and the Black family over there have the same zip code, that doesn't mean we don't still live in two utterly different cities. They stay on their side of the bridge and we stay on ours. Literally everyone follows that unwritten rule, so when someone ends up on the wrong side of town, people notice. I don't think it's wrong for me to assume that the only reason a Black man would have to come over here is to sell drugs or kill somebody. It's a common sense and a well-supported fact, and the better my record is as The Watch, the better my chances of joining the force.

"I hear you ma'am, thanks so much for letting me know." I cut her off, just to get her to stop all of that absent-minded droning. "I'll check on that and see what it is he's all about. Where'd you say he was again ma'am?"

"Just a little ways down from my house. I can see him from my window. He might not be up to anything, but I'm here in this big house by myself and so-"

"Well, I'll do what I do Ms. Thompson. And I do understand why you'd be worried."

"You know I really do appreciate that Mr. Garrett and be careful: It seems like the world's set out to make ya'll good guys the bad guys these days."

"I hear you ma'am, and don't mention it. See you Sunday. Alright. Bye" Hanging up, I turn to my family, with Leah looking at me expectantly. "I gotta call. Django's wandering around where he shouldn't be. Be back soon, love you guys." I reach down to ruffle Emerson's hair.

Artie bumps down the stairs, finally dressed, and says, "We'll still play football later?"

"I promise we will, as soon as you guys get outta school today." The boys high-five each other as if they've just accomplished something absolutely extraordinary.

"Be safe." Leah actually stops sweeping for long enough to place her painted purple fingertips against my chest and press her lips briefly against mine in what I guess you would call a kiss, though there's something empty about it.

Clipping my Glock 22, equipped with a maxim silencer to my belt, I grab my coat and head for the front door. The second it opens, my cheeks and ears are met with a mean, icy January blast. The sky is depressingly gray, the scene unsettlingly quiet. Tennis shoes dangle from the telephone wires above me in front of our house, their laces wrapped tightly around the cords, hanging on for dear life.

Walking to the edge of our driveway, I see a hooded figure at the edge of the street, his hands shoved deep into his pockets. My heart thumps against my ribcage and I actually feel the adrenaline coursing through my veins. It's stupid, but whenever I get a call I enter this fantasy world. I pretend like I've got a badge on my chest and like the whole force is counting on me.

It's not that I want him to have anything on him, but if he did have a gram or two of contraband in his pocket, or a weapon, and I just happened to be the one to bust him, that probably wouldn't hurt me if I mentioned it in the interview later. I walk in silence behind him, as the wind bites at my ears, gradually closing the distance between us. The guy pauses, glances quickly over his left shoulder and sees me standing there. He's got to be what? 6'4? At least. He doesn't move and neither do I. I don't know what the kid might pull out of his pockets, but I do know I don't want to die today.

Sliding my hand under my coat, my fingers find my gun. A few more steps close the distance between us even further. He turns away and keeps walking, a little faster this time, black Nikes shuffling quickly against the concrete. Speeding up, I call out to him and his steps quicken.

"Hey!" I call out to him again. In my mind I say, 'Dilson PD!' But in reality, the words, "neighborhood watch. Can I speak with you?" He stops to glance over his shoulder again, before turning his back and hurrying down the sidewalk at an even faster pace. "STOP RUNNING!" I match his pace and begin to gain on him. As I get closer I'm halfway expecting a bunch of gang members to come around some corner to his defense and beat me to death. I'm just about close enough to reach out and unfortunately up (because of his height), to grab his shoulder when he turns, and we make eye contact for a fraction of a second before his eyes flash down to the gun on my hip. His eyes go so wide I can see the white above and below his pupils. He yanks his shoulder away and slips out of the jacket, so

I'm left with just a fist full of his red zip -up hoodie, which slips through my fingers toward the ground.

He narrowly avoids losing his balance before breaking into a full-on sprint in the direction of the bridge. With his hands deep in the pockets of his jeans, he's got no balance at all, and is apparently too dumb to know how to tie his own shoes. Predictably he trips, and is catapulted forward, face first into the sidewalk.

As I close the gap between us, his body remains unmoving on the cold ground. In seconds I'm standing over his sprawled, motionless form, fighting to fill my burning lungs with oxygen. His jeans are too short for his tall frame and I can see his dry ashy ankles peeking out from under the denim. For the first time I get a glimpse of his face and see that he's young, maybe 16 or 17 years old. A bag of M&Ms is poking out of one of the pockets in his jeans. Still trying to re-inflate my lungs, and with one hand on my gun, I begin to question him. "I'm not gonna hurt you, I just wanna-" his body suddenly springs to life as he lunges upwards and plows into me knocking the wind straight out of my lungs.

My body slams against the stiff, icy grass, the bulk of my weight falling on my left knee. He towers over me. I can hear him breathing, and I get a glance of his broad chest heaving as he does. Lying flat on my back, I realize I've just lost whatever upper-hand it is I thought I had before. Gasping for breath, I struggle to lift myself off of the ground. From my sitting position in the grass, I instinctively pull my gun out of the holster, bring it around to the front of my body and pull the trigger twice.

Two bullets pierce his back as he turns to run. The kid drops instantly like a stone in water, his head landing face first into the ground. My hands are shaking, and my chest is tightening up. As I try to stand, the ground beneath my feet seems to tilt sideways with the sole intention of knocking me down again. The world spins as I limp towards the still mass before me. His white shirt is stained by two growing crimson splotches. My body is numb. My head is spinning and pounding and banging and throbbing. I must be dreaming. I do not feel cold. I do not feel guilt. I do not feel fear or anger. I feel nothing. I feel absolutely nothing.

Looking down at my hand I realize I've got a death grip so tight on that gun, my knuckles are turning white. I want to drop the thing, but my fingers won't let it go, so I use my left hand to peel each stiff frozen finger from its locked position on the weapon. The gun falls from my fingertips and lands in the dead brown grass next to the dead brown boy I just murdered.

SAMUEL NOBLE

❝And then I was like, 'I don't know babe, I don't usually do that kind of stuff on the first date' and she was all, '*Awwwww*, I don't *either* Carter, I've never understood why people throw themselves around like that.'" Carter makes his voice all obnoxiously high-pitched and nasally when he imitates Amber. His voice, which is actually, surprisingly and almost creepily similar to hers, echoes off the tile bathroom walls of the 2nd floor boys' bathroom.

Blankly staring at my reflection in the mirror, I periodically offer Carter empty nods as he continues describing last night's adventures to me, blunt between his fingers, clouds of marijuana hanging around his head.

"And then I said, all romantic-like, 'I don't want to do *anything* you want to do baby.'" He cocks his head to the right and places his hands over his chest dramatically. "I like you for you, ya know babe? Not just for your body." He blinks his long black lashes at me and I can't help but laugh picturing him doing the same to her last night.

"And then dude, do you know what she said next, Sam?"

I suck my cheeks in and bite them to stop laughing at Carter's excessive blinking. "What'd she say next?"

"She said: (in an obnoxiously nasally Amber voice), 'Well *I* want to do whatever *you* want to do.' And she's leaning all forward like she *wants* me to see her tits, and I'm just sitting there next to her on the bed, thinking to myself: 'have I just like, solved the biggest problem in my life? Is all I have to do to get in bed with this girl is pretend like I *don't* want to get in bed with her?' And *then,* guess what happened?" Carter asks, grinning at me from across the empty bathroom.

"Umm, I'm gonna go out on a limb here and say you had sex with her."

"Damn right!" Carter says, humping the edge of the sink. "And I gotta date with another girl, that red-head Marsha this weekend. Guess what I'm gonna tell her?"

"That you don't want to have sex with her?"

"Bingo!" he yells, "and she'll come right to Daddy," Carter says holding his arms out in front of him. I've never understood what it is that goes on in a guy's head for him to think it's OK to refer to himself as 'Daddy.'

So, I go, "I really just can't see a girl liking it when a guy calls himself Daddy."

"Your mom didn't seem to mind when I said it to her last night." Carter's incredibly quick with the comeback and looks at me like he's dead serious. His expression is so unmoving, I feel my heart jump in my chest.

Panic must've actually flashed across my face because Carter goes, "Kidding man! Kidding!" He throws his head back and cackles.

I sigh and rest my palms against the cool sides of the sink, staring at the mirror in front of me again.

Carter's studying me intently from across the bathroom.

"Sam man, you need to get yourself some of that, or you'll end up like Steve Carell."

"Some of what?" I ask like I don't already know.

"Pussy." He blows rings of smoke out in front of him and we watch them disappear.

"Oh." I really don't want to talk about this. "Well what the fuck does Steve Carell have to do with it?"

"He was in that movie *The 40-year old Virgin*, remember?"

"Oh. Right." So much for changing the subject.

I swear, in high school it'd be more acceptable to be 300-pound, one legged male ballerina than it is to be a 17-year-old male virgin. "Oh right." I repeat, "Good movie."

"You're a rare breed Sam," Carter says squinting and shaking his head. He lifts the blunt again and before touching it to his lips he says, "A rare, rare breed."

It's ironic to hear Carter talking about me being a rare breed. Carter's a 6 foot 4, ridiculously skinny, half-White, half-Korean pothead with long dark dreadlocks that fall halfway down his back, and a body covered in weird Buddhist tattoos. The whole reason why we're standing around in this bathroom, is so he can smoke for a second between classes. We're standing on opposite sides of the room, so I don't have to smell as much like pot as he will when I go back to class or when I get home. My parents would kill me if I walked in the house smelling like weed. Carter's parents on the other hand, don't care at all that their son is pretty much perpetually high as fuck.

"You do though, Sam."

I lift my eyebrows like I'm confused. "Girls, man! You need girls! You're light-skin. Girls like that kind of shit. There's this house party this weekend at Stephanie's and it's gonna be EPIC. Perfect place to hoe some hoes."

I think I may be the only straight high school male in America who isn't interested in hoeing hoes.

"You've only got a few months left, you know man; and you *can't* graduate from high school a virgin. The party's gonna be dope but I wish it was summer, not the middle of January." He pauses, then says, "You know why I wish it was summer?"

"Why?" I ask, pretending like I don't know.

And Carter's like, "Because of them ass-hugging shorts and skirts man. Sometimes I'm just sitting there thinking to myself, damn, whoever decided that it's socially appropriate for a girl to walk around in public with shorts *that* short deserves a freaking medal!"

"Whatever, man. I gotta go or McAllister's gonna kill me," I say, turning to leave as I realize the smell of weed is starting to make it from his side of the bathroom to mine.

"Oh yeah, say hi to that little faggot for me. This weekend though bruh!" Carter's back to humping the sink again, "This weekend you become a man!" The door closes behind me as I try to purge that image from my mind, but there's no point. I know full well I'll never be able to look at a sink the same way again.

White people line the lockers in Uggs, chatting and Snapchatting and talking about those cringeworthy ABC shows like *Pretty Little Liars* and drinking Starbucks and stuff. White people. You see fortunately and unfortunately, I live in the Black part of Dilson, but a side effect of being adopted by two White, middle class parents is that they did anything and everything they could to get me in the 'good White school' on the other side of town. Sure, I don't have to worry about stray bullets flying through classroom windows while I'm taking a pop quiz, but going to school here makes me the token Black boy. For some reason, the few other Black kids who go to this school act according to the stereotypical and grossly inaccurate White ideals of how a Black person should act. The unfortunate product of this mental oppression is as follows:

1. Rapping between and during classes
2. Dabbing often and unnecessarily
3. Obsessing over Jordan's
4. Engaging in endless arguments such as 'LeBron vs Steph Curry' or 'Kendrick vs Cole'
5. Retweeting/Reposting memes and videos courtesy of WorldStar Hip-hop

What makes life difficult for me is that I don't do any of those things. Except for the WorldStar thing. And I mean, I have dabbed before. But my brother and I have never been like that. After decades of systematically steering Black people to the East side and piling them up in public housing, in 1968 the towns were incorporated in some warped demonstration of false unity. But the schools show it all. If my adoptive parents weren't White, I know I wouldn't be here.

As I'm walking down the hallway avoiding eye contact, the worst thing possible happens; Lily Jackson, the HOTTEST girl in school, turns the corner and begins to walk in my direction. As Carter would say, she's wearing these 'ass-hugging' yoga pants, and a low cut black T-shirt. She's like the baddest field hockey player in the history of Wyatt High, the smartest girl the entire state of Alabama has ever seen, and definitely not a hoe. Lily Jackson walking opposite from me is the worst thing that could possibly happen, because now we have to have that super awkward couple of seconds where we pass each other and I don't know whether to say hi, or wave, or nod, or smile or look away, or propose, or just suddenly pretend to be really super interested in my iPhone, like I just got a text message or something, when obviously I totally didn't. The icing on the cake is that I can't get that image of Carter humping that bathroom sink, and at this point, if I were Aladdin and had a genie, my one and only wish would be to have a textbook or something to hold in front of my jeans.

So, Lily and I are getting closer and closer to experiencing the pinnacle of awkwardness with every step, and I'm already reaching around to grab my phone from my back pocket, when the statistically speaking least probable thing happens; Lily smiles at me, with inexplicably straight and blindingly white teeth and says, "Hi Sam."

And I'm so caught off guard, and so surprised that Lily Jackson even knew my name, and even more puzzled by the fact that she knows it's me she's looking at and not my identical twin brother Gregory, that all I manage to do is laugh awkwardly and say, "Yeah." And then, the moment is over, and Lily's already passed me by and I'm standing there feeling like an idiot and remembering once again that I am actually the most awkward human to ever walk the face of the earth.

As soon as I open the door to the classroom, Mr. McAllister's humorously effeminate voice pierces my ears. Mr. McAllister is incredibly young, incredibly gay and incredibly fascinated by the law of supply and demand. I usually spend his macroeconomics class a.) Doodling, or b.) Scrolling through Instagram with my phone under my desk. For whatever reason, Mr. McAllister feels compelled to wear a different combination of brightly colored bow-ties and plaid shirts every day of the week, tucked neatly into identical pairs of uncomfortably tight skinny jeans.

As I take my seat in the back of the class, a couple of kids look up at me, sniff, grin, then nod or wink knowingly. They all smell weed on my clothes and have come to the conclusion that I must've been smoking. Bruce Jameson, a mediocre wrestler who always has a buzz cut and dresses in all black takes in one deep breath through his nose, then reaches his hand out the side of his desk for a low-profile handshake. Naturally, I wouldn't want to touch Bruce's hand (wrestlers are notorious for catching stuff like staph infections), but I reciprocate because it'd be awkward if I didn't, since a couple of other kids are watching me.

As I slide into my desk, the kid on my right, whose name I don't remember goes, "You high man?" And I just stare at him, trying to figure out whether or not the kid's asking me this because he's assuming the Black kid just *must be* on drugs. Then the kid's like "Can you hook me up with a bit of the shit?" He's sitting there nodding his head when it occurs to me that this kid thinks I'm a drug dealer. I'm surprised at how open he is about asking me, right there in the classroom with the teacher standing there in the front of the room, and I'm trying to figure out whether I should be flattered or offended when McAllister yells my name from the front of the room.

"Noble! Michaels wants to see you in the principal's' office. Immediately."

The kid, who probably thinks I just got busted for doing

something I don't even do, shrinks back in his chair and looks away from me, pretending like he wasn't just asking me to sell him drugs. I know exactly what this is about, and it's got nothing to do with drugs.

7:30 am in front of the school:

"Bro, you're trying to get me killed, aren't you?" Gregory asks, dropping his shoulders.

Shaking my head, I say, "C'mon Gregory, stop being a spaz man, just run down there real quick and get a couple bags of chips, it won't take that long." Gregory and I had both forgotten to pack our lunches that morning.

"Sam, don't you get it?" he protests, "I. Can't. Be. Late a-gain, on account of me needing to do this thing called GRADUATING in May. Why can't you do it?"

"Dude, I told you already, I've got a take-home test to finish up before first hour. You're not gonna be late. CVS is only around the corner. Cut through that neighborhood off of Seventh if you need to," I reason with him.

"You are trying to get me killed! First you want me to miss the bell, get another tardy and gamble my chances of getting my diploma, and now you want me to risk my life by walking through that White neighborhood, and past The Hagnotizer's house?! Do you want me to end up like JP?"

Neither of us can keep from grinning on the outside and crying on the inside at that one. I guess you could say The Hagnotizer is like the Boo Radley of the Peasant Run housing development. Gregory and I don't live there; but, we've heard the stories.

Like eight years ago, this short blondee kid named JP, (I don't know what the letters stand for) was out in his front yard with his friends playing football, when a bad pass sent the ball across the street and into The Hagnotizer's yard. The Hagnotizer is like 4 feet tall, and 100 years old, with black beady eyes and a horribly fake gray wig she's worn since the at

20

*least the 1970s. (Not that I've ever seen her, but that's what I've heard).
When little JP made the unfortunate mistake of venturing into her yard to
get the ball, as if on cue, she stepped out of her front door with a plate of
cookies balanced on the palm of her hand. Any half-smart human being
knows that it's statistically more likely for Kanye West to actually become
the president of the United States than it is likely for a warm-blooded all-
American boy to turn down an endless stack of chocolate chip cookies. The
Hagnotizer knew this better than anyone. The story goes that she'd waved
him on and ushered him in through the front door. They say he was in that
old house for hours. JP didn't talk to anyone for a couple of weeks after that.*

*He went to our middle school and whenever I saw him, he always had
this blank, distant empty look in his eyes, like old hag had hypnotized him,
hence her name. He never acted quite the same again, they say. Anyway, in
10th grade, JP slit his wrists with the blade of one of those handheld pencil
sharpeners. Which granted, was like 7 years after he went into that house so
there isn't necessarily all that much evidence of it being a cause and effect type
of situation. But still, it's unsettling.*

*Obviously, Gregory isn't really afraid of the Hagnotizer, he's just too
afraid of getting another tick over the limit on his attendance record.
Gregory's shoulders are slumped forward, until he sees Amanda Bentley out
of the corner of his eye. Amanda Bentley is like Gregory's own personal Lily
Jackson. I don't think she's all that, but he's been hitting on her since like
the 3rd grade when she sang "Footprints in the Sand" at the school talent
show. He straightens his shoulders and stands up taller.*

"OK, I'll do it, but you owe me," he says, catching me by surprise.

*"OK," I shrug. "Here, I'll even give you the money." Gregory eyes the
20-dollar bill as I press it into his hand.*

"I get to keep the change though."

*"Whatever," I agree, rolling my eyes. "As long as I don't have to eat
that mystery meat in the caf."*

With that, Gregory turns, pulls his red hoodie up over his head and shoves his hands, one squeezing the now crinkled up 20, into his pockets.

So, in all likelihood, Gregory ratted me out for 'making him go' to the store and missing class, and being late, so now we were both busted. A hand slaps my back hard, and a voice that's suddenly right beside me yells "What's good nigga?" way too loudly for a high school hallway. The only thing worse than a guy who calls himself Daddy, is a White person who thinks it's OK to use the N-word. "Yo, you see the game last night, man?" he questions me, again far too loudly for a school hallway.

"Nah man, but I heard it was a great game."

"Bro, you didn't see any of it? It was a great game!" Ant is one of those White guys who has so many Black friends he starts to think he's Black too.

"Alright man, I gotta run," I say, as I remember where it is I'm supposed to be going.

"OK dude, yeah. Text me." With that he pulls his blue hoodie back over his head and stalks down the hall away from me.

As I transition from the shiny linoleum of the hallway to the deep blue carpet covering the office floor, I make accidental eye contact with Principal Michaels. It is the nature of this eye contact that leads me to believe that the news I am about to receive in this room will be a lot worse than the suspension I expected. I look at her and she looks back at me and her face is crinkled up and her eyes are red, and I see the feeling that she is feeling in her eyes and know that whatever it is that she is about to tell me is almost as horrible as I am awkward.

MONAY DAVIS

❝If I'd had any say in it, I sure as hell wouldn't have given myself such a Black-sounding name," I say to my Jay as we make our way down to Starbucks along the bustling streets of Atlanta. It's one of those days that looks a lot nicer than it is. Like if you were inside and looking outside through a window you'd think it were a warm, breezy, clear-skied day, but just one step outside, and a single breath of cool air hitting your lungs reminds you that despite how it may look, it's January, not June.

"I know, right?" Jay agrees, adjusting the rolled-up sleeves of his blue dress shirt so they fit snugly around his broad brown forearms, "I've never understood why Black people willingly choose to send their sons and daughters into the world with names like DeShawn, Jamal, Ebony, and Shanice. It's not that there's actually anything fundamentally wrong with those names," he says, backpedaling, "but it just seems like, you know, you're setting your kid up from birth to be tossed in the wrong pile when it comes to applying for jobs."

"So true," I say nodding. "Have you seen the Sharkeisha video?"

"Sharkee what?" he says, laughing and unknowingly flashing his bright white teeth as he steps in front of me to open the door. Jay is classy like that— a real gentleman.

"I don't know, I saw it on YouTube."

"Oh, you know what?" he says pointing a finger at me, "I think I know what you're talking about. It's that video of uh, that Black chick sucker-punching that girl." His face cracks into a wild grin, "And then there's someone in the background yelling 'Sharkeisha noooooooo!'"

I'm nodding and we're both cracking up as we walk up to order from the front counter. He stops laughing, replaces his wide smile with a straight face and says, "You know that video is like really old, right? Like it's not new at all. It came out years ago."

"Ohh...Yeah. I mean I figured. I'm 32 now, you know. Too old for social media."

"What's your email address?" he asks, "it ends in 'aol' doesn't it?"

"Yeah, why?" I ask.

He smirks. "Nothing, don't worry about, it just all makes sense now," he says. "Two Frappuccinos. I want one caramel, one vanilla." Jay always orders for the both of us. "I'm sure there'll be some Barackiesha's here soon," he says, turning towards me. "Actually, I bet there already are."

"It's not just Black folk though," I say. "A few months ago, I was at this dinner and there was this young White couple there, and the wife was like massively pregnant, so I asked her how far along she was, because the silence was awkward and I kinda felt like I had to, and she goes 'seven months' and then I made the mistake of asking them if they thought of any names yet and-"

"They're gonna name her Sharkeisha?" Jay cuts me off with a corny guess I suppose he thought would come out as a funny joke as we grab our drinks and start table hunting. His long legs

24

and even longer strides have me struggling to keep up without spilling my Frappuccino as we strut across the coffee shop to our usual two-seater in the corner by the window.

"Ha ha, no," I laugh. "They're gonna name her M-L-E."

He looks at me like, clear brown eyes gazing and squinting into mine like I'm crazy, "I don't get it." He shrugs, defeated.

"M-L-E pronounced Emily," I say, trying my best to keep a straight face.

"Oooohhhh," he says leaning back in his chair with realization. He smirks, "White people," he says chuckling. "What'd you say?"

"I know. It's worse than North West. So anyway, I said "That's a *beeauuutiful* name, and so unique."

He smirks, "At least the second half was true."

"Yeah, I mean it's not like I could say 'hey that's a horrible baby name. That'd be like telling new parents their baby is ugly, even if it's true."

"Yeah, that's a no-no," he says taking a sip of his Frappuccino.

"Yeah, I say sipping my own coffee like I'm not wondering what it would feel like if his strong hands were wrapped around my waist instead of that paper coffee cup.

I take a minute to look at my co-host. He's got a strong jaw, dark skin and glowing white teeth. Put simply, he's incredibly photogenic. You'd never guess he was 35 years old. I sigh, taking in the moment and the smell of my Frappuccino and absorbing the mellow scene around us.

This Starbucks is situated right next to the ANN (Atlanta News Network) headquarters, just a five or six-minute walk down, and nestled just outside of the heart of downtown Atlanta. Inside it's quiet, but not too quiet, busy but not too busy: there's just enough noise and busyness to remind you that you aren't alone in this world, but not so much that you feel overwhelmed or invisible.

This is always my favorite part of the day, just when it can barely be qualified as early afternoon. After a stressful, hour long live show pretending to care about depressing and repetitive news stories, I get to come here, exhale, drink coffee, and talk to a beautiful man.

Jay really is a very attractive guy: There isn't really another way to put it, you know? Like there's a reason why he's a prominent face of daytime television. They don't just put anybody on TV. But after three years of co-hosting *Yesterday with Jay and Monay,* after all the early groggy, and intimately make-up-less mornings we've spent together we've never shared so much as a kiss on the cheek.

I sigh, leaning back and sinking further into the cushy seat. As I do, I stretch my stiff knees under the table out until the side of my foot hits something. Jay looks up from his iPhone.

"Oops sorry," I say.

He laughs gently, "It's cool," he says without moving his shoe. And the two of us just stay like that; the side of my heeled shoe leaning against his black ones, and soak in the moment and the coffee and silence. Even just the simple non-awkward silence between us, the on and off eye contact is *really* nice. Non-awkward silence isn't the type of thing you can have with everybody.

"I swear, the longer I live, the more I realize that, even in the year 2017, some White people simply can't wrap their minds around the fact that a Black woman could actually be wealthy, successful, and classy AF," I say as Jays leans forward to sip his Frappuccino.

"I know," he agrees, swallowing, Adam's apple bobbing. "Especially not stereotypical, southern American hillbillies and rednecks."

I stifle my budding laughter because I'm hyper-aware of the fact that Jay and I are the only Black people in the entire Starbucks, employees included. Jay, who's unapologetically Black and proud, so much so that it's dangerous, keeps talking because he doesn't give two shits about whether or not White people hear him being racist.

"Before I moved to Atlanta, everybody told me how the city was so progressive, and that it was this major metropolitan area, and they were right," he says swallowing, "but, what they forgot to tell me is that the actual state of Georgia, is as racist as any place."

An old White lady on our left is eyeing us up from a few booths away. Normally I'd tone it down some just to avoid a conflict, but now that Jay started going in, it's too late for the glaring eyes of angry White people to pull him down from his soap box.

I chime in. "The last thing White people expect a Black woman to have is money, and I see that in their faces when I leave the house with a Luis bag or walk around the mall in Louboutins or pull up to the drive-thru window in a BMW," I say, louder than I'd like to. My cheeks are getting hot and I can practically feel the people's eyes drilling holes into my back, but I keep going. "It's the same look every time, like they're in shock, caught in a web of their own disbelief. The bottom jaw drops open a little too far," I say, giving him demonstration, "eyebrows crinkle cynically and their head always cocks to the side as if to say "OMG is she Black?? A Black woman with *that* purse wearing *those* shoes driving *that* car? It's a look of resentment, but I've gotten used to it."

Jay is grinning a wide handsome smile that tells me he's been in similar situations. He holds his Frappe with one hand, fingers wrapped loosely around the cup, other hand hovering over his iPhone, which awaits his touch against the table. His brown eyes shine as they catch perfectly, the rays of sunlight wafting in through the window against his smooth, dark skin.

"How do you think I feel?" he begins after a long swallow. "When I walk down the street people automatically think I'm a threat. Women grip their purses tighter and Moms squeeze their children's hands like they're scared I'm gonna run over and snatch 'em up. Heck, when you're a Black man, even driving is a crime." I can tell that he's trying to sound calm and keep the conversation light-hearted, but I can see that on the inside, some of those things really get to him. His voice is strained, like he's honestly just tired of constantly having to prove and defend himself.

"That's true," I add, calmer and quieter, "Black women don't usually have to worry about getting randomly shot by cops. I mean, at least not as much."

Jay gives me a pained fake smile and looks down into his coffee, and my heart aches. I wish we could live some place where we didn't have to live like *this*. Always worrying about getting pulled over for driving, shot while obeying orders from cops, or strangled on the street for selling cigarettes. To lighten the mood, I tell him one of my stories.

"Yeah, so about the stuff I was saying earlier about nobody expecting a Black girl to be rich, there was this one time where I left my house with a Louis Vuitton bag, red bottoms and that Corvette I bought last year." He looks up, like he may or may not be interested in what I'm saying, but is just glad we stopped talking about Black guys getting shot. "So yeah, I was strutting across this Walmart parking lot and there's this couple standing by this beat up old minivan and the wife is like struggling to get this screaming little kid out of the back of the car, but the guy's just standing there. And so, the wife is yelling too now, and she's like 'Ben, help me get your kid out of this car!' And she's all stressed out and shit and that's when I realized what the guy was staring at. It was my car, and you know what? Staring isn't even the right word, I mean the guy was practically lusting after the car. Some White people probably haven't ever seen cars like that."

Jay nods, without looking up as he scrolls through Instagram. "So, to be honest, I was kind of flattered. I slowed down to give him some time to admire the fruits of my labor, but the wife was obviously getting irritated. She looked at him, then looked to where he was looking, and at this point, I was only a few steps away from my car, but I saw out of the corner of my eye as the wife leaned towards her husband," I lean in towards Jay for emphasis, "and said in what I guess she *thought* was a whisper voice: is she Black?' And I just stepped on up to that car and opened the driver's side door and looked at them like "Yasss bitch. Yasss she is."

I'm smiling and hoping for a reaction from him, but he just gives me the 'cool story bro' look, and the moment gets awkward. He purses his lips together, and against my will, I find myself wondering what they would taste like. Be professional. We *work* together. He cracks a smile and for a second, I'm worried that somehow, he might've been reading my thoughts.

"You know what you should call that?" he asks.

"Call what?"

"That look they all give you with the mouth open and the eyes squinting, and the head tilted to the side." He looks adorable trying to imitate the look. I shrug.

"The ISB," he says slyly.

"ISB?" I ask.

"Yeah, Is She Black?" It's definitely stupid, yet somehow funny. We both laugh a little, then sit in silence for a moment in the corner of the coffee shop. His eyes linger on mine and I wish I knew what he was thinking. Men are absolutely impossible.

I sip my Frappuccino like a White girl and shift my attention to the large flat screen TV bolted high on the wall showing the news. Fox unfortunately. I'm genuinely considering asking one of the baristas if they can change it to MSNBC or at least to CNN or something. Then the young boy's face plastered on the screen catches my attention. He looks familiar. It's something about his facial features, his caramel skin and the way his clear round eyes are set in his face. His eyes are grayish blue. I've seen those eyes before. I've seen that face before. I'd know it anywhere. Jay's calling my name from across the table, trying to get my attention, but my eyes are glued to that boy's face. I stand up out of the booth and walk closer to the screen, mesmerized. I know him. Don't I? And then a caption pops up at the bottom of the screen and oh shit, I know him. Unarmed. Gregory

Noble. Shot. Fatally. My heart feels like it's falling out of place. My throat tightens as if it's being forced shut and pressure builds inside my body, pushing outwards against my forehead, eyes and ears. His name is Gregory Noble. My vision goes black then comes back then goes black again. Nausea builds inside of me and the room swirls around my head. I know that name. I know those eyes. I know him. Gregory Noble. My body goes hot, then cold, then numb, then limp, then everything goes black.

HUNTER GARRETT

My heart is beating so loudly, I'm worried even the dead kid might hear it. My lungs must not be working properly because I'm not getting near enough oxygen to my brain. I just killed someone. I mean I just fucking killed someone. How do I explain this? I can't stay here. I need to go home. Before I can think, my legs start moving and I'm headed towards the house, straight into the wind. It blows against my face and into my eyes, drying them to death. My lungs ache and burn as the weakness in my body makes me feel like I'm running in slow motion or underwater.

As I approach the start of my driveway, a sharp pang strikes somewhere deep in my left knee. Toes drag behind me against the ground weighing me down, but my good leg just keeps on going. A wave of dizziness hits me, then the earth seemingly jerks and jumps and shakes and spins and I'm thrown off balance and back into the grass again. Flat on my back, I look up at that rumbling gray sky, low hanging telephone wires and those damn shoes swinging in the wind, laces flapping wildly, taunting me. The laces wave and slither as the tongue bobs up and down like that of a laughing mouth.

I lie there, my body stiff and frozen against the ground. Tears are streaming from my eyes, wrapping themselves around my face and running straight back to tickle the inside of my ears. Gasping for breath only invites bitter cold wind in to burn my lungs as my heart pounds, echoing out against my ribcage and into the ground below me. My arms hardly have the strength to push my body upright and my legs are bound with lead weights, but somehow, I hobble through the sharp falling rain pellets to the front door. It opens, and I'm face to face with Leah and the kids about to leave for school. There's a couple of seconds where all four of us just stand there staring at each other. My chest is heaving, I'm out of breath, and tears are drying up on my face.

The boys stare at me, heads tilted upwards, eyes open as wide as their hanging mouths. I can't think because my mind is just as frozen as my numb fingers, so I say, "He's...he's dead." Leah locks eyes with me, and I can tell she understands what just happened.

She turns to Artie and Emerson, stumbles on her words then says, "Uh... why don't you go in the kitchen and have some ice cream? Emerson, get you and your brother some ice cream, would you?" Artie and Emerson look at their mother like she's crazy, then look at each other.

"It's 8:00 in the morning and... we'll be late for school," an obviously confused and worried Emerson says, adjusting his glasses. "Dad are you cry-"

"ICE CREAM!" Artie shrieks, inadvertently quieting his brother. Ignorance is bliss.

Leah eyes Emerson and he squints right back at her as she nudges him, and he leads his little brother into the kitchen. She looks at me and her eyes say it all. She knows.

"Where's the body?" She doesn't sound scared. Her tone is clam and the way she says 'the body' sounds...clinical. Like he isn't a person anymore.

"In that field at the end of the neighborhood. It's kinda hidden by trees you know?"

"Yes," she answers so quickly she just about cuts me off. She nods and crosses her arms, pulling her thin gray sweater tighter across her body. "He attacked you." She says it like she saw it with her own eyes. "You were doing your job and he attacked you." I'm shaking as she grips my bicep tightly and pulls me closer. I lean down so her lips are at my ear. "You need to make it *look* like that's what happened." She lets go of my arm and shoves me towards the stairs. I look at her over my shoulder and she nods as if to say, 'go on.' Bowls and spoons clank from the kitchen.

I barely manage to stagger up the stairs and drag myself into the bathroom, locking the door behind me and dropping my black jacket on the floor. As I'm gripping the edge of the sink, my fingers are just beginning to thaw when my stomach rumbles wrong. My knees hit the floor before the toilet, just as sour acid forces its way back up and out of my mouth, splattering against the porcelain bowl. My insides keep twisting and squeezing and convulsing and I vomit until there's nothing left to come up, but even then, I retch again anyway.

"Daddy? Are you OK?" The sound of his footsteps pounding up the stairs seeps in below the crack under the door, and bounces off the walls, filling the room.

"I'm fine," I lie. It comes out like a croak. Vomit drips from my chin and onto my white shirt as I reach to flush before attempting to let go of the rim of the toilet seat and stand on my own. Against all odds, I'm able to steady myself and make my way back in front of the mirror. Walking even that short a distance without collapsing is exhausting.

I'm a mess. My face, beard and shirt are all smeared with tears and vomit. Even though my body is still freezing, rain mixed with sweat coats my body, soaking my hair and pushing it up in odd directions.

"Dad...What happened?" I can tell Emerson is right outside of the door now. "Dad?" I can tell he's starting to panic. His socked toes peek out from the space under the door. I imagine his cheek pressed all the way up against the door as he waits for me to open it.

"Emers-" I'm about to say something before I hear Leah call him back down the stairs to leave for school. He lingers at the door for a second before I hear his tiny feet stomp softly down the stairs.

My face is filthy, but unmarked. I do know what I have to do. Bringing my shaky hand in front of my face, I ball it into a tight fist and slam it into my left eye, hard enough to leave an impressive shiner. My face throbs and reddens as the pain sets in. Again, this time I go for the bottom lip where cuts are notoriously bloody. The impact splits the lip and blood flows immediately, dribbling from my chin, to mingle with tears and vomit before dripping tiny red beads around the sink. I feel like Edward Norton in *Fight Club*. Is this even believable? Won't they see the marks on my hands and know I did this to myself? Releasing a slow, shaky breath to help handle the pain, I promise myself that one more should do the trick. Inhaling one last time, I clench my fist, and slam my meaty hand straight into my mouth.

As blood pools between my cheeks, I lean forward to spit into the sink. Thick mucus hangs on like a string from my mouth. There's a soft clank, as the fluid finally detaches itself from my lips. A small white fragment rests beside the drain drenched in blood. Grinning in the mirror, I notice that one of my front teeth is chipped to a jagged edge. Blood is smeared around my mouth and chin, and beads of red stand out starkly against the white of my shirt. Damn, I look like I just got into it with somebody.

When I bust out of the bathroom door, Leah stands at the bottom of the stairs and gasps as she covers her mouth with her pale thin fingers. I blow past her and plow through the front door. The first thing I see are those fucking shoelaces dancing in the wind. Limping across the yard and down the sidewalk, and across the parched brown grass, I end up right next to the body. His lips are already turning a chalky white, and his left arm is bent backwards against the ground in a painfully awkward position. I run my hand up my neck and over my chin to pick up a little bit of blood. Kneeling beside the body, I smear a generous amount onto the toe area of the kid's right shoe. I'll say he kicked me. Damn, there's no way this is going to work. Slipping my shaky hand in my back pocket, I grasp my iPhone and dial three numbers. It happens just like it does in the movies.

"911, what's your emergency?"

"I was just attacked. It, it ended with me shooting him. He's dead."

SAMUEL NOBLE

When Gregory and I were eight or nine, some lady in Pennsylvania (who was apparently a friend of our parents) died so our Mom and Dad took us with them over the weekend to go to the funeral, and while we were there, our Dad took us to Valley Forge. Valley Forge is a historical park, 20 miles southwest of Philadelphia where George Washington and the American Continental Army spent an exceedingly unfortunate and freezing winter during the Revolutionary War. Of course, at eight years old, I didn't care about any of the history. All Gregory and I cared about was the epic demonstration the guys dressed up like Continental Soldiers did for us while we were there.

It was freezing, but Gregory and I were starstruck by the fake battle taking place right in front of us. When it started to rain, Mom and Dad, tried to get us to go inside, and I was fully onboard with that idea, but Gregory wouldn't budge. He was fascinated by the uniforms and the weapons and the fake cannons, fake rifles and fake deaths. His eyes were glued to the action on the field, and he looked like he would burst into tears if our parents tried to take him away. So, Mom and Dad went inside and watched us from the window, and even though the battle wasn't actually all that fascinating to me, I stayed out there with Gregory in the now pouring rain, just because I could tell it was all that fascinating to him, and because that's just what brothers do. On the way back to the hotel in the car, Gregory declared that he wanted to be a soldier. Seven years later, he was following through on that proclamation. It was his plan to join the Armed Forces as soon as he graduated. And I'm telling you all of this because I'm standing in Principal Michaels' office right now and she's literally giving me the worst news of my life right, and ironically, all I can seem to focus on is the miniature toy soldier on her desk and why it's there.

My ears do hear the words she is saying, yet my mind is unable to process them, my heart unwilling to believe. Ms. Michaels has never looked as hideous to me as she does right now. She seems way too tall, way too pale and far too skinny. As the ugliest words continue to fall out of her mouth, all I see is how her crooked nose seems to curl over her hairy top lip. How did I not notice that before? I've been here plenty of times. My body sways to the left and the room closes in on me, the thickening air making it too hard to breathe. She must be joking. I ask her if she is. She says nothing, just shakes her head and blinks out a couple more tears.

"The police showed up at your parents' address. It was on your brother's ID and…I just got the call. They don't know exactly what happened," she whispers, "just that he's… gone." This must be a prank. It has to be some sort of intricate plan to punish me for telling Gregory to skip school this morning. It's some sick genius way of teaching me a lesson, and keeping me here until graduation in May. It has to be.

Her phone starts to ring, and she starts to reach out like she's going to answer it, then pulls her hand away like she just remembered she's having a serious conversation. "So…your parents are waiting for you in the attendance office," she says to me. She says it so matter-o-factly, almost like I'm an inconvenience to her, a piece of gum stuck in long flowing hair she'd prefer to just cut off altogether rather than take the time to pick through it and save what she can.

As I return to the linoleum floor, my body feels heavy, my head full. Dead brothers don't just get found in the grass with bullet holes in their bodies. This can't be real. It just can't be. It's a dream or a hallucination. There's no way this is actually happening. I feel like I'm standing off to the side against the lockers, watching myself drag my feet down the hallway.

I must have drifted off in McAllister's class, and when I open my eyes, I'll see a plaid shirt and a bow-tie and a circular flow diagram. All I have to do is wake up. I have to wake up. But denial is the first stage of grief isn't it?

"Hey Gregory," a soft voice calls from behind me. Unfortunately, Wyatt high is such a small school that you can't go anywhere without seeing someone you know because everyone knows everyone else.

"Oh. You are Gregory, right?" I turn around to see Amanda Bentley, the "Footprints in the Sand" girl standing behind me outside of the girls' bathroom. She's wearing a loose purple sweater, tight black jeans and white vans. Her dark hair tumbles over her shoulder. She's OK, but has nothing on Lily Jackson.

"Uhh... No... I'm uh, I'm Sam." My throat is tight and burning as I clear it and try not to cry, blinking tears out of my eyes.

"Oh shoot, I'm sorry. I thought that I saw you walk into the office a couple minutes ago and I was gonna catch you on the way out...But I mean, I thought you were Gregory so..."

"No. Yeah it's cool, I mean, you know, people confuse us all the time. No biggie." I can't bring myself to repeat to her what

Ms. Michaels just finished telling me.

"I bet," she says, "I mean you guys really look *exactly* the same. For real, like usually I can tell twins apart."

I just nod and smile and try to keep from telling her that 'looking exactly the same' is what identical *means,* when I notice that she's got some type of small board behind her back and looks kinda embarrassed. "Can I like pass a message along?" I ask, as if he'll ever get it.

Her cheeks go bright red. "Oh uh, I dunno." She shrugs and brings the board around to the front of her body and I can see that it says 'PROM?' in big orange letters against a white background. "I was going to ask him. I think I still want to tell him myself." She looks up at me shyly. "Can you keep a secret?"

I want to tell her *Gregory's dead. You're too late.* But I don't. Instead I just nod and say, "Sure. Yeah, of course," before walking away, head low, heart jerking in my chest.

Somehow, I make it into the attendance office. The secretary looks up at me when I push the door open, pity etched across her face; I don't need it. She's blinking her concerned eyes and opening her mouth when I look away and see my parents standing just in front of the wall of windows. Dad's got his arm wrapped around Mom, as she leans into him, his lips pressed against her forehead. Her puffy red eyes glance up to meet my own. Mom runs to me and pulls me close, soaking my shoulder with tears. I'm so numb I can hardly bring myself to hug her back, but for her own sake, I do. I don't ask any questions like how or why or when, because to me, Gregory is still alive. Dad ushers us out of the door and into the whirling winds and bitter cold of January. The sky is so gray, it's almost as if God knew ahead of time that today would be the worst day of my life, so he painted it that color on purpose.

Dad gets in the driver's seat and Mom climbs in on the passenger side. I go out of my way to walk around the back of the car and sit in the seat on the left side because Gregory sits in the seat on the right, and I can't just go on taking his stuff. "Buckle up," a deep voice says from behind the wheel. I look at him like he's crazy.

"How can you..." I begin, "how can you actually be worried about stuff like that right now when, when..." Again, I can't say it.

"Oh Sam..." Mom begins before trailing off. Dad says nothing, just starts the engine and pulls away. I make no attempt to buckle my seat belt.

My iPhone buzzes in my pocket. Still, I'm hopelessly optimistic that it'll be a text from Gregory that'll say something like; 'GOT YOU GOOD DIDN'T I?' and I'll laugh and cry and text him back promising to never make him do anything again.

The text is not from Gregory, and it says:

> **Carter**: Hey saw you in the hall with Bentley
>
> **Me**: Yeah
>
> **Carter**: She has a nice ass
>
> **Me**: ...
>
> **Carter**: Ask her fine ass to the party this weekend
>
> **Me**: You know that's Gregory's girl
>
> **Carter**: Sucks 2 b him. U snooze U lose. I'm gonna invite her on your behalf

He has no idea that Gregory is dead. My body gets hot, throat clenches and goes dry and I want to punch Carter in the face.

I just say: Whatever. Gotta go.

The air itself in the car feels dense with melancholia. Mom sniffs every couple of seconds, and the side of her head shakes against the side window like she's still crying. Tucking my phone back into my pocket, I ask "Where are we going?" Mom and Dad exchange looks and say nothing. I stay quiet and give them time to think, remembering that Gregory wasn't just my brother, he was their son too, adopted or not.

I'm staring at the top of Dad's balding head peeking over the top of the seat when he says, "We have to identify him." It's the way he says this that frightens me the most. My Dad is strong and tough and stern, but when he says this his voice falters and cracks against his will. For the rest of the car ride I keep my mouth shut. There is nothing left to say. We drive past drab, decrepit and run-down houses, their walls brought to life by faded graffiti. We pass fields of dead grass and people fighting to ride into the wind on their bikes. We drive by family-owned stores and mom and pop restaurants, and the sky doesn't get any less gray. The further we drive, the less I think this is a joke.

Eventually, we pull into the parking lot at Garner-Scott Memorial Hospital. Garner and Scott used to be separate hospital systems until they merged a couple of years back, bought up a bunch of smaller hospitals and became a massive hospital system that serves like half the state of Alabama. There's a Garner-Scott West, a Garner-Scott East and a Garner-Scott North and South. We're at the South one right now.

I feel as if I'm in a dream as we walk in silence from the car to the entrance. Somehow, I haven't shed a single tear yet, though my heart hasn't stopped aching since I left the principal's office. Inside, the lights feel way too bright, and I linger behind near a wall of magazines as Dad talks to the lady in scrubs at the front desk. She takes in the sight of us, surprised as most people are when they see two White parents with two Black boys. Well... one Black boy.

When Dad waves for me to follow him, I do, and the three of us stand in the chilly hallway silence, waiting for the elevator. The doors open to reveal a dark-haired, sobbing young woman standing in the corner blowing her nose and sniffling. She tries to hide her face in her hands when she sees us at the doorway. She's so beautiful, that I feel like I just have to know what it is that's made her so upset, but I don't get the chance, because she suddenly rushes through the elevator doors and past the three of us. In the elevator, Dad pushes the 'B' button, and we begin our descent into the depths of the hospital. There is no music. We stand in silence, falling lower and lower and lower underground, until we're well beneath the surface of the earth and far away from the life and lights of the world above us.

The elevator doors slide open to reveal a brick wall in front of us. "She said to the left," he says gesturing for us to exit. Now at 17, my height has finally caught up to my father's. I follow him down the dark narrow hallways, staring at the back of his bobbing balding head as we walk. "I think she said it's a right next," he mumbles as we turn a corner and come face to face with a set of guarded double doors.

The guard, a young Hispanic dude, looks up at us. "Who are you here for?" he says it like it's a question he's forced to ask far too often.

43

"Gregory Noble," my father whispers back. I've never heard him say his name that way before. It comes out low and crackly like he can't believe he's saying it. He lifts his hand and shows the guard a small plastic badge, the scrubs lady at the front desk must have given him earlier. The guard gives a satisfied nod, sighs and steps backwards against the door, pushing it open and giving us room to step inside and merge with the darkness. Ceiling lights flicker on and a low humming sound fills the chilly room. I notice I can see my own breath as I watch Mom stifle a shiver next to me. Two walls are filled from floor to ceiling with white, body-sized compartments reaching several feet back into the wall.

"Over here," a voice calls to us from the left corner of the room. The old mortician wears a full length white coat, small round, wire rimmed glasses, and even in his old age maintains a full head of stringy silvery hair. He hardly acknowledges us, just waits for us to join him in the corner, before reaching out for the silver handle and yanking it towards him. A black body bag emerges from the section in the wall. Mom, Dad and I stand over the bag, crowding the tiny space, bracing ourselves for what we're about to see.

"OK," the mortician says as if this is a daily routine he's grown far too accustomed to over the years. With that, he reaches for the zipper at the far end of the body bag and pulls it downwards. The center of Gregory's face peeks out from in between the edges of the bag before the mortician's bony white hands pull the edges back and the entirety of his face emerges from the depths of the bag. My mother cries out. I've never heard a human being make a sound like that before. She falls to her knees, littering the floor with her tears.

Looking down at my twin, I see a mirror image of myself. A

dead version of myself. His lips are white, and his skin is darker than it should be, but worst of all are his eyes. They're completely open, bulging from his stiff lids and looking straight up into the ceiling. A pained gasp comes from beside me. I look up and lock eyes with my father. He's crying. Never in my life, have I seen my father cry. Not when we went to that lady in Pennsylvania's funeral or when our uncle, his brother-died. Up until right now, I honestly believed that maybe my father just wasn't capable of crying. Like maybe at some time in a man's life he just gets so strong and so tough, that crying just simply isn't a thing he can do anymore. But right now, he's standing there in front of me, tears streaming down his face, and I'm the one who can't bring myself to shed a tear. Somehow, this moment still doesn't feel real. "That's him," Dad whispers through shaky breaths, "that's Gregory."

MONAY DAVIS

❝OK. I'm just going to need you to give me one more *hard hard* push, alright hun?" She says it like it's a simple, painless request. Somewhere even, in the back of her tone is a hint of annoyance, probably at the fact that my inability to push a baby out of my body as quickly as she would like.

I'm lying on my back in a hospital bed, chest heaving, sweating screaming, gripping the rails on either side of the bed so hard my hands are going numb. Even through the pain, I can't help but feel ashamed by the fact that I can only wonder what it would be like to have done things right and have a man's hand to squeeze instead.

The doctor between my legs is yelling at me to PUSH! at the top of her lungs. The pressure is unbearable. There's no way my body was made for this.

"I can't. Oh, my Go—" The room is closing in on me. "I can't do it, I can't, I can't, I can't!" Giving up isn't something I even really do; but in this moment, I'm thinking that maybe this just isn't *possible,* you know? And it's up to me to communicate this fact to the doctors around me and then maybe they'll realize they're just gonna have to cut me open or something. So, I say it again, looking directly into the doctor's eyes, "I *can't* do it. I *CAN'T!"* The woman shakes her head and I can see the outline of her now pursed lips beneath her surgical mask

"Honey, you don't have a choice." Her eyes burn into mine. She's right. The baby is coming whether I want it to or not. Sweat and tears soak my face and gown as I writhe on the bed sheets beneath me, trying to no avail to cope with the burning sensation at the meeting of my thighs. It feels as though somebody has their fists around my inward parts, as if to wring out my guts in jagged, twisting motions. Nine months of morning sickness, wild cravings, and stretch marks all led up to this excruciating, disgusting and beautiful moment.

When I asked other moms whether or not pushing a set of shoulders out of your vagina hurt, they all told me the epidural was like a magic bullet. "Get the epidural they said," "you'll be fine," they said. Now I'm finally here in the moment, and I'm unfortunately aware of the fact that what those women didn't tell me about giving birth is that getting an epidural saves you from the pain, but not from the pressure. The pressure is unbearable. I feel as if my body is going to split in two under the pressure of that malleable little skull. I'm screaming and yelling and pushing as hard as I can, wondering who the hell would willingly get pregnant a second time after going through this just once. Laying there, legs wide open, I begin to wonder if at 16, my body just isn't ready for this kind of stress. I scream, gathering together every last grain of strength in my body. Maybe I'm not built for this, maybe this isn't for me. I Push. Maybe…

Suddenly I hear it; the most beautiful sound on God's green earth. The sound of *my* baby crying. There's silence as the baby suddenly stops crying and the doctor dips down a little lower so all I can see are the blondee flyaway hairs atop her head. I'm propped up on my elbows and straining my neck to see what's going on…it's too quiet…. Babies aren't supposed to be this quiet, are they? My heart is thumping in my chest, partly from the rush of delivering the child and partly from the rush of fearing for that child's life, seconds after birth. I'm just about to gather up enough strength to ask if it's okay when the doctor stands up, holding a naked little human, drenched in mucous and fluid. He's the most gorgeous little baby I've ever seen.

"A little boy," she says as if that isn't obvious. Every inch of my body is flooded with relief and joy at the sight of him. I scarcely have the energy to keep from falling flat against the bed sheets as I reach out for him with what little energy I have left, desperate for the feeling of his tiny body in my arms and against my chest. But the younger dark-haired nurse takes him away from the doctor, cradling his screaming body in her arms and whisks him away and out of my sight behind the curtains. Panic strikes deep into the vessels of my soul. "Wa— wait! Where are you going with him?! He's mine!"

But there's nothing. No answer from her, and no cries from my son drift beyond the curtain to where I'm sitting. Just an "Oh my! There's another one!" But I don't know what they're talking about; and at this point, I don't really care. I'm thinking about how I just want to lay back and sink into the bed, becoming one with the sheets, and how badly I just want them to give me my son back. "OK momma, just keep on pushing!" It takes me a minute to realize that by 'momma' she means me, and that by 'another one' she means a second baby. I'm stunned as I watch her reposition herself between my legs at the foot of the bed.

After what feels like literal hours more of screaming and pushing and feeling like I'm going to die, another little boy pops into the world. Their cries ring out, coming together to form a flawless chorus and making a sound so glorious, no set of twins could ever beat it.

And then nothing else mattered. Not the pressure or the pain, or the doubts I had, or the people who lied about the epidural, or the fact that I'd just pooped on this table in front of several other people. I can understand how it's possible for the Duggars to have 19 kids and counting. It's those stupid hormones. All that matters to me right now are two boys and their tiny fingers and toes and soft curly hair and round little hat-covered heads nuzzled against me. And I'm thinking to myself, *how can a nose actually be that small?* And I'm wondering how it's possible that all humans come into the world so utterly perfect, only to leave it beaten wrinkled, marred and ugly. His hands are clenched tightly and one of their mouths form an adorable miniature 'O' as he yawns, then leans his head against my body. The other opens his eyes and looks up at me and in that moment, my life is complete. They're gray. As gray as storm clouds. I named him Samuel, and his brother Gregory.

The unmistakable feeling of a man's hand stroking my face tears me from this moment. Opening my eyes, I see Jay leaning over me, his usually clear eyes looking strained and tired, his strong jaw, now covered in a thin layer of stubble, clenched with worry.

"Hey," he whispers, "you're OK, you're in the hospital." He smiles a smile that's meant to be reassuring but those kinds of smiles are usually the most unsettling.

"Wha—What happened?"

"You fainted in the middle of a Starbucks and banged your head pretty good on the edge of a table on the way down. Doc says you do have a slight concussion," he says, pulling his hand away from my face and reaching out to hold my own.

"What time is it?" I croak.

"Umm..." he says, reaching into his pocket with his free hand for his phone. "It's 7:00 pm, so you've been out for a good 8 hours."

Leaning forward to sit up in bed and looking over at Jay I can tell something's bothering him. "What's up?" I ask.

"Oh, no, uh. Nothing. No, it's just that uh, when you woke up just now you were saying some guy's name...Sam I think it was." Looking closely, I see in his expression that there's something else there in the background. Jealousy? Just a hint maybe? Or am I being overly optimistic that he thinks I was calling out some guy's name and is a little *jealous* about it? As bad as it is, that thought causes butterflies to take flight in my stomach.

But now what do I say? I can't tell him, *oh yeah so, I actually got pregnant at 15. And Sam? He's my son and his brother Gregory is the kid making national news for getting shot by some maniac with a gun. I was young and gave them up to focus on myself.* What would he think of me? So, I say, "Sam's my, um dog." And I regret it as soon as I say it because I don't have a dog and Jay knows this. And because I shamefully, in an effort to bury the facts of my existence, pretended my own son is actually a dog.

I'm hoping he'll just go with it and let me slide when he says, "Uh. You don't have a dog."

"My dog...that I used to have I mean. He died."

Jay's eyes dart left, then right, then they land on me and I can tell that he knows that I know that he knows I'm lying. My eyes search his for answers but find none.

"You want Jell-O?" he asks, standing up and looking for an excuse to leave the room.

I don't want him to leave, so to stall I say, "Why Jell-O?"

"I don't know, it just seems like whenever people are in the hospital, the person with them always goes and gets them Jell-O from the cafeteria."

"How many people have you been in the hospital with?" I ask playfully, lifting a brow.

A hint of a smile plays on his lips before his mind reminds his mouth that he's supposed to be mad at me for lying and he sort of frowns in my direction. "Jell-O or nah?" he asks.

"Blue if they have it."

"OK," he says, avoiding eye contact as he closes the door behind him.

"OK" I say, even though he's gone.

I'm alone again with my mind and my thoughts, filling the room with guilt and regret. I wanted to do what was best for my boys, but a I look up to the tiny TV showing the news in the corner of the room, I'm reminded for the second time today that one of them is already gone, and that what I really wanted was what was best for me.

HUNTER GARRETT

When I was a kid in the 90s, my father took me to the park. It may seem like nothing to you: for most people, a memory of going to the park with their Dad probably isn't out of the ordinary enough to even become a memory. But I remember this day, because for me it was out of the ordinary.

My father never took me anywhere. Mom always assured me that it was because he was a police officer and always busy saving lives, but even then, at 11 years old, I knew it wasn't true. At night, I fell asleep trying to push the truth out of my mind. The youngest of five athletic older brothers, I was pale, bird-chested, skinny, so blind I couldn't see the board from the front seat of the classroom without thick glasses, and allergic to everything. The runt of the family, my father didn't take me anywhere because he was ashamed of me.

But that day was different. That day he had come in from playing football with my brothers in the backyard, startled me with his deep voice as I sat on the floor of the TV, tossed my baseball glove at me, and told me we were going to the park to play catch. I jumped up so quick I nearly slipped, but even at that pace, I'd noticed the genuine surprise on my Mother's face, which was followed by a reassuring smile as I passed by her saying, "Yes sir," on my way to grab my shoes, glove in hand.

At the park, I dove for every grounder, leapt for every air ball. I wouldn't let not one of my father's hits get past me. So,

I'd caught and fielded every last one, and he hadn't said a word. Instead he'd just toss the ball into the air in front of him with one hand, swinging the bat effortlessly with the other.

I followed the ball closely with my eyes, jumped and stretched my arm to the sky, when it bumped the top of the glove and dropped into the grass. My father shook his head and said. "You're not trying, are you Hunter? You just don't know how to work hard at anything. That's your problem." He turned away from me, dropping the bat to the ground, and my shoulders slumped forward under the sun, when a Black man burst out of the bushes across the street from us and bolted across the field. A couple of cops on foot came up quick behind him and the one in the front hit him hard across the head with a heavy club.

When that cop socked that Black man upside the head like that, people scattered, grabbing their kids and making a beeline towards their homes and cars. But my father, who had appeared behind me, grabbed my shoulders, held me still and said, "Watch this Hunter." He said it all excited like we were about to watch a cool fireworks show or something like that. So, I watched as three cops jumped on the guy who was lying face first in the grass and beat the living shit out of him in broad daylight. The guy was screaming and yelling, and the cops just kept hitting him and hitting him and hitting him and kicking him until his face was covered in shiny blood and he lay still in the grass. I'd never seen blood on black skin before. I thought he was dead until I heard him cursing as the cops handcuffed him and dragged his limp body across the grass before stuffing him into the back of their squad car. I'll never forget what it is my father said next. He said: "You see? Aren't you glad we don't live by all of that? And that we have great cops keeping an eye out for us?"

"Yes sir."

"Now let's see if you can learn how to catch," he said, slapping me on the back.

"Yes sir," I said, jogging further out into the field for the next hit. And as I bent my knees, squaring up to catch the ball flying towards me, I knew I'd be a cop someday.

Boy is it different when you're the one getting arrested. The frozen grass is hard and cold against the left side of my face as a bony knee pushes the entirety of a massive screaming cop's weight into my lower spine. Looking up, I see Ms. Thompson's small wrinkled face peering through a window and looking down at me from her home. We make solid eye contact before the curtain falls back into place.

At first, I try to protest, pushing back against the cop's weight, telling him that I was provoked, but I'm no match against his booming voice and crushing body mass.

I feel like I'm in some crime show on TV. I've watched so many episodes of CSI and Law & Order, that I can almost recite the words with him:

"You have the right to remain silent. Anything you say can and will be used against you in the court of law. You have the right to an attorney. If you cannot afford an attorney, one will be provided for you."

The cop bangs a set of metal cuffs hard against my wrists, binding my arms around the back of my body, and lifts me off the ground by my forearm. I'm ushered into the back of the black squad car. I've never been in a cop car before. It smells like urine and marijuana. The seats are torn up and worn down. Strings of gray fabric burst out from the tears and slits in the leather. As I rest against the filthy seats, I try not to think of all of the violent criminals who have been here before me. Rapists, thugs, sex offenders and murderers have all leaned back against these same seats and looked through the same side windows. I glance upwards and into the rear-view mirror. I see myself and I realize I am the murderer.

When I get out of the car in front of the police station, I feel like a felon. A woman is walking with her young son, and even from across the street, I can tell her eyes are glued to me, to me stepping out of the back of a cop car. She wraps her arms around her boy's shoulders and pushes him to the side of her body, further from me as if she's scared I might just run over across the street and snatch him up. For a second, I wonder if that's how Black guys feel all the time; like everybody sees a handcuffed, criminal version of themselves.

I'm pushed in through the double doors of the police station and to a room in the back. I strain my neck to see the clock on the wall behind me. It's 8:47. Damnit. I'm praying that the chief doesn't see me when as if on cue, he rounds the corner strutting across the room at his full, towering height.

He stops and cocks his head at me, lifting an eyebrow. Something about his super low haircut and the precision in the way he speaks makes me think he's ex-military. He points a thick, tan finger in my direction, and suddenly I just feel like a wannabe-cop, wishing I could just melt into the floor and disappear without anybody noticing. Or maybe he just won't recogni—.

"Garrett?" His booming voice simultaneously crushes my worthless optimism and draws the attention of everyone else in the room. "You're early. I thought we'd scheduled the interview for 10:00."

Why does he have to talk so loud? People stop filing papers and delivering coffee orders to look up at me.

The chief seems unfazed by all the attention (something I'm sure he's used to) and is still waiting for my reply. "Uhh, yes sir, it is." I try to reach out to shake his hand, but I can't because they're in handcuffs behind my back. His eyes widen, and his brows scrunch up, before he squints in confusion.

"Um, what's going on here?" He steps to the side and leans over so he can see my hands bound together behind me. "And what happened to your face?"

One of the cops at my side goes, "Says a Black man charged him out in the Pheasant Run neighborhood. In self-defense, he fired several shots and killed him." Before the chief can say anything, face still frozen in stunned silence, I'm pushed away from him and down a narrow hallway. How did they buy that story so easily? They just honestly believed it happened exactly the way I said it did. The cop ushering me down the hallway must somehow misinterpret my confusion and amazement for a look of fear and trepidation, because he pats me on the back and says, "Don't worry man, this is all just protocol, you'll be fine," and cuffs me to a metal table and chair before walking away

The tall thin Black man sitting across the table from me asks a lot of different questions:

"What is your full name?"

"Hunter Garrett."

"What is your date of birth?"

"June 14th 1982."

56

"What is your occupation?"

"I'm a watch guard for my neighborhood."

"What is your address?"

And on and on and on.

I feel like it's some sort of sick revenge on the universe's part that I've got to sit here small and ashamed, answering to a Black man. And this went on and on and on until the Black guy is replaced by a fat woman with dark hair who waddles over to me and says, "Give me your hand." So, I do, and she gently presses each finger on my right hand into a black ink pad, before rolling the finger onto a white card, and starting over with my left hand.

A buff, blondee-haired cop in a uniform way too tight for his bulging muscles comes over to me, uncuffs me from the table, then leads me into a room that looks to be a combination of a closet and a bathroom because it has a mirror and a sink, but no toilet. Then he says, "Put these on," and hands me a bright orange jumpsuit.

"You've got to be kidding me. I don't actually have to put these things on, do I?"

"Does it look like I'm kidding?" When the cop says this, the collar of his uniform is so tight I'm worried his thick neck might burst it open. He leaves the room and shuts the door behind him. I can see the back of his blondee head through the tiny window in the door as he stands guard.

Stripping down to my underwear, I examine my pale, skinny body in the mirror. I look starved, my eyes are sunk into my face as if I haven't slept in days. Basically, I look like shit. My wrists are sore, purple and bruised from those tight metal cuffs, and

I'm standing here almost naked in a quiet, empty bathroom in the back of a police station, about to put on prison people clothes. The only thing I can think is, how did I get here? This morning started out so perfectly... How did I get *here?*

The eyes that stare back at me in the mirror grow red as I realize why this happened. Thompson. I never would have been here without her. I knock the side of the sink with my fist. If she hadn't called... I lean forward, hands on either side of the sink, head down, forehead pressed against the glass. And the kid. In my neighborhood. He shouldn't have been there. He shouldn't have been there, but he was, and because of him I'm here.

I'm seeing red and before I can think about it, I stand up straight and my fist shoots out in front of me and slams the glass mirror, shattering it to the floor. I hear a scream that I figure must've come from me, since I'm the only person in the room. And then I'm on the ground, in only my underwear, lying on shards of broken glass and gripping my cut-up, blood covered right hand when the thick necked cop busts through the door, hand on his gun.

SAMUEL NOBLE

Never in my life have I stared at a wall for so long. My body is frozen, my eyes glued to the tiny cracks and lines hidden in the interlocked bricks stretching from the floor to the ceiling. I want to cry. In fact, I feel like I am, but I know that I can't be because my eyes are dry.

My brother is dead. He's the only person I've ever known personally, like had a relationship with, who's died. Well I guess that isn't quite true. (There was that uncle who died.) But I didn't really know him that well, just that he loved playing spades and drank too much. And I guess, to be technical, he wasn't really my uncle anyway. My heart jumps as I realize that now, I'm truly alone because in this moment, the only blood relative I've ever known is lying in a body bag in little drawer dozens of feet below some random hospital in Dilson, Alabama.

Something wet hits my hand, which is resting in my lap. It's a tear. I realize my cheeks are wet, so I guess that means I am crying. My vision blurs and I lose sight of the tiny cracks and lines in the wall as my sobs rack my body, and they just keep coming and coming, flowing harder and faster and stronger than I knew tears could, and I am wondering if humans ever run out of tears to cry. There's so much pain and agony in the world just waiting to be felt, and cried about, that I doubt it. Out of the corner of my blurred vision, I see my mom notice me crying. When she pulls me against her, I don't care if I look like a five-year-old boy, I just close my eyes and soak her shoulder with tears.

I can close my eyes, but not my ears. In the small square room in the back of the local police station, the man's southern draw ricochets off of the four brick walls.

"We received a call at around 7:45 this morning from a night watchman in the Pheasant Run community." He's talking slow and proper and careful like he's walking on a frozen lake and is afraid the wrong movement might send him straight through the ice and into painfully cold waters. Mom says nothing, so the man keeps talking, just as slow as before. "He told the operator that there was a suspicious man in the neighborhood, whom he'd approached nonviolently only to be physically attacked and pinned to the ground."

"What could he possibly have been doing over by Pheasant Run at that time of morning?" Mom cuts him off. Without opening my eyes, I know her expression is laced with fury. My mother hasn't ever been the type to hold back her anger. "He should have been in school. He should have been..." she trails off.

I squeeze my eyes shut even tighter. I want to say, *he was there because of me, because I told him to go to some stupid store, and he didn't even want to go, but he did, because I asked and that's just the type of brother he was, and now he's dead and it's 100% my fault, because he wouldn't have been in Pheasant Run at all if I hadn't made him go.*

"The caller," the cop drones on, "then confessed to fatally shooting the man in an act of self-defense."

"He isn't a man, he's a 17-year-old boy and his name is Gregory. He's our son," Mom says through her own tears.

I lift my head from her shoulder and look at my mother in that moment: her eyes are red and puffy, though still exuding a look of strength and seriousness, trained squarely on the uniformed man across from us. Dad just looks distracted and is staring in the direction of the officer, but I can tell his eyes are focused on nothing, just above his head. The man nods and opens his mouth as if he's about to speak, but I cut him off.

"What was his name?" The man shoots me a bullshit excuse for a confused expression and lifts an eyebrow. "THE. MAN. WHO. KILLED. MY. BROTHER." I spell out to him in the strongest voice I can muster.

He makes eye contact with me, swallows hard. I'm sure I look like a complete mess. Then he says, "Hunter Garrett."

Hunter Garrett, I think to myself. That name just *sounds* racist. The way the syllables sound when spoken aloud make me cringe and my face feels like it's on fire. I imagine a massive, pale, potbellied man, with a fake leg and a hook for a left hand. He's hairy and bald and he smokes a cigar and puffs it out slowly right into my face, and then laughs, when he does. His teeth are crooked and yellow, and his beady little eyes squint up from behind his dirty round glasses as the most horrible sound in the world erupts from his insides and explodes from his mouth as he giggles like a madman. He lives alone in a tiny run-down shack with no electricity at the edge of the earth. He has no wife and no kids and sure as hell doesn't know what it means to have a brother, or he wouldn't have killed mine.

And then I see him holding his gun out in front of his body and laughing that hideous, obnoxious laugh as he pulls the trigger. I see him standing there over a body, his stomach bulging so far over his belt buckle he can't see his own shoes.

Then I see Gregory. I see his red sweatshirt and his black Nikes and his dead brown face and his dead brown eyes staring upwards the way they did in the morgue at the hospital and suddenly I'm filled to the brim with anger and despair and I know I'll never forget that name.

And then I'm back inside the little brick room, staring at those tiny cracks and lines while Mom and the cop keep on talking. He says something like "Will you be pressing charges?" And mom says a couple of cuss words then stands up abruptly, knocking my head away from her shoulder. Slamming her hands against the table between us and the cop, she says, "*What?*"

The cop stares blankly at her, wrinkly white skin crinkling on his face as he purses his lips slightly and swallows.

"What do you think? He *murdered* our *son.*"

"Of course, ma'am, of course," the cop says more quietly than he'd spoken before. There's silence, and then he adds, "But you do understand that Mr. Garrett acted in self-defense. I highly doubt that he had any malicious intent."

Mom gasps in disbelief of the fact that this man is sitting here defending the man who killed Gregory. I look to Dad, but he doesn't say anything, and his expression remains blank. I can tell by the uncoordinated expressions on Mom's face that she doesn't know where to begin.

But she knows what I know, and what I know is that we live in one of the most racist towns in America. Here, it's unlikely he'll even lose his job. The laws weren't made to protect Black men. And even though my middle-aged, middle class, sweet, stay-at-home Caucasian Mom *knows* this, she can't and won't ever quite understand it. It isn't her fault; this ignorance isn't a result of her own doing, but a product of inherent White privilege. In this case, her White privilege is not needing to understand things like that, because she won't ever have to experience them. But I listen to her anyway. I listen to her trying to understand, as she speaks as though she understands.

"Acted in self-defense?" she repeats slow, low and monotone. "You mean he *claims* he acted in self-defense." The cop stares back at her in silence, shifting his eyes to my father who says nothing. She continues speaking calmly and loudly at the same time, slowly leaning forward near the officer's face. "And he *claims*, that he was in fear of his life." She throws her arms into the air, hair now flashing around her shoulders with her movements. "Well of course!" Her tone is starting to scare me a little. "Of course, it was self-defense and he," (she uses air quotes for this part) "feared for his own life! They all do! They all do, don't they?" Her eyes are wild as Dad looks on. "YOU KNOW he shot him because he was Black." There's silence as Mom slowly lowers herself to her seat.

"Ma'am," The officer says holding his hands out in front of himself. I understand, I understand. We'll be in touch." A deep piercing shriek fills the room. At first, I'm sure it's the verbal manifestation of Mom's frustration with the fact that this officer is acting like we're talking about planning a summer vacation and not pressing charges against the man that killed my brother, but when I look at her to confirm, I realize that she too is looking around trying to figure out what body that scream came from. And all three of our heads jerk to the right. The dreadful sound is coming from outside the sealed door to the room we're in. I glance at the cop who looks down away from me and think to myself that if Hunter Garrett screamed, that's exactly what he would sound like.

He clears his throat and continues, "In the meantime, I need you to sign this," he says, sliding a sheet of paper towards my parents. "You have to confirm that it's OK for us to release a few of the details of the case, like your son's name, while we're waiting on the examination." Mom signs her name on the line at the bottom of the page, pen scratching roughly against the wood table below. Something still feels so surreal about the moment. Like it hurts, but it's like an unreal kind of hurt. Like a slow, steady, swelling, rising up of pain in my belly, radiating out towards my heart and pushing tears from my eyes. My insides feel worn out, like my emotions themselves just ran a marathon. And somewhere, somehow, in my heart, I'm still clutching my phone in my hand, hoping for a text from my brother, though my mind knows it will never come.

MONAY DAVIS

When Jay wraps his strong brown arm around my waist, I find myself wishing harder than I'd like to admit that he wasn't just doing so just to keep me from tumbling down and ending up in a heap at the bottom of the stairs leading to my apartment. My head pounds, and as I fumble in the dark to get my keys in the door, a wave of lightheadedness washes over me and I feel my body sway to the side.

"Whoooaa, you alright there?" he asks. My arm is draped over his shoulders as he half carries me into my dark apartment and over to the couch in the center of the room. He sits beside me as the blue glow of the TV casts odd shadows on his face. I leave it on to avoid coming home to a dark, silent apartment, so it feels less like I'm coming home to a depressingly empty flat. My noodle-like limbs melt into the couch like butter on warm toast. Giving the silence a chance to help my body relax, I notice how badly my head is throbbing, and how much I can feel the bruise behind my left ear pulsing. Jay just sits there beside me, as I spend what little energy I have left on turning my head towards him. Through the darkness, I can only see the side of his face illuminated by the blue glow of the TV, but half a face is all I need to see that something's on his mind.

"Mo… I need you to tell me what that was all about earlier." As if on cue, he shifts his body weight on the couch so that he's facing me, left leg bent at the knee and resting on the couch, right foot flat against the hardwood floor. His concerned eyes pierce mine through the darkness, jaw clenched tightly.

"What do you mean?" I ask.

"I mean… with you fainting like that in Starbucks. As soon as you saw that kid on the TV, you were like, mesmerized or something. And about Sam the 'dog,' he shakes his head. "I know you too well. Don't *lie* to me Monay." The emphasis he puts on the word 'lie' makes my heart sting with guilt. There's silence and the TV screen goes dark for a second as it transitions to a commercial, and the blue light disappears from around his face. His dark skin blends in with the darkness around us so that for about two seconds, all I can see are the whites of his round, clear, pleading eyes.

"I…" I trail off. I want to tell him, but I'm afraid of what he'll think of me. Another Black girl who fucked around and got pregnant in high school. I'm more than that. I'm not ratchet or ghetto, or a whore. I'm successful, and that's the version of me Jay knows. That isn't me. What happened back then…that isn't me. It's shameful. I wouldn't want him, or Robert or anyone else who watches my show to see me that way. I made it out of there, out of the hood, against the odds. I'm not a statistic and he'll never know how *hard* I worked to get out and to get rid of that reputation, or how much it hurt to leave my family behind because all they could see when they looked at me was a teenage girl who opened her legs too soon.

If I told him I was that girl, the got-pregnant-in-high-school-girl, the gave-her-baby-away-girl, he'd look at me differently. He wouldn't respect me. Jay wouldn't understand the struggle. How could he? He isn't from the hood, he doesn't know struggle, he's from the wealthy white suburbs of St Louis. If I tell, he'll judge me verbally, and in his head, he'll shame me too.

But in this moment, sitting here next to him, I just can't bring myself to lie. His eyes silently search mine for answers as I search his for any hint of how he might react. He slides his hand across the seat of the couch between us and covers my hand with his "Gregory Noble... the boy who died..." I begin. He nods for me to continue. I take a massive deep breath before I say, "He's my son."

Jay goes quiet. The only sound in the room is of the lady on the news droning on in the background and the barely-there sound of his hand sliding backwards across the couch and away from mine.

...Yesterday at 7:45 am in Dilson Alabama, a young Black teen was fatally shot...

"Your son?" he says, looking down at my belly like he's halfway expecting me to be pregnant right now. "The kid who got shot down in Alabama is your son? You're shitting me," he says, almost laughing. "He was like 17, you're only, what, like 33 right?"

...The name of the teen's killer has not yet been released...

"Jay I'm, I'm not joking. Gregory is my son."

...brief physical altercation with a neighborhood watchman...

"You did say you grew up in Alabama..."

...The victim, 17-year-old Gregory Noble, was unarmed...

"Yeah. I went to high school there."

...The events leading up to the teen's death are unclear...

He's nodding his head like maybe he's actually starting to believe me. "So… you were, like, what? 15 or something?"

"Something like that…" I trail off.

He looks at me, an expression I can't quite discern plastered on his face. "So was it um…" He's searching for words and talking with his hands, trying not to say the wrong thing or the right thing in the wrong way.

It was like consensual or were you…" He swallows and cocks his head to the side, looking at me for help.

"It was consensual," I lie. He nods.

"Damn Mo," he covers his face with his hands, then reaches out to touch my arm. "Are you OK? I mean after what's happened to him?"

"I don't…. I mean, I didn't know him, you know? So, like, it's a really weird feeling like I should be crying and depressed right now, but I just… I don't know. I'm just not. He's a stranger. Was."

"That's really rough." Jay looks at me, and I can tell by the cynical squinting of his eyes that he doesn't believe what I'm saying to him about not feeling anything.

"Well I gave them away right after birth because I was so young I couldn't take care of any kids," I blurt out.

He cocks his head to the side, and more of his face is shrouded by darkness. "Wait, *them?*"

Jay doesn't ever miss anything. "Yeah. Twins. Identical."

"Is the other one's name by any chance…Sam?" he asks hopefully.

"Yeah," I say with a small laugh. "You peeped that, huh?"

He sighs heavily as a wave of relief washes over his body. "I peep everything."

He smiles. "For a second, I thought that Sam was... some secret boyfriend of yours," he laughs as his gaze falls downcast, showing off his long, dark lashes.

Curious about his sudden change in demeanor, I ask, "Would you care if it was?" with more boldness and confidence than I'd intended. I shrink back, look down, and swallow hard through my sudden nervousness. I feel like I'm somehow imposing on him by probing his personal feelings and desires this way.

"I would," his deep voice gently disrupts the silence that was quickly closing in on us. His eyes linger on mine and he moves his hand further up on my thigh and I feel my heart jump in response. He looks away briefly, swallowing hard, just as I did seconds ago. Then he looks back at me with more confidence than he had before, locking eyes with me, more certain of what he's saying than he is when he stares confidently into the camera as he speaks to millions of people as he continues. "I would care...if it were another guy I mean."

"How so?" I ask, fishing.

"Mo, I-," he presses a little harder with his hand, which is till resting on my thigh, looks away, laughs one of those you-don't-get-it-do-you? laughs, tightening his jaw a bit and shaking his head. But what he doesn't know is that I do get it. I just want to hear him say it. And I don't know exactly what 'it' is, but I know that 'it' is something that will let me know I'm not a sorry, hopeless romantic and that this thing I can't define hasn't been one sided for all this time.

The light from the TV casts a solemn, blue glow on the side of his face. He runs his other hands once or twice along his own thigh. His lips move several times as if he's fully intending on saying something, but he's uncertain, as if the right words are simply evading him. His eyes move from my own, down to my lips, then back up to my eyes and when he starts to lean forward, my heart jumps in my chest and I get a whiff of whatever cologne he's wearing; and as I'm closing my eyes, I'm thinking that, while him saying something profoundly romantic and cliché would have been a great story, whatever's about to happen next will definitely work too.

But right when I'm thinking that this is about the time our lips should be touching, I feel his head rest in the area between my right cheek and shoulder, and his strong arms wrap tightly around my body. He's not kissing me, he's hugging me. So, I hug him back, a bit disappointed until I wrap my arms around him too, and I feel his body relax, and his soft sigh against my ear, and his heart beating almost right against mind. "I'm glad you're okay," he whispers.

The sound of the newscaster in the background fades away, and it's just us, and I don't know how long we stay like that, because I'm too lost in the feeling of safety and warmth, and protection, and the sensation of one of his hands gently stroking my back, to think about it. When we pull away, all I can think is to never, ever again underestimate the intimacy of a hug, as my body buzzes with anticipation.

"Why are we sitting in the dark?" he asks, our eyes still firmly locked.

I lift my eyebrows and shrug slightly, as if to say wordlessly,

"I don't know."

He gets up, and within three long, invisible strides through the darkness, is on the other side of the room flipping the switch. We both blink and squint as our eyes adjust to the rush of light flooding our retinas. I'm looking at him standing there by the switch in the kitchen, still in his casual, tan colored pants, and now wrinkled, purple dress shirt, sleeves rolled haphazardly about his forearms, when he says, "It's late. I think I should go."

In an effort to prevent him from becoming aware of the fact that those words caused a literal pang in my heart that practically pushed it out of my chest, and into my stomach, I say, "OK. Yeah, yeah, yeah, you know, you're right. Thanks for everything."

I start to stand up to walk him out, relying on the arm of the sofa beside me to make it to my feet, when he says, "No no, you stay sitting, you need to rest. Do you want the lights on or off?"

"Off, thanks," I say. The room goes dark at the same time that I freely allow my body weight to plop down against the couch. "You're the best."

And he smiles with those pristine white teeth, which practically glow against the dark air of my apartment, and says, "Good night Mo."

"Good night." The door closes behind him, and for the second time that day, Jay leaves me alone in a room staring at a TV plastered with my son's face.

I regrettably turn my head in its direction, just as the picture changes suddenly to a bird's eye view of people swarming the city streets and the woman's voice continues to narrate the scene.

And now, thousands of Black Lives Matter protesters have taken to the streets to express anger, frustration and concern over the events that took place this morning, an event they're calling "another Ferguson." On the ground in Dilson is Senior ANN reporter Ryan Benchman. Ryan, tell us what it is you're seeing there on the ground in Mobile."

I'm standing there, alone in my apartment in front of the TV, watching thousands of people yelling and holding signs in the air to protest the death of my son, who I don't know any better than they do.

... And the Dilson Police Department is on their toes tonight, hoping to prevent the violence, rioting and looting that took place in Ferguson in 2014. So far, all protests have been peaceful. I'm Ryan Benchman, back to you Maria.

HUNTER GARRETT

"Neighborhood watch," I say as the man scribbles notes down on a large pad, with the black ink pen that he holds between his large, pale fingers. I see the corner of his mouth smirk. To a real cop, the term 'neighborhood watch' is probably a joke. I find myself looking at his badge and uniform and wishing they were mine. When he sets the pad and pen aside, his silver wedding band bumps gently against the wooden desk.

"So, you want to be a cop, huh?" he asks. I don't know if it's objective reality, or my own insecurity that makes me feel like he's puffing out his chest, taunting me with his badge.

"Yes sir," I say, nodding.

"Alright," the officer says, his head bobbing atop his thick neck, in what I assume his version of a nod. "Thanks for coming by. I'll make sure I get this to the chief." He gestures to the notepad, "And if he's interested, we'll get ya in here for an interview."

"Thanks officer," I say, as we exchange a firm handshake.

"OK, take me from the top," says the officer sitting at the table across from me. He's much shorter, and older, and has a lot less hair on his head, than the cop I met with just weeks ago. A middle-aged, bearded man in a suit with a full head of hair sits next to him. He's looking down and never makes eye contact with me.

We're sitting in a poorly-lit interrogation room with thick brick walls on three sides and a full length dark window on the fourth wall. I'm pretty sure it's one of those things where I can't see what's on the other side for the life of me, but I'm damn sure whoever's on the other side can see me.

"Walk me through what happened this morning," the short, uniformed guy prompts me. I don't really know what to say, so I just start talking, starting at the beginning like the guy said.

"I was... with my family when I got a phone call from the old lady down the street. That's not unusual, since, like I said, I'm the Watch. Now this lady is really old and lives all alone in that house. When she told me some Black man was hanging around out front, I didn't think it was a big deal. But like I said; she's really old, and all alone, and I could tell it was bothering her that he was out there, so I told her I'd go take a look, and see what he was about." I pause before continuing, and dictating slowly, "It's my *job*."

"And at what time did you receive this call?" the bearded, suited man interrupts, hardly looking up from the pad and pen in front of him.

"Uhhh, well, the kids hadn't left for school yet, so I guess it had to be around 7:45." The men nod in unison, signaling me to continue. "So, I grabbed my gun, which I am *licensed* to carry concealed in the state of Alabama." I pause to let that sink in for a moment. "And I stepped outside, started walking, and I saw him. He was a big dude too. And fast. He turned around and looked at me, then picked up his pace. His hands were in his pockets and I thought he might've had a gun on him or something." The short cop holds up his hand, so I stop talking.

"And at this point his back is to you?"

"That's right."

"And about how far ahead of you was he?"

"Maybe 30 yards." I say attempting to gesture with my hands when I'm reminded by the sharp pain that my right hand is wrapped in layers of bandages and that my wrist is cuffed to the table leg in front of me. The two men continue to scribble notes in chicken scratch on their yellow pads.

"Go on," says the bearded guy in the suit.

"OK so yeah, I, I uh, thought the guy might've had gun on him, so I called out and told him to stop running, and to put his hands up. That's when he broke into a sprint and got it so there was a real distance between us. I tried to catch up, but like I said; the kid was fast. His shoes must have been like untied or something, and he fell down face first which gave me enough time to catch up to the bast— to him." A lump forms in my throat. The men exchange looks but say nothing, so I keep on talking.

"So, yeah, after he fell, I caught up to him. I was standing there about to ask him what he was doing in my neighborhood when the guy just like leapt up off the ground, ran straight into me, and knocked me flat on my ass. So, he's got me *pinned* to the ground and he's just going at me, like kicking me in the face and stuff." I uncross my arms from around my chest to be sure they can see the dried blood that got smeared onto the orange jumpsuit as I put it on. Neither of them seems to care.

"And so, I was really kinda out of it for a second and I honestly thought he was gonna beat me to death. For real, it was like, instinct to reach over for my gun which was on my belt and I pulled it out in front of me. As soon as the guy saw it, he turned to try to run, but at this point there's blood all in my mouth and eyes and my head is throbbing so hard I can't see, and I can't think straight, so I pulled the trigger in self-defense, and in fear of my life." The room is utterly silent. Neither the cop, nor the guy in the suit has anything to say.

"But, just to clarify, the kid did have his back to you when you shot him?" The guy in the suit is drilling me with those beady little brown eyes. My breath catches in my throat and my body heats up. "It that correct?" the cop asks from beside him.

"Yes. That's correct," I confirm, out of options. The two men squint and look at each other again. The one in the suit gives a small nod.

"OK Mr. Garrett. That should do it. You get one phone call."

SAMUEL NOBLE

❝As we step into the house, flashes of this documentary I watched years ago flood my memory. It was about this theory that there's this measurable energy that people emit, like some type of unique spiritual noise that people give off and we all go around sensing it unconsciously all the time, but we just aren't really aware of it on a conscious level. Except for when it's gone. I'm saying all of this because when I step into the house, the force and pressure of the absolute silence nearly pushes me back out the front door. It's usually so much louder, and more alive in here. Like either Gregory is singing, or he's playing the piano, or playing with the Xbox, or the TV is on or *something*. There's always *something*.

But the only noises in the entire house are the sounds of our wet shoes squeaking against the floor as the three of us begin to move around the house. Mom announces that she's going to head upstairs and get some rest. Neither Dad nor I say anything, but I watch as he walks slowly into the family room, sighing as he sits down on the couch. As I turn lifelessly into the kitchen, I'm expecting to hear him turn on the TV to watch some golf or daytime TV like he usually does on Saturdays, or when he stays home from work. But it's silent when I open the fridge, scan the shelves to see that there isn't anything good to eat; just some pomegranate juice, some cheese sticks, and a few containers of yogurt, and it's silent when I close it as well, a few seconds later.

I look over my shoulder to see what my Dad is doing sitting there in silence, but he's gone: I no longer see his bald head poking up over the back of the chair. As I move away from the empty fridge, through the thick, dead-silent kitchen towards the family room, I realize it isn't completely silent. There's soft sniffling coming from where Dad would be if he were in the chair, and as I step around in front of the chair, I see my father still sitting on the edge of the gray seat cushion, bent forward at the waist, with his head down, cradled in his hands.

At first, I can't tell if he's crying or praying, and then I realize he's doing both, when a tear falls to the wood floor by his shoes, and I notice his lips whispering words of scripture into the silent house around us.

I feel awkward. I've never seen my Dad pray before, and not only do I feel like I'm imposing, but seeing him cry now is reminding me of the way he covered his mouth with his hand when he saw Gregory peeking out of that body bag. And I'm seeing Gregory's pale, dead face all over again, and I can feel hot tears begin to burn the corners of my eyes and blur my vision, so I try backing away from him in silence. When my left foot hits the charger plugged into the wall, and knocks it to the floor, my Dad bolts upright, obviously startled by the noise.

He must have noticed the tear that's now made it all the way down to my chin, because he takes a half a step forward and gathers me into his arms, and when he does, I just bury my face against his shirt and cry. Like shaking, sobbing, snot producing, uncontrollable crying.

And then we step back, and he says, "I love you son," and there's a pause, and with his eyes he's telling me, '*and I know this hurts, and it doesn't feel real, and it's the worst thing that could have happened, and fuck that cop for fucking up our lives.'* But his mouth doesn't say any of that. His mouth only says, "Get some rest."

The clock ticks as I walk towards the stairs. It's funny how you can only hear those kinds of sounds when it's ultra-quiet. When I get to the top of the stairs, I hear my mom's muffled voice drifting out of her closed bedroom door. Moving through the still darkness of the hallway, her words grow louder as I approach her door. She's whispering and yelling at the same time. Like her voice is intended to be a whisper, but her words exit her mouth at a forceful, rage-tinged clip.

"That security guard or night watchman or whatever murdered my son. He murdered him. Murdered. There's no way around it, there isn't. There just is not." There's a pause like the person she's on the phone with is talking. "I know, that's what I'm saying, and I said that to the cop there today, and Mike didn't say anything. Nothing. Sam was so upset, and Mike just sat there, staring into space." There's another pause, then a sigh.

"Yes, so I know Mike won't really be any help. I know he loves his kids, but I just don't see him really wanting to go and say what needs to be said. If I had to be honest with you, I'd say he's really an All Lives Matter person. And I don't see him challenging this to the degree of calling this murder. I just don't. So, something has to be done...something else has to be done. That guy...he doesn't deserve to live."

My heart beats fast, as I back away from her door, walk down the hallway, and close my bedroom door, sealing myself in the darkness of the room. Tears wrap around my face as I lay on my bed staring up at the ceiling fan. I have an essay to write. How is it possible for me to have homework to do when my brother is dead?

The world is a lot like the ceiling fan. It doesn't care about your personal life, your problems, or people you know dying. It just keeps turning and spinning and turning. I just lay there. Time passes. It's silent around me, but in my mind, all I can hear are my Mom's words replaying over and over again. About my Dad and how he isn't going to do anything to fight for Gregory. My iPhone buzzes from my nightstand. It's Carter.

Carter: Dude. Wtf is going on?

I don't know why Carter is texting me like he doesn't know what's going on. It's 2017. I'm sure that if he's been on any form of social media today, or turned on the TV, then he knows exactly what's going on.

Me: What?

Carter: I just turned on the news man

Me:

Carter: They're saying Gregory is…

Me:

Carter: They're saying he got shot

Me:

Carter: Fatally

Me: Yeah…

Carter: What happened? Are you okay?

Me:

Carter: Do you want me to come over?

Me: Can I just come to your place?

Carter: Yeah of course man

I slide slowly off the bed, pull on the pair of jeans I wore to school today, slip on my black Vans and a black sweatshirt and head downstairs. Mom is now pacing around the kitchen talking to someone about 'the body' and Dad is just sitting there at the table staring at a wall looking the way I probably did as the police station. Mom freezes, stops talking and looks at me as I enter the kitchen.

"Samuel. How are you doi—"

"Fine." I cut her off as she reaches out to me. "I'm going to Carter's." It's such a normal and appropriate thing for me to do, yet in this moment it seems wildly inappropriate for me to say or do such a thing.

"OK."

"OK. Bye," I say reaching for Dad's car keys and heading for the door and stepping out under the dark sky and into the warm air. Dad's silver Honda Civic is parked in front of the house.

Carter lives in Pheasant Run, the community where Gregory was killed this morning. Pheasant Run is only a few miles south from where we live, so it'll only take a few minutes to get there. As I approach Carter's community, I know that if I turn my head to the right, I'll see the CVS. I don't look though. I can't. Driving through the dark neighborhood, with one-story houses lining either side of the street, I know one of the guys in one of the houses is the guy who slaughtered my brother. My hands grip the steering wheel and my body heats up, as my heart burns with a sick combination of anger, guilt and despair. I'm not going to cry right now. I'm not going to cry.

Stepping out of the car and into the dark of the night, I

knock my knuckles twice against the Zhus' front door. Carter answers immediately, like he was standing right there waiting for me.

"Hi," he says, almost like it's a question.

"Hi," I say stepping into his house.

Carter's eyes are clear and wide and searching my own. Briefly, we hug. It's just for a second, before we each step backwards and continue into the house.

In the family room, Carter's Mom, Dad, and little brother Matthew are all sitting on various couches and chairs, eyes glued to the TV. My brother's face is taking up the whole screen, but once again, I feel like I'm looking into a mirror. I can tell from the part of his shoulders that aren't cut off, that it's a picture of him in his ROTC uniform from a couple months back. I wonder how they got it.

"Hi Mr. and Mrs. Zhu." Carter's dad is Asian, and his mom is White. They turn and look at me in silence, just staring.

On the TV, the news lady says, *"Several hours ago, authorities released the name of the deceased teen, named "Gregory Noble..."*

Matthew kicks his legs to swivel his chair in my direction. He looks at me, confused, before craning his neck to look at Gregory again, then back at me. I don't think he's ever met Gregory before; he only rarely ran in the same circles as Carter and I, outside of the boring empty summer months when he had nothing to do.

The news lady keeps talking, *"The teen, who was unarmed, was shot twice and pronounced dead on the scene."* She promptly and nonchalantly moves on from discussing the death of my brother to the dangers of the Kylie Jenner challenge, like neither topic is really that big of a deal. A strip of wetness runs down my right cheek.

Finally, as if awakened from a trance, Mrs. Zhu jumps to her feet, runs over to me and says, "Awww honey," like I'm a five-year-old who just fell off his bike and scraped his knee. Before I can say anything, she pulls me against her squishy shoulder, and is holding the back of my head against her, and even though it's awkward and uncomfortable and she kind of smells like broccoli, it somehow feels good and safe.

I stay there for a few seconds, and then Carter and I are on the stairs headed up to his room, my body weighed down with every step, when Carter goes, "Dude... what the hell happened? They're not telling us anything on the news."

Carter's sitting there on the carpet of his bedroom looking at me and I notice for the first time that his eyes are red like he's been crying, which is weird because Carter doesn't cry. And I sit down on the floor beside him, and don't say anything for a few seconds, shaking my head because so far, no one else even knows why Gregory would have been in that field this morning.

"I asked him to run to the CVS before school to pick up some stuff for lunch, because, you know, we forgot to pack them today." Carter's nodding, leaning forward and listening intently.

"And ummm, yeah, he texted me that he had picked up some stuff, so I figured he'd be heading back soon enough to make it to class on time." Carter's concerned eyes continue to pierce my own like he's still waiting for me to answer his initial question.

"After I left the bathroom, you know, you were there too, and went to class, the teacher told me to go to the office, and when I got there, she said Gregory had been…shot. And killed."

"The CVS right there?" Carter says, gesturing in the direction of the CVS down the road from his house. And I realize Carter doesn't know that Gregory got shot and killed, essentially in his own backyard. I nod and let him put the pieces together on his own. "So, it was this neighborhood… my neighborhood?" I stare at him in silence.

"Wait…" Carter scratches his head. "Watch guard… was his name… Hunter Garrett? I mean the guy that shot him. They haven't said who killed him yet on the news."

"Yeah. That's what the cop said." I say, recalling the image of him I'd made up in my head earlier.

Carter jumps to his feet and says, raising his voice, "The guy who shot Gregory is Hunter Garrett?" He's holding his head now, watching me nod when he says, "I know him! He lives right there. That's the shoelace house, he lives in the shoelace house!"

"What are you talking about man?"

"The shoela—, remember that time last summer when me, you and Carter were hanging out and we found that pair of shoes behind the school, so we were all trying to get those shoes up there and finally Gregory got them up there? On those telephone wires?"

Suddenly I do remember. "That's where Hunter lives?" I ask.

"That's where Hunter Garrett lives."

MONAY DAVIS

I want to cry and be upset and mourn and suffer and curse all cops the fuck out like a mother should when her unarmed son is shot and killed, but I can't. I'm filled with emptiness instead of pain, which is worse, I think. My heart beats slowly through the thick layer of guilt surrounding it. I feel like I didn't know him, and I didn't. I didn't know him at all because I handed him away the second he came into the world. I don't feel upset at all. If anything, I feel angry, pissed at myself, and it's impossible to ignore the fact that if I hadn't given him away he'd be here right now.

I'm frozen against my bed, looking up through the darkness at a ceiling I can't see. I feel like the weight of my dead son's coffin is pressing against me keeping me pinned flat against the sheets. When water flows from my eyes and backwards towards my ear and the pillow below, it's because I haven't been blinking and my eyes dried out, not because I'm crying…I really don't do that.

I gave him away because it was *too hard for me* to look in his eyes and *too much of a burden* for me to care for him at 16 years old, and because *I was ashamed* of the fact that I'd ultimately made the same mistake so many Black girls do; getting pregnant in high school. It was all about me the whole time, my own hopes and goals and aspirations, my success, and how I didn't want those two tiny sets of feet to crush my hopes and dreams.

But he's dead now. Dead and gone. I never even told him I loved him. Did I love him? The death of my son means little more to me than the death of a stranger. And his brother, Samuel is out there alone, sleeping in a house with parents who aren't even his parents, going through it alone.

I lie in silence until the alarm on my phone goes off, startling my heart out of its guilt-induced sluggishness and sending it into a rapid fluttering frenzy against the inside of my hollow, empty chest. I guess I crawled out of bed, took down my twists, and fluffed them in front of the mirror. I guess I got dressed in the usual suit and heels, and drove the same 20-minute drive to work I do five days a week. I'm assuming this is the way it went anyway (it's the most plausible), because the next thing I really remember is sitting at my desk in the nearly empty studio.

I'm staring at a pile of notes and stories for this morning's show without really seeing any of it. And I'm thinking about how it's super early in the morning, yet my feet are already growing sore from my heels.

And I hear, "You know, maybe you should have him on the show." Jay startles me from across the room. At 6:00 am we're already in studio E of the ANN building in Atlanta preparing for our 7:00 am show. He's dressed up nicely as usual in a pale blue button-down shirt, and a gray suit and tie. By the time we finish the show the sun will be shining through the full-length window on the right, but this time of morning it's still dark out, the stage lights are not yet lit, and the only light in the studio comes from a few dim, circular lights embedded in the ceiling high above us.

"What? Who?" I'm just now starting to snap out of the trance-like state I've been in since my alarm woke me up out of bed an hour earlier. In my mind, I'm still lying there drowning in guilt and what ifs.

"Your son," he says. It shocks me for a second, before I remember our conversation from last night.

The thoughts of him cause a wave of nausea and weakness to spread across my body. "Oh umm. I don't know about that," I say, steadying myself in the chair by pressing my palms flat against my desk and exhaling slowly whilst trying not to spill my emotions all over the studio floor.

"What?" he yells, peeking his head out of one of the closets in the back of the studio. "I can't hear you from over here."

I bet he knows exactly what I said, but I amuse him anyway. "Oh," I say, louder this time, "I don't know about that. Like I said, I have no rights. I didn't request any visitation. He doesn't know me."

Jay ducks back out of the closet and starts walking towards me, "I know, that's what I'm saying. It'd be perfect because I know you don't have any rights, and this way you'd be able to meet him, but as an interviewer and not as like…" He's been walking towards me the whole time he's been talking, and even though the studio is almost empty, and he's practically right in front of me, he still whispers the last two words, "His *mom*."

"Oh. Right. I mean, I guess so, I say, feeling numb. I can tell by the slight expression of anticipation on his face, that he spent time thinking up that idea and was expecting a response from me, so I say, "Yeah, I mean that's not a bad idea, it could work I suppose."

"I mean, he knows he's adopted right?" he says, partially satisfied with my forced verbal appreciation of his idea.

"Uh yeah yeah, I mean his adoptive parents are White, so yeah, I mean he'd have to know that." I try to add a little laugh at the end of it, but it comes out more like a pained croak or gasp.

Jay stops, halfway across the studio, feet firmly planted against the smooth wood floors and says, "You let two White people raise your Black sons?" He's appalled. His blatant expression of unadulterated disgust makes my heart throb with pain, embarrassment, and regret. I swallow hard...I don't have an answer. His expression softens, probably in reaction to the pain etched into my own.

He resumes walking and says, "I mean, you don't need custody rights to have him on the show. I'm sure Fox and MSNBC will be all over the kid soon. It's big news, you know, I mean they're already comparing it to what happened with Mike Brown and Trayvon.

"Yeah, I heard that. And 'the kid'? His name is Samuel, remember?" I really wish we didn't have to talk about this right now. I know I told him and myself that it didn't hurt but I didn't know that meant he would take it as a green light to talk about this so freely.

"Oh. Yeah...sorry. Samuel," he says in a small voice, heading towards me with a mug of chamomile tea. "Still though," he continues, "They're planning protests for Gregory all across the country today."

"Who?"

"The Black Lives Matter people. It's a really big deal," he says, setting the mug on my desk.

"Hmm. I bet. They haven't released his name yet, have they?

I mean the guy who shot him?" I ask Jay. I've avoided the news altogether since last night.

"They have I think," he says softly taking a seat beside me. I find myself way too aware of his scent. "You weren't joking about what you said about Black names though," he laughs, interrupting my thoughts, and leaning his arms on the desk in front of us, the sleeves of his light blue dress shirt rolled up to his strong forearms as they always are. He leans in.

"How do you mean?" I ask, focusing on his face.

"I mean Gregory and Samuel aren't exactly your run of the mill Black names." He puts air quotes around the 'Black names' part.

"Oh, so you're saying I should have named them DeShawn and Tyrone? And if I ever have a little girl her name should be Barcakeisha?"

"Barackeisha Obamaneisha," he says and we're both giggling at our stupid inside joke.

"Ain't nothing wrong with the name Tyrone though," he says all serious.

"No, no, no, I know a couple of decent brothers named Tyrone."

Jay shrugs and says, I don't actually know that many Black people to be honest." I'm about to tell him his privilege is showing, in that he doesn't know many Black people because he grew up in one of the wealthiest, and Whitest suburbs of Atlanta. But instead, both of us are quiet for a moment as he looks through the stack of news stories we're supposed to cover this morning. From the silence surrounding us, emerges time for me to think.

Maybe he's right. Maybe I should have Sam on the show, so I can have some sort of connection with him in this dark time. Even if he has no idea who I am, at least I'll know that I had some form of contact with him and offer a bit of consolation. It's no substitute for not being there for 17 years, but at least it's something. And maybe then I wouldn't feel so guilty.

"Ugh... #OscarSoWhite again?" Jay exclaims. "Didn't we literally just talk about that?"

"Maybe you're right," I ignore him. "Maybe I should have Sam on the show."

"Hey Robert!" I call to the older man who works behind the scenes setting up interviews and getting in contact with people we might want to have on the show.

He peeks his bald head out from behind the wall surrounding the small office-like area in the back and says, "Yeah Mo?"

Jay watches silently from beside me, waiting to see what I'll say next. "Could you get me in contact with the parents of Samuel Noble?"

"Already on it," he says, nodding his head, I arch my eyebrows in surprise. Did Jay tell him? I look at my co-host without turning my head towards him and watch as he gives me the subtlest head shake, indicating a 'no'.

I'm squinting at Robert trying to figure out why he'd have a reason to be 'already on it', when he says, "I know how passionate you are about race relations. Plus, I know I had to jump on the opportunity before the other stations did." I don't appreciate Robert talking about my son like he's some, opportunity for high ratings but then again, he doesn't even know I have a son, and I'd prefer to keep it that way, so I say, "You're the best, Robert." And he nods and disappears back behind the wall.

THE END

"Hello?" Her voice sounds tired and unsure through the phone.

"Hey, Leah. It's me."

She lets out a slow, shaky sigh. "Hunter, oh my gosh baby, are you OK? Where are you? What's going on? You gotta tell me what's happening?" She is throwing questions at me rapid fire and sounds like she's about to start crying.

"Shhh, Leah I'm OK, I'm OK. I'm at the police station. They just questioned the shit out of me, but I'm alright." In part, I'm reassuring myself with my own words.

She's definitely crying when she says, "So what's happening though? I mean what's next? Are you coming home?"

I wish I could hold her right now because I can't help but imagine her lying there in our dark bedroom alone. I hate myself for having caused her this much pain, and the thought of her crying makes me want to do the same, but for her, I keep my voice strong. "So, what's happening next is uhh, I'm going into court tomorrow morning and the judge is gonna decide based on, I don't know, something, whether or not he's gonna give me a chance for bail and how much it'll be."

"OK" she says, and I can tell she's trying had to pull herself together. "Can I do anything? Do you need clothes?"

I look down at my oversized orange jumpsuit. I don't want to tell her what I'm wearing right now, so I just say, "Oh, no. I have clothes." But despite my trying, I can tell by her silence that she's picturing me standing there in a prison uniform. "But there is something… I say, "I need you to call Mrs. Thompson and tell her to call the police station so she can act as a witness for me in court tomorrow."

No words come from the other end of the line, just the sound of her breathing and then a soft, "I can do that."

"How are the kids?"

Immediately, her tone lightens as she says, "They're good. Just want to know where their Daddy is and why he wasn't home to play football with them after school like he promised. Artie begged me all day long for ice cream after I made the mistake of spoiling them this morning and Emerson's just really looking forward to that trip to the Aquarium this weekend," she laughs, "he even made me stop by the library to pick up a book about fish."

I wish she could hear me smiling through the phone.

"Tell me I can tell him you'll be there when we go this weekend." There's a hint of a pleading tone in her voice.

"I'll be there."

SAMUEL NOBLE

Literally every set of eyes turns silently toward me and drills holes in my body as I walk down the hall to my first hour class. There are so many eyes drilling so many holes that I'm honestly worried there won't be anything left of me by the time I get to McAllister's door. The sea of eyes just stares at me, watching expectantly like they're waiting for me to burst into tears and fall on the floor. Some of the eyes are paired up with wide open mouths, just hanging there catching flies. Girls look at me, tilt their heads to the side and pout at me like I'm a little boy who just lost his teddy bear or something. Every time I make eye contact with a guy, he just looks down or away from me as soon as possible, but I can practically feel their eyes turning back towards me to drill more holes as soon as I pass them by.

Then the bell rings and life instantaneously returns to the halls of Wyatt High. The buzz and gossip of teenagers fills the narrow hallways as hundreds of students rush to their first hour classes. It's like they all forgot about me and Gregory that quick, and I'm reminded of that ceiling fan, and how it just kept on spinning just like the earth and all the people on it just keep on keeping on, no matter who lives and who dies.

Carter and I make eye contact as he stands stiffly against a row of faded metal lockers. Today, I don't care if I'm late for class.

"Hey man," I say.

"Hey Sam. How are you?" He's speaking a little slower than usual and sort of over-articulating his words like he's talking to a kid.

"Still here, aren't I?" I try to make it sound light-hearted, but it comes out suicidal. "You?"

"Hanging in there," he says, nodding. "You ready to turn up this weekend?" he asks as his tone returns to that of the Carter I've known for years.

"Turn up?"

"Yeah, the party dude, remember? Nonstop 12-hour grind!"

"Oh yeah. Right. I'll be there."

"Cool," he says, looking relieved. Then we go in for the bro-hug and he holds me for a half-second longer than normal. The most physical contact two guys can have without being accused of being gay; it's a wordless, 'I'm here for you.' I turn and watch Carter rush down the hall to his first hour English class.

My macroeconomics class has carried on without me for at least a full five minutes, but McAllister doesn't say anything to me, just gives me the same sad eyes I saw dozens of times in the hallway. As I weave through desks to my spot in the back of the class, everyone sits in complete silence. The kid on my right who asked me for drugs yesterday does everything in his power to not lock eyes with me. Instead he just flicks his pencil back and forth between his fingers nervously.

The class stands in unison as the recording of the Pledge of Allegiance plays over the intercom, and my body feels so heavy, I don't know if I've got the strength to stand through the whole thing. As usual, no one recites it with Principal Michaels. We just stand there in silence, eyes glazed over, with our hands over our hearts. Then something new happens. The real Principal Michaels comes over the intercom and says, "Please stand for a moment of silence in honor of Gregory Noble," and in that moment I feel like I might actually burst into tears and fall on the floor. But I don't. I just stand there, wrapped in the heaviness and tension filling the room, until the moment (which was really more like 30 seconds) of silence is over.

Mr. McAllister, who's wearing a hideous red and green plaid shirt today (which clashes horribly with his blue bow-tie), is walking down each row collecting some paper from each of the students. It's an essay- the one I didn't do.

"Hey... Sam," a deep, raspy voice calls from my left. It's the kid who thinks I'm a drug dealer. Looking into his deep sad brown eyes, I remember his name. It's James.

"Yeah?"

"I'm sorry for your loss." No one's ever said that to me before. Ever. There's never been a reason to. And now that there finally is, I have no idea how to respond. I mean what is it that I'm supposed to say to that? 'thank you'? As in 'I'm thankful for you being sorry for my loss?

That makes no sense. I just give him a half-nod and look away. Out of the corner of my eyes, I watch his fingers go back to fidgeting with his pencil.

"Samuel." I look up to see McAllister standing over my desk holding out a hand. "Your essay?" Oh right. The essay.

"I don't have it. I'm sorry," I say, but really I'm not sorry. I couldn't care less about some essay on the history of economic thought.

McAllister's face softens, and he says, "Have it here on Monday," then struts away from me in his tight red skinny jeans.

The rest of the day passes like a blur. A lot more people give me sad eyes and say, "I'm sorry for your loss," and even on the 14th go-round, I don't know how to respond.

In the cafeteria, I sit down next to Carter at our normal spot at the round table in the corner by the window. The cafeteria is filled with gray round tables and chairs that are way too tiny for the kids who use them. It's almost like whoever chose these tables and chairs for the cafeteria forgot they would be for high schoolers and not elementary school kids.

"So, about dat party doe." Carter says, his mouth full of cafeteria mac and cheese. I'm starting to catch on to the fact that Carter and I must have kind of wordlessly agreed not to talk about Gregory at all. I open my brown paper bag packed with the usual turkey and Swiss on sourdough with chips, an apple and a bottle of water. I can tell he's not genuine and is just trying to lighten the mood and not focus on the reason why the chair to his left is empty.

"Oh yeah, it's tomorrow?" I ask, even though I already know the answer.

"Yep. Tomorrow night man. I'm even willing to miss Morgan Freeman's *Through the Wormhole* to be there, and that says a lot because his voice is freaking awesome."

"Doesn't he also narrate that show *Cosmos* something or other?"

"Nah dude, that's Neil deGrasse Tyson. They don't look or sound anything alike besides the fact that they're both Black."

"Oh, so you're saying there are two different Black guys who host two different shows on outer space? Maybe we really are making progress," I say sarcastically.

"Yeah man, you should know that. I mean, you're Black. Don't all Black people like, know each other or something?" he jokes.

"I'm not all black." For whatever reason, I always feel the need to point that out to people. Even though I don't know who my birth parents are, and my adoptive parents have never been willing to shed much light on it (whether that's because they honestly don't know who they were, or because they just don't want me to know who they were, I'm not sure). I can tell by the color of my own skin, by how curly my hair is: I'm not all Black.

"True. That's true," Carter says, food hanging out of his mouth.

Before I know it, the day is over and I'm walking home from school alone. I've never walked home from school alone before. The silence pushes against my ears for the entirety of the 10 minutes it takes me to get from the double doors of the school to the front door of my house. No one is downstairs, but I can hear my mother's muffled cries coming from her bedroom, as well as the sound of my Dad shushing her, and I imagine him comforting her with his arms wrapped around her body. Both of them must have stayed home today from work. I was given the chance to stay home too, but opted to leave because sitting here listening to my parents cry would have been way too depressing.

Inside the house, I feel like I'm finally feeling the burden of all those holes people drilled into my back weigh on me. I drop my backpack by the door and head straight up the stairs. With each step, I feel like my heart is getting heavier and heavier, falling lower and lower into my chest.

The sound of her sobbing makes me sick. I shove my face into my pillow, so my parents won't hear me crying. Then there are footsteps and a knock on my door, then the sound of it creaking open. I scramble to sit up, my face wet, to see Mom and Dad standing in the doorway, his arm wrapped around her shoulders.

"Hey… Sam." I don't think they can tell I was in here crying, because my Mom says, "How you doing?" and steps away from Dad and into my room to sit on the edge of my bed. She reaches out to me, but I shrug away before she can touch me. She lets her hand fall back into her lap. Dad crosses his arms and leans against the door frame of my bedroom. "We got a call from ANN," he says, "you know that show *Yesterday With Jay and Monay*?"

They're talking about this morning news show hosted by these two people Jay and Monay. It's kind of like the Today Show. "Yeah, I've seen it a couple of times." I say, trying to keep my voice from cracking.

"Well she, I mean they want to have you on the show Monday. Do you think you'd want to go?" he asks.

"We'd have to fly to Atlanta," Mom says.

What the fuck? Immediately blinking the tears from my eyes, I turn to Mom. *How could she be asking me if I want to be on a fucking TV show?*

"Why would I want to do that?" I can't stop shaking my head at her in disgust.

Mom swallows. I partly regret whatever expression must

have been on my face, because I can tell by looking at her that it cut deep. "I-I... I'm sorry Sam," she pauses. "It's too soon. I don't know what I was thinking. I shouldn't have asked." She lowers her head with every word.

My heart drops slightly, just knowing that I hurt her, but just as I open my mouth to apologize, she stands swiftly from my bed. Offering me a sad smile, wrapping her arms around herself as if to retain body heat, and leaves the room, closing the door behind her.

MONAY DAVIS

"Hey Mo," Robert calls from around the back of the studio, "I have Mrs. Noble on the phone. She wants to speak with you."

Wow, that was quick. I don't know how Robert gets his hands on people so quick. "OK, that was quick, I'm coming on back," I say, as I stand from my desk.

I'm not sure how the conversation with my secret child's adoptive parents is going to go, and the uncertainty must show pretty obviously on my face because Jay gives me an encouraging smile and says, "You got this," while making a fist with his right hand. I chose parents for Samuel and Gregory before they were even born and had almost no interaction at all with the Nobles. They were there the day the twins were born, which was the same day I gave them away.

"Hello Mrs. Noble," I say as professionally as possible, gesturing for Robert to leave me alone in the office.

"Hi Monay, it's been a long time." Her voice sounds speculative, like she doesn't know what it is I'm up to. Like she's scared I might be trying take Sam away from her or something.

"It has been. Almost 18 years. I'm sorry for your loss."

"Same to you." She returns, and it takes a moment for me to realize that she's referring to the fact that I lost a son yesterday too. I don't know what to say next, so I say nothing, and she says, "So you want to have Sam on your show?" in a slow suspicious tone.

"Yeah, that's right. It'd be great to fly you guys out here Sunday and have you on the show Monday morning," I say, in the way I would to any guest we might have.

There's silence on the other end until finally she says, "You know that's against the rules... Of our contract, I mean. No contact."

Unfortunately, she's right- I basically signed away my rights to a relationship with my own children. For the first time since Gregory's death, I feel a sharp pang of pain in my heart that settles like a rock in my gut. "That's true," I say, choosing my words carefully, "but don't think of this as me having contact with Sam. Think of it as him giving the world his perspective. I mean this is a huge deal. There are riots taking place across the nation and people want an inside look. Also, this is strictly...business. It's strictly professional." I swallow hard, shocked in part by the ease in which I have just effectively dismissed the nature of my relationship with my son. It wasn't hard for me to do. It was too easy. There's silence, so I take it upon myself to fill it. "I mean I'd understand that you lost your son yesterday, so..."

"We lost our son yesterday," she corrects me. "And you're right. Sam's always been...like hyper aware of race and vocal around those issues," she says. "I'm just worried about..." she trails off and I know exactly what it is she's worried about; me.

"Mrs. Noble, you don't have to worry about that. Sam won't know anything, and I won't try to, you know, send any messages."

She sighs through the phone, "OK. I'll talk to him when he gets home from school and see what he says. I'm on board, but ultimately it'll be up to him."

"Of course," I say, suddenly feeling an unexpected burst of excitement.

"OK, and I'll just call this number back?"

"Yep, that'd be fine," I say, as the rock in my stomach transforms into a swarm of rushing butterflies. I'm going to meet my son.

"OK then, bye," she says.

"Bye," I say, hanging up the phone.

As I walk out of the office my face is plastered with a huge grin. Jay stands to his feet as I emerge from behind the wall and into the studio, as I try miserably to rid myself of the massive smile.

"So, how'd it go?"

"It went OK, I mean she's actually OK with it. She just has to check with Sam. Jay, I think I'm really gonna meet him!" I almost feel like I'm talking through tears of joy. Where did all of this come from? At what point did I start caring so much?

"What if he says no?" Jay asks.

"Huh?" I say, confused.

"What if...Sam says no?" he clarifies.

The swirling butterflies in my stomach turn back into a rock and the smile is all but ripped from my face. What if he does say no? What if he doesn't want to go? What if I'm selfish and insensitive for even asking him?

"Oh Mo, I'm sorry, I didn't mean to- I'm sure he'll say, he'll say yes," he backpedals, but for me, it's too little too late.

"We're live in five," Robert gives us our daily five-minute warning. Jay reaches to put his hand on mine, but I pull away and plaster a smile on my face. I, like most other hosts and entertainers, only ever let the world see the happy version of myself.

HUNTER GARRETT

Thin, spidery cracks litter the walls around me, and the ceiling above. I'm lying on my back against the thin cot in my cell, thinking about how badly I want to be outside right now with the boys, catching and throwing and tackling. With every sigh, a puff of visible air is expelled from my lips. 'Dragon breath,' Artie would call it. For me it's simply serves as evidence that it's the middle of winter, and these cells aren't heated in the least. And somehow, *I* am here. For the second time today, I find myself asking that unanswerable question: How did I get here? My hand, still wrapped in layers of gauze throbs against my chest. I don't know what time it is, but it's got to be late. It' silent, and I hear no commotion coming from the door that leads back to society.

"Hey!" a shrill voice screeches from the cell across from mine. I sit up and stare into the darkness as my heart pounds in my chest. I thought I was alone here. As I stand to my feet, a wave of dizziness washes over me, but I fight through it and make it across the room, reaching an arm through the bent, damaged bars of my cage to switch the lights on. They flicker and hum, before a dim light floods my space. In the cell across from mine is an old man huddled on the floor in the corner. He groans and covers his eyes in response to the sudden brightness coming from my cell. "When the hell did you get here?" I ask.

The man croaks out a laugh, pushes his long, stringy brown

hair away from his face with his dirty stubby fingers and says, "A long time. I've been here a long time." The guy is barefoot and has a beard that reminds me of the one Tom Hanks had in Castaway, and it's matted and sprinkled with pieces of food. From where I'm standing I can only imagine what he smells like. "You know what I can do?" The man continues, grinning, his eyes as wide as a madman.

I just stare at him, cradling my hand against my chest, while he pulls a few strands of his greasy hair into his mouth and starts *chewing* on the strands long enough for him to reach with his teeth. In between his chewing, he repeats, "You know what I can do?"

"What can you do?" I ask, my words twinged in disgust. When he spits, strands of wet, clumpy hair fall from his lips, some of them sticking to his wiry gray beard. The man suddenly jumps to his feet, and leaps to the front of his cell, his feet pounding against the cold concrete below us. When he jumps, my heart does too, and I'm startled backwards, stumbling a few steps away from the bars in front of me.

When he wraps his dry, bony hands around the bars, gripping them so tightly that his knuckles turn white, and puffs air out of his mouth and nose to keep the unruly strands of hair framing his face from falling into his eyes, I decide to stay far from the front of my cage. I'm honestly afraid I might catch something from him. "They tell me I can see things. I can see things!" he says. "They say I can see what's coming!" The guy has his face against the bars and his bony hands and overgrown, black fingernails are gripping the bars.

"See things?" I dare to ask, trying to suppress my brief flash of panic. This guy's right- he must have been in here for a really long time. I look towards the door leading to stairs that go up to the main open area of the police department. I'm halfway expecting to hear someone bust through the door to see what all the clanging and yelling was about, but nobody does.

"The future!" the man says, jumping up and down and throwing his hands into the air. And he starts to ramble: "I remember when I was a boy, in New Orleans, and there was this girl, across the street. And and and, I had a dream! I had a dream and I told her what I saw because she was, she was in it, she was in it."

The more he says, the more frantic he becomes. He's rambling, and his words aren't making any kind of sense. And for the first time all night, I'm genuinely happy to be locked in a cage where this maniac has no way of getting to me.

He continues on in fragments: "In my dream she got raped. There was this man, and he tricked her, said there was a puppy that was sick or whatever or he had candy or whatever, and she went and told her parents, and they thought I was crazy, they thought I was crazy! Then it happened, and they knew when it happened that I could see things." He's going on and on without even breathing. Each word just runs right into the next. I'm still standing in silence, when he says, "I saw you this time. Do you know what I saw?"

"Wha-," I begin.

"He kills you! He's gonna fuckin kill you!" He twists his hands back and forth on the bars in front of him with so much force the friction must be burning the palms of his hands away.

What the fuck? Is this guy threatening me now? His wild eyes pierce my own as I try to clarify his comments, "Hold on, hold on, who is it you think is going to kill me?"

The man puts a hand in his stringy hair and balls it up in a tight fist as if he's trying to pull it out. "Your son! They told me it, it's, it's gonna be him! I saw it!" Then the guy starts laughing. He's hysterical, like the Joker. He just laughs and laughs a loud cackle that ricochets off the cement wall where we're being kept. My heart jumps in a way it never has before, and I feel my body heating up.

"How do you know I have a son?" I ask, taking my first step in his direction.

The guy just keeps on howling. He's lying on the floor now, back resting against the cold cement, bare feet dancing in the air, but gives me no answer.

"Who told you that?" I demand, stepping up towards the front of the cell to grab the handlebars of my own cage. The guy stops his rolling and howling cackling and looks up at me from the floor of his cell. His expression changes from one of madness to one of fear, and his eyes get really big and round.

"It's the voices," he says softly at first, and then louder, "it's the voices, the voices, the voices!" until he's screaming and chanting it over and over and over.

"Hey, what are you doi-," I start to say, and then the guy cups his hands against his ears like a bomb just went off. And then he's crying and saying it over and over, 'It's the voices, the voices." Then he's on his knees, leaning forward and banging his head against the concrete. I yell at him to stop but it's like he can't hear a word I'm saying. He keeps going, banging his head again and again against the concrete floor, and when he lifts his head, his forehead is smeared and covered in blood and I think it's all finally over until he slams it down again.

SAMUEL NOBLE

 " *We have just received breaking news. The Dilson Police station has just released the name of the man who has confessed to fatally shooting unarmed teenager Gregory Noble. The shooter, 33-year-old Hunter Garrett, the night watchman for the pheasant run community.* "

I'm sitting on the stringy brown carpet of Carter's bedroom looking at the TV, when he goes, "Hey, man, want me to turn that shit off?"

It's been one day since Gregory died, and honestly at this point I feel so numb and empty, that I don't give a shit whether or not Carter turns off the TV. My brother isn't coming back either way, so I just shrug without looking away from that ROTC picture on the screen. The bed springs creak as Carter leans over and reaches for the remote on the bed next to him. The picture changes and I recognize the film immediately. It's *To Kill a Mockingbird*, the old black and white film with Gregory Peck from the 60s.

"This OK?" he asks softly. Before I have time to shrug again, the doorbell rings. I look up at Carter who says, "Oh," like he isn't surprised, then proceeds to look at me even more suspiciously, before jumping off the bed, pulling open the door to his room and bumping down the stairs. That was weird. Something's up. Standing to my socked feet, I follow Carter out of his room and lean against the railing of their stairs, looking down into the foyer where the front door is.

Carter takes a deep breath, exhales, then opens the door. Standing there in tight jeans and a black hoodie is none other than Amanda Bentley.

"Sup, Amanda?" he asks casually.

"Hey Carter." She lifts her head as if she knows I'm there and makes three seconds of eye contact with me that are just too real. The pain I feel inside of my body must be written across my face because when she looks at me, I can see that her eyes slowly fill with tears. I'm not sure if he knows that she saw me, but Carter opens his arms and embraces her in a warm, yet platonic hug. He leads her up the stairs, arm still wrapped around her shoulders in a 'just friends' kind of way.

All three of us are sitting on the floor in Carter's room, and *To Kill a Mockingbird* is still playing in the background. Amanda and I are sitting next to each other with our backs against the bed, and Carter's on the other side of the room against the wall. I can tell by looking out of the corner of my eye, that Amanda's eyes are glued to the TV, and Carter's to his phone. I'm trying to figure out why the hell he would have invited her over here.

"Wanna smoke?" she asks, leaning over to unzip her backpack. When she moves, her scent wafts towards my nose. It's light and sweet, maybe like vanilla or something.

"HECK yes," Carter says, dropping his phone on the carpet next to him and rubbing his hands together. Amanda pulls a Ziploc bag of weed and a lighter out of her backpack as Carter jumps up and runs across his room to open the window. I just watch, unsure; I've never smoked before. Amanda rolls a blunt and lights up. She's holding it gently between her fingers, and is just bringing it to her lips when Carter tells her to smoke out the window so his parents don't know he's smoking in the house.

She rolls her eyes at him like it's such an inconvenience to her, and says, "My parents wouldn't give a shit." As she drags her feet across the room, she leans over, until her head is out the window, pushing her butt out and resting her elbows on the sill. Carter looks at her ass then lifts his eyebrows at me, grinning. I shake my head at him and pretend like I wasn't looking too.

Carter walks up behind her, holds out a hand and says, "C'mon, don't hog it." She tips her head up at him sideways, her dark hair tumbling over her shoulder as she does, and passes the blunt to him. He pulls it from between her two fingers and leans towards the window, and brings it to his mouth.

She turns her head and studies me sitting there on the floor fidgeting with the corner of my phone case for a few seconds, resting her chin in the palm of her hand, elbow still against the window sill.

"You wanna try it Sam?" she asks in a tone somewhere between gentle and teasing.

"Umm…" I trail off.

"You ever done it before?" she asks.

Carter snorts with his back to me and says, "Nope."

Amanda ignores him and waits for me to answer. "Um no," I admit.

"Well, there's a first time for everything. It's not gonna kill you, I promise."

"Nah, I'm alright," I say.

Amanda drops her shoulders and pouts at me. "Don't be like that, just trrrryyy it," she coos.

111

"Really, I'm good," I insist, picking up my phone to pretend I'm looking at dank memes.

"Don't mind him, he's just a lil' pussy," Carter says laughing. And she laughs with him. He passes the blunt back to her. He walks back across the room to pick up his phone. Somehow even without looking up from my phone, I know she's looking at me again.

"It's trending on Twitter." Carter's voice is dead. I feel Amanda move her eyes away from me.

"What is?" she says.

"#GregoryNoble. It's fucking number one right now. People are saying all kinds of shit. They're mad as hell."

I almost don't believe it. Wordlessly, I tap my home button, and swipe haphazardly until I find the Twitter icon. Upon viewing the trending topics, I realize it's true. There are hundreds of thousands of tweets talking about 'justice,' and 'murder' and 'police brutality,' and there's pictures of him everywhere and I'm trying to figure out how they found all these pictures of my brother, and I'm scrolling so fast my thumb stiffens up. I don't even realize that Amanda has stepped away from the window sill, until she sits next to me again and pulls her own phone out of her bag as I take it all in.

There are dozens of memes, pictures of his face, plastered with words he never said, and criminal histories that don't exist. There are RIP hashtags and Black Lives Matter hashtags and Fuck Black Lives Matter hashtags and people saying the cop deserves to die and people saying Gregory deserved to die.

I refresh the trending page over and over. And then I see a Tweet with a video pop up. And I click that triangle on top of that blurry image, and some cell phone footage starts to play. It's from high above this grassy field, in what looks like a neighborhood. It's like someone was holding their phone out of a second-floor bedroom window. It's blurry, but I see that across the street there's a kid running in a red sweatshirt, and I recognize it. It's *my* sweatshirt. The one Gregory would always steal from my room.

And I watch, through that shaky cell phone camera lens as my red sweatshirt tumbles to the ground, as Gregory's legs flail in the air behind it. And there's yelling and when a man runs into the frame, I see that it's coming from him. He's slender, with long legs, and he's hobbling towards Gregory like he's got a bad leg, and when he gets close to him, my brother jumps into the air, and knocks the man down, and then there are gunshots. And the person holding the phone curses and ducks, so that briefly all I can see is a window sill. Then I can hear the person holding the phone breathing hard and then when they gather the courage to stand back up and when the grassy field comes back into frame, I see my red sweatshirt laying in the grass, and a few feet away is a body in a white T-shirt with two darker red spots expanding on the back. The person recording cries out, and I know they're shaking hard because the phone is moving around like crazy. But I've seen all I need to see.

I close the app, and I can't help it. Hot tears are rushing down my face and chin and I'm shaking. When I look up, I notice Amanda is looking at her phone and crying too, and Carter's on the other side of the room covering his face and wiping his eyes. Somehow, spontaneously, Amanda's warm body is against mine, and then I feel her wrap around my shoulders pulling me closer, and I just fall right into her until I'm leaning over so far, my head is practically in her lap. My body is trembling and so is hers and tears are blurring my vision and mucus is clogging up my throat. Carter's leaning forward with his hands holding his head between his knees. There is so much pain sealed up in Carter's room, I'm scared it'll bust the door open. Her hand is rubbing my back as we all sit there crying tears for Gregory. I don't know how long we stayed that way, but eventually, I feel my breathing return to normal and I slowly push myself out of Amanda's arms, and when I look at her face, it's red and wet and our eyes lock. I feel an urge to take away the pain that she is feeling in any way possible, and before I can think at all, my mouth is against hers and her lips taste slightly salty from her tears, and my body has never felt so warm. Then I remember about Gregory and jazz band, and *Footsteps in the Sand* and I pull away from her. Her eyes are still closed. I'm on my feet and the room is spinning, and why did Carter invite her here in the first place?

"Carter, can I talk to you?" My voice is cracking like I'm 12 years old again, as I stumble into the hallway. Carter's looking at me stunned, still wiping tears out of his eyes.

"Dude, why the hell did you invite her here?" I say, shoving him away from me. Carter's eyes pop open and even through his tears, he gives me a knowing look.

He laughs a groggy laugh and shrugs it off, saying, "What?" as if this is funny to him. I shove him again, harder this time. As he's thrown of balance, he looks at me, obviously startled.

"That's Gregory's girl!" My voice is still cracking, my cheeks wet. I know Amanda can hear me clearly from just down the hallway.

"Dude," Carter begins. His eyes are red, but he hasn't wiped that ridiculous grin off his face. Soon I'll have to do it for him.

"If Amanda was hot for Gregory, then she's probably into you too man. I mean let's be real here: You're fucking identical twins."

My body is hotter now than it was when I kissed Amanda, only this time, not in a good way. He's still smiling. I'm going to hit him. I'm really going to hit him right now.

I don't hit him. Instead I say, "You're so immature. And me and Gregory are different people, Carter. He was a much better human than I'll ever be. Don't fucking talk about him." And I push past him, grab my bag off the floor without making eye contact with Amanda, shove my feet back into my shoes, and bump down the stairs to leave.

HUNTER GARRETT

What is it with these gray skies? The wind comes, only to bite my ears, blur my vision, and burn my lungs. I'm standing in an open field; a field where every last strand of grass is dead. A pained screech, comes from nowhere. I spin around to its source and see a man standing in the distance. He's wearing a black leather jacket and jeans. The screech erupts again from his direction. Before I can choose to or not to, my legs take me in his direction. I'm running straight into the wind, breathless. Those loud, pained screeches keep filling up the field, bouncing off of the mountaintops in the distance. I'm behind him now. He has short red hair and his shoulders are bent forward too far to be normal. Again, the scream. The man doesn't move.

It's almost like the icy wind has frozen him to death. From behind him, I see on the ground, the edge of the red sweatshirt. He's standing over a body. It's the kid. His eyes are open so wide, I can see more white than I even thought a human eye had. His skin is so dark, his lips so chalky. His mouth opens to form an 'O' as the scream erupts from his dead body. He's alive. His eyes don't blink. I reach out a hand to touch the shoulder of the man in front of me. His feet stay planted, and his body square, as his head swivels like an owl's until he's facing me. His body is still facing the direction of the screaming kid on the ground. It's something out of a horror film. My body is robbed of every last ounce of oxygen as I stumble backwards and land on the dead grass. The man standing there is me, only his eyes aren't green like mine, they're black.

His eyes drill into mine, and he says, "Jump." The words linger in the cold dry air and the kid on the ground screams again. Then, the man throws his head back and lets loose a booming cackle that bursts from his chest. He's laughing like a monster, like some sort of insane, madman, maniac. He just laughs and laughs and laughs, his chin held high, his black beady eyes staring up at the sky. Then he gasps, and clutches, and crawls at his throat. He's gasping and gagging as his face goes red, then purple then blue, and his eyes bulge from their sockets. He grips his throat as he desperately gasps to get air back into his lungs. It's too late for him. He falls to the dead grass, and when his hands fall limply to his side, and I see what it is that killed him. It's a pair of dirty white shoelaces, tied around his throat, digging into his skin. The world spins around me as I stare down at myself laying strangled in the grass. The kid screeches on.

"Rise and shine Garrett." A gruff voice shatters the quiet air around me, and painfully bright lights burn my pupils even through my closed eyelids. I have no idea what time it is, but I'm damn sure it's too early to be waking up. Fuck. My back aches as I strain to sit up. The thin cot did little to keep the metal screws and imperfections on the bed frame from digging into my back overnight. I'm jolted fully upright and awake when a grinding, creaking, incredibly loud sound assaults my ears. Looking over, I identify the source of the noise, as a guard finishes sliding open the heavy, rusted metal door of my cell. Still squinting as my eyes adjust to the brightness, the guard says, "Let's go. Time for your bail hearing."

Shuffling to my feet, a cop gripping my elbow all the while, I emerge from the depths of my cell.

"Hey," I ask, turning to him. He ignores me, but I continue on anyway. "What was up with that guy in the cell last night?"

He pauses, turning to me, lifts an eyebrow and frowns. Then he says, "You were the only one we had in there last night."

I'm too confused and embarrassed to say anything else. There's no way that hobo banging his head against the floor was all in my head. Either this guy's fucking with me, or I'm going crazy...

The courtroom is not one of those large rooms you see on Judge Judy, but instead, it's a tiny space with a man in black, and a row of wooden benches.

In the front row of benches, all the way at the end is Ms. Thompson. She looks small and wrinkled as usual, and her wig is pushed too far forward, her shoulders sloping forward obviously burdened by the weight of the brutal aging process. As the cop leads me past the wooden rows, I lock eyes with her. The woman drills her eyes into mine, then nods the tiniest nod she could possibly give for me to still know it was a nod. Then she turns away from me to focus on the judge at the head of the room, and so do I.

MONAY DAVIS

I fucking love Atticus Finch. There's no other way to put it. The guy is an amazing and compassionate father, an epic lawyer and such an anti-prejudice person that he was willing to sacrifice his own career and reputation to defend a Black man in racist Alabama of all places. And yes, it's fair game for me to call Alabama racist because I grew up there- so I would know. Anyway, I've admired Atticus Finch ever since I was a little girl watching *To Kill a Mockingbird* on the floor in front of the TV with my mother. I would have named my kid after him, but let's face it; Atticus is kind of a funky name, so I settled with Gregory, like for the actor who plays him, Gregory Peck. Jay sighs from beside me.

It's Friday night and we're sitting side by side, shoulder to shoulder on the couch at his place watching the legendary film right now. "I don't find this interesting in the least," he whines. My shoulders drop, and my mouth falls open. I cannot believe what my ears have just heard. I refuse to. Jay might as well have just told me he's a Donald Trump supporter.

"How- what? How could you say that?" I say, stumbling on my words and making disorganized gestures to the TV.

"I mean it's in *black and white*," he says, exasperated and completely serious.

"But Jay, it's a cuh-lassic though."

He shrugs, "So what? That doesn't mean it's actually a good movie."

"Uggghh." I groan letting my head fall back against the couch cushion. "You don't get it, do you?"

"Get what? I mean the Black guy-."

"Tom Robinson. The Black guy's name is Tom Robinson," I correct him.

"Yeah, whatever. He dies in the end anyway."

"But that's not the point. I mean don't you get it? What Atticus stands for I mean? He stands for reason and morality and equality at a time and in a place where such principles are almost taboo in regards to race."

He stares at me blankly, and I know my words are going in one ear and out the other, but at this time I feel the need to continue. "And all of Atticus's beliefs and characteristics are constantly contrasted by the racism and hatred and bigotry that plagues Macomb County. And all of this," I say making a wide grand gesture, "is chronicled through the eyes of a small child. Don't you find that beautiful Jay?"

He's smiling at me and holding eye contact. Again, my heart flutters. *Brrrrriiinnnggg!!* My ringtone rushes in to ruin the moment. My body goes hot as I realize whose calling. It's Robert, who mentioned just as I left the studio, that he'd be calling to let me know about the interview.

"It's Robert," I say nervously, looking at Jay. He nods, encouraging me to answer. I take a huge deep breath, filling my lungs to the brim with air, before exhaling slowly to relieve my mounting nerves.

"Hello?" I answer.

"Hey Mo, it's Robert," he says as if I don't know.

"I know. I have your number saved in my phone," I say lightheartedly. Then there's silence. "So…" I pry, "any news?"

"I'm sorry Mo, but apparently the kid said no. He just wasn't feeling it."

Trying to ignore the fact that my heart feels like it's falling from a cliff, I swallow, straining to find the strength to make it sound like I'm OK. "I'm sorry to hear that, but thanks for letting me know Robert." My eyes meet Jay's and he offers me an empathetic look, placing his hand on my shoulder and running it down to my elbow and back.

"Yep, sorry Mo. Just wanted to let you know though. Good night."

"I'm glad you did. Good night Robert. See you."

As I hang up the phone, my heart feels so heavy, I'm worried it might act as an anchor and weigh me right down to the floor. Wordlessly, Jay reaches out and pulls me toward him, so my head is pressed against his muscular chest. His strong arms around my body feel like a healing cast surrounding my heart.

"I'm sorry," he says, and his deep voice causing his chest to vibrate. He pulls away and we look at each other in the semi-dark room, so close that the tips of our foreheads are almost touching. He lifts his head a little and the tip of his nose just barely brushes my own.

I let my eyes wander downwards from being locked with his to following the perfect lines that make up his strong jaw, to his brown lips and lower still past his chin, to the silky skin of his neck and collarbones, when I notice his Adam's apple bob in his throat; the unmistakable result of a hard swallow. And when I look back up toward his eyes, his head is angled slightly downward; his eyes are resting on my soft skin of my breasts peeking out from the top of my partially unbuttoned shirt. He looks up at me without moving his head, giving me that *look*, and instantly, my breath is gone from my lungs, stolen by the sheer intensity of his gaze searing into my eyes.

Then I find myself, partially against my own will, heart now fluttering haphazardly in my chest, saying "Jay."

He responds immediately with a breathy, "Yes?"

"It's late," I say, not wanting to rush into something I won't ever be able to take back.

HUNTER GARRETT

"Hey, Leah?" I say through the phone.

"Hunter? Oh my God, how'd it go?"

"50 thousand." I say as calmly as possible. The judge posted my bail at 50 thousand dollars." I can't even believe the words coming out of my mouth. There's no way. She doesn't say anything, so I keep talking to try and make her feel a little better, "But thanks so much for calling Ms. Thompson. She umm, she showed up." What I really meant to say is that she lied on my behalf. "I think that was a big reason why I got bail at all."

"Hunter." She cut me off there's a strange flare to her voice.

"Yeah? What is it?"

"Hunter I…." Then she starts giggling and the giggling just gets louder. Even though I don't know what she's laughing about, her giggles make me smile.

"Leah? What is it?"

"After we got off the phone last night, I started one of those GoFundMe pages."

"Go what? What the heck is that?"

"It's," she's still giggling softly, "like one of those website thingies where people can donate money." My silence signals her to continue. "And Hunter, baby, people did. People did donate money." My heart flutters. I dare to ask.

"Like…How much?"

"Like enough for us to get you out of there. Today."

The details of the next several hours are grossly unimportant. The next important thing that happened was me stepping into the passenger seat of our car, Leah at the wheel. I know I probably smell like shit, and I haven't brushed my teeth in 24 hours, but she gently grabs my face and kisses me anyway. Even though I saw her just yesterday, I feel like it's been ages since she did that.

"Where are the boys?" I ask, turning towards the empty back row.

"In school. It's Friday."

"Oh. Right," I sigh, a comforting feeling of normalcy rushing over my body. Even though I spent the last 24 hours in a jail cell, the world around me just kept on spinning as usual. It's incredibly good to know that.

"Let's get you home," she says, examining my obviously exhausted face.

"I love you." I say without thinking. Sighing a sigh that I know must smell horrible, I lean over against her anyway, I'm so fucking tired. I feel her smile as we pull out of the parking lot and head home. The skies are crystal clear for a change, as we drive past tall office buildings. It's midday, and most people are at work, so the roads are relatively quiet. I lift my head at the faint shouting I hear in the distance. As we make a left turn through downtown, the shouting gets louder. And when we turn the corner I see something that makes my whole body tense up and holds my gaze even through the rain-stained car window.

Thousands of people flood the streets, most of them Black. They're screaming and chanting something I can't decipher through the sealed car windows. They're wearing T- shirts and holding signs that all bear the same infamous and senseless message "Black Lives Matter."

"What the-," I begin.

"Hunter, it's OK. Don't worry about any of this." She cuts me off as we drive slowly past the raving negro savages blocking the streets. Just as she says this, my eyes catch sight of a large sign held high above the rioting crowd. 'JUSTICE FOR GREGORY' it says. And right beside those words there's a picture of the boy I killed.

"You knew about this?" I ask. She doesn't say anything, just grips the wheel tighter, and stares straight ahead, but I roll down the window to hear what it is they're saying.

Only a few yards away, and with the window down, I hear them clearly chanting, "Justice For Gregory! Justice for Gregory." Shit. So much for my fantasy about the world having maintained its balance of normalcy for the past few hours. The people keep on screaming, thrusting painted posters into the air. A row of well-armored officers stands stiff and tall in a line, keeping the protesters contained. A large Black woman screeches and curses at a motionless cop. She reaches out with a meaty arm as if to push him backwards, but before she even touches him, the cop sprays something straight into her eyes. She howls and stumbles backwards, as other Black people erupt into screams and rush the row of cops. Just then, a building takes the place of my view of the scene. But even though I can't see anymore, I can hear their words. I can hear sirens, and the sound of pepper spray cans hitting the ground, and I can hear them saying, "Hands up, don't shoot. Hands up. Don't shoot."

The further away we get from the crowds, the softer the chanting becomes. Eventually, the sound fades completely away, and silence lulls its way back into the car. A new concern dawns on me, and I turn towards my wife. "Leah? Did they… Did they like say my name on TV?"

"Ummm yeah," she says, "they did," and suddenly, this car is too small. This car is way too small, and there is not enough oxygen. I feel beads of sweat forming on the surface of my skin.

"Leah." My voice breaks. "Did they… I mean, do you think they know our address?" I ask, gesturing in the direction of the house as we pull into the driveway. I'm so glad we're finally here, because I swear this car was starting to feel way too small, and way too hot

As I emerge from the vehicle, a light flapping sound catches my attention. When I turn around, the first thing I see are those laces flapping in the wind against that clear blue sky. And for whatever reason, it's in that moment, as I'm squinting up into the sun, that I remember that the whole reason why that kid tripped and fell in the first place was because his fucking shoes were untied, and if they had been tied, he wouldn't have tripped, he wouldn't have charged me, and I never would have had to shoot him in the first place. My hands move slowly toward my throat when I remember what I dreamt last night.

SAMUEL NOBLE

It's an impossibly warm Saturday night, considering it's January, and I've got my bedroom window open to let some of the evening breeze inside. I did absolutely nothing but binge-watch Netflix shows all day from the safety of my twin-sized bed. I'm proud of myself though: It's the first time since Gregory died that I went a full day without crying. However, the absence of tears didn't keep a hazy cloud of darkness from weighing over my room all day. It followed me when I got up and left my room, to take a shower. It was there when I stood in front of the bathroom mirror to brush my teeth, it hung, drooping right over my shoulder when I went downstairs to rifle through the cabinets looking for food, and it returned with me as well, when I retreated back up to my bedroom for the day.

It may be true that had I left my room, maybe to interact with some other human being, the cloud may have stayed there in the room, and I'd be free from it, (even if only for a brief time until I returned.) But it's taken me so much of the day to process everything that happened last night with the video, and kissing Amanda, and almost punching Carter, that I just didn't feel up to bracing the wrath of the outside world.

It's 8:00 now, and even the unorthodox comfort that being alone brings can't convince me that I haven't been... I've been in here alone for too long. So, I drag myself out of bed. Somehow, even under the added, burdensome weight of the cloud above me, I manage to crawl out of bed, pull on a pair of jeans, a black T-shirt, and a jacket. When I get downstairs, Mom and Dad are sitting on the couch watching *House of Cards*, but when I walk past, I hear them pause the show. Silence. And then Mom goes, "Hi honey," in a tone ridden with artificial maternal sympathy. It's like she is too tired and too broken to keep putting this 'everything is okay' mask on, whenever I come around.

"Hey," I say without looking up, as I reach for Dad's car keys.

Before I can ask him if it's OK for me to use the car (I know that he'll say yes), he says, "Sam? Is that you?" and I can tell he's forcing it too, trying to be funny. "Haven't seen you all day," he chuckles. "I was starting to think you'd got lost in there. Like your room had just swallowed you up."

"Heh. Yeah," I say, "Can I use the car?" I ask, holding the keys up.

"Where you going?" he asks.

"Out with friends." This is the most ambiguous answer I can think of, and I can tell Mom isn't satisfied, but she doesn't pry. I think she would have if Gregory was still alive.

"Sure," he says. Everyone treats you differently when they feel bad for you.

I've always hated January. It gets dark too freaking early. The streets are dead and quiet as I let the window down a little and breathe in that crisp evening air. As I turn the car on, opting to keep the radio off, all I hear is the sound of the tires rubbing over the loose gravel at the end of the driveway as I cut the wheel and start down the road to leave the neighborhood.

The gentle chorus of the evening silence is interrupted by the introduction of some other, far away sound. The further down the road I drive, the louder it gets, and I can just barely distinguish that it is human voices that are responsible for the sound, though they are still too far away for me to know what's being said. As the faint shouting continues to emerge from the darkness, though I can't decipher the entire phrase, a single word stands out to me. Gregory. They are definitely saying Gregory. Justice. Justice for Gregory.

Their words become clear at almost the exact same times as the crowds come into view. I slow to a crawl and watch what has to be thousands of people crowding the street downtown, yelling and thrusting signs into the air. The chanting is entangled with the sound of glass breaking and wailing car alarms. In the distance, I see what appears to be a man standing on the roof of a car, stomping and leading some type of chant. There are *so* many people, moving in so many different directions, and the moment feels unreal. I duck, startled even from the safety of the car, as a helicopter rumbles overhead, shining bright lights and scanning across all the people below.

Cool air rushes in on my face as I prepare to screw up today's 'achievement' and start crying. But I don't. I don't cry. It's something else I feel right now. It's anger. It's anger for the fact that my brother's gone. Anger for all these random people out here protesting for and defending someone they don't know anything about, holding pictures of someone they never saw with their own eyes. I'm pissed that people are out here standing on cars, and screaming, and cursing out cops, breaking shit, and destroying our own streets and stores, like it's going to *do* something. Don't they know? This won't *do* anything, because right now, Hunter Garrett, the man who killed him is probably sitting in his filthy house on his filthy couch in front of the TV, laughing as he watches Black people once again take it upon themselves to destroy their own shit.

And suddenly I'm just so fucking mad, because it isn't fair. Black people get killed by cops every day, and this is all that ever happens. There's outrage, there's hashtags, and protests, and stealing and cursing at cops, and then in the morning, somebody has to come and clean up these streets. When it's over, somebody has to heal the community, somebody has to pick up the all the broken pieces left behind by all of the broken Black people who have mourned and cried and screamed. When it's over, somebody has to do twice as much work to try to go back and convince White people that we're not violent, we're not thugs, we're not dangerous, we're just tired. And we're tired of being killed. In the middle of the road, I stop the car, put on the emergency brake and bang my hands against the steering wheel, I guess because that's what angry people do in movies. There are no tears. Just me yelling and hitting that stupid wheel in front of me. I tell myself to breathe, and that I'm OK. I'm good.

Somehow, I pull away from the chaos, and in seconds, I'm back on a calm and quiet road, then pulling into Stephanie's driveway. When I open the car door, it feels like the music is so loud it's vibrating the whole house, including the driveway beneath my feet. A single thought runs laps in my head as I approach the front door is; *Please say Amanda is there, please say Amanda isn't there, please say-*. The door opens before my knuckles make contact with it to knock. It's Amanda. I'm pretending not to notice her ass-hugging black yoga pants when she says, "Oh…Sam. It's you." In a really disappointing voice. I know she heard everything Carter and I said about her last night, and half of me wants to tell her to never touch me again, and to stay away, but the other half wants to say I'm sorry about what I said, and that I didn't not like kissing her because I did. But I don't say anything. I just step forward into the doorway, expecting her to step backwards into the house, but she doesn't. She stays put, which means, that now our bodies are uncomfortably close together. I'm standing under a cloud (of marijuana) looking into her eyes, trying to figure out why she's standing so close to me, and I can tell by the wideness of her eyes that she's trying to figure out the same thing. She smells the same as she did last night, like vanilla.

Then Carter's voice rises up from the crowd. "Heyyy Sam," he slurs his words. "You know there's an empty room upstairs, right man?" And it just rubs me wrong. I sidestep Amanda to keep from knocking her off her feet, rush into the hot, crowded room, pushing drunk and high teenagers out of my way, grab Carter's left shoulder to hold him still, and bash my fist straight into his right eye.

MONAY DAVIS

I mean we were like legitimately, completely pressed against each other, and we were so completely alone and so completely *close*, breathing the same air, sharing the same heat and the same thoughts… and I can't lie: I panicked. I couldn't do it. It's been hard for me to get that close to someone for a very long time. The events of the night have been playing over and over again in my mind since I left his place, alternating with the unavoidable, insuppressible disappointment at Sam's desire not to come in for an interview. As much as I tell myself that it doesn't matter, that I did what I could to reach out, and that it's the thought that counts, I know it isn't true. And even though he's ignorant to the reality of the situation, his rejection gnaws at my heart. As I step into my apartment, I lean back against the door, using the weight of my body to shut it. Slipping out of my heels, I hear noise from the TV drift in from the den. The weather channel is on this time. Sometimes denial is the best medicine.

I'm hungry but too tired to do anything about it. It's just after 1:00 am, late enough for me to go to sleep and just wait until morning. I feel like I'm floating as I pass through my kitchen, across the smooth wooden floors of the TV room and into my bedroom. I flop against the mattress, every inch of my body tingling; partly from the remnants of the sparks and electricity Jay and I made just minutes before, and partly from the pain induced numbness and sense of defeat surrounding me.

It takes no time for me to escape into sleep, seeking refuge away from my pain.

Clouds of marijuana hang over my head, as I lay slumped, my blood alcohol content, obscenely high for a 15-year-old. It's one of those too hot days in May, and the lower level of the house is humid, and dozens of us reek of distilleries and weed. My head is pounding and covered in sweat, so I press my cheek against the cool white walls to ease the persistent throbbing wracking my skull. I need something to take the edge off.

Against all reason, I reach up to grasp the edge of the couch and pull myself up onto my wobbly knees, standing momentarily in a bent position as I wait until I feel steady before standing fully upright to refill the first red solo cup I see on the floor. As soon as I bend down and reach out for it, the wooden floor under my feet seems to slant sideways and my vision goes dark around the edges. A couple of people gasp as my body goes limp and I head for the floor.

I fall not to the floor, but instead into someone's warm arms. "Whoa there." A southern drawl comes from above me from a set of lips I can't see on a face I can't see because my face is pretty much buried in his chest, his arms wrapped around my waist. "You look like you could use a rest." The faceless voice speaks again, his hot breath tickling the tip of my ear. He's supporting 90% of my weight as I lift my head to look at him. I'm too drunk and too high to take in his features and the only thing I really notice are his super green eyes, and bright red carrot-colored hair.

Through my drunken haze, he looks nice enough to me that I mumble the words, "M'kay. I want to sleep," before carelessly allowing my head to roll right back into his chest.

I also trust him enough to let him drag me up the stairs to a bedroom at the end of the hall on the second floor. The carpet feels soft and fluffy under my bare feet as he leads me over to a bed against the back wall of the room, toes dragging, my arm draped listlessly over his shoulders. It's unfortunately ironic how we remember ever second of every detail of everything when something bad happens to us. The mattress feels like a weightless cloud under my dead, sloppy-drunk weight. As soon as my body falls against it, my arms fly limply outwards.

"Thanks," I slur from my sprawled position, expecting him to leave.

My breath comes slow and easily now that I'm comfortable, weightless. My heart calms as well, locked safely away in my chest, my eyes shielded from the harsh lights they had to hide from just moments before. The music is now only a faint muffling that drifts up the stairs and seeps through the cracked open door to the bedroom and my mind cherishes the silence as the pounding in my head begins to fade. I'm protected and at peace in this sphere of darkness and semi- silence; safe enough to drift off…

My eyes are closed, but I know I didn't hear his heavy footsteps leaving the room, or the soft creak of the door closing behind him. Struggling to open my heavy eyelids, even in the darkness, I see his skinny form standing at the edge of the bed. I watch his silhouette sway as he backs over to the door, closes it silently, then creeps back to his position, leaning over me. Even after however many drinks, and a couple hours of sitting in a pot-filled bubble, I know this is bad. I struggle to sit up, but he reaches out and pushes me back against the bed. His outstretched arm catches the moonlight flowing through the window for a brief instance, and I catch a glimpse of a little tattoo on the underside of his wrist inked to look like the scowling face of a tiger against his pale milky skin.

"Shhh," he says with a bony finger pressed against his lips as the bed creaks under the weight of his mass moving onto the bed to straddle my body. I open my mouth to scream, but he moves his warm, meaty hand over my lips, sealing in the sound. "Shhhhh," he says again, the whites of his eyes drilling into mine against the darkness. "Don't make me hurt you." He moves his hand slowly down from my mouth and wraps his fingers around my throat. He squeezes tighter and tighter, his eyes wild with the thrill of it.

"Shhhhh," he repeats, even though I haven't said anything else. This time he's so close to my face I can smell his breath. It doesn't smell like pot or alcohol, but like... potato chips; the guy is stone cold sober. Keeping one set of fingers wrapped around my throat, he slides the other down my body, between my breasts and over my stomach until he gets to the top edge of my jeans. He unzips them, the whites of his eyes, glued to mine as he does so. When I try to scream, he tightens his grip around my throat until I retreat back into silence. I struggle against the hand ripping my jeans from my body, but it makes no difference. When I try to sit up, the hand shoots up from my waistband to wrap around my neck and knock me backwards against the mattress.

I hear his belt unbuckle. I hear it hit the floor. And I watch as he removes his other hand from around my neck and spread my legs. I kick wildly, trying to get him off of me, but he just shifts his weight over me and pins me against the bed, one hand still sealed firmly against my lips. I strain against him, struggling to sit up, or roll over, or something, but my strength is no match for his mass.

He forces himself inside of me. It was the worst pain I've ever felt in my life. Hot tears rush out of my eyes as I continue my attempt to fight him off through my drunken haze, but my skinny arms slapping haplessly against his chest do nothing to stop his thrusts, and the deepest pang strikes my soul with each one.

I'm finally able to scream, as neither of his hands are covering my mouth, but now I realize it doesn't even matter. To the outside world, I'm a girl pinned under a man against a bed in a locked room at the end of the hall on the upper level of a house filled with two dozen other kids listening to music loud enough to rattle the Eiffel tower. In defeat, I slump into silence against the bed and let my arms fall beside me. My tears run all over my face and sideways back into my hairline.

He leans down and kisses my cheek as I cry. My body is so frozen and

135

paralyzed with fear that I'm not even sure my heart is still beating. And then he makes the most repulsive sound my ears have ever witnessed. It's like some sort of a snort. It's deep and hideous, and loud enough to fill up the entire dark and silent room.

"'Scuse me," he mumbles, like he's trying to be polite.

And then I guess he's done because he moves from on top of me and his feet hit the floor with a soft pat, and I just lie there listening to the jingling of his belt buckle and the zipping of his fly and the creaking and soft thud of the door closing behind him.

The hint of light from the early morning sun seeping into my bedroom and past my eyelids summons me both to an awakened state, and back to 2016. The sexual sparks I went to be with bled over into my dreams as they often do, and brought back unfortunate memories I never wanted to remember, let alone relive. Rolling over onto my stomach gives me the illusion that maybe, if I press my face against the pillow hard enough, I can snuff out all my past experiences, extinguish the lasting pain from my mind and smother away any remaining memories.

When I sit up I push all the darkness out of my thoughts automatically. It's something I've learned to do so well, I've had no choice. Pain and baggage like that is far too heavy to have to lug around every day and I've gotten almost too good at setting it aside.

Driving to church Sunday morning, I'm replaying all of this over in my head. How Jay hugging me Friday night sent all those memories rushing back at me full speed. Suddenly I felt like that 15-year-old girl again, being suffocated by a monster. I don't know his name, or how old he was, or where he went to school. I'd never seen him before, and I haven't seen him since. I remember that tiger tattoo, and I remember that animalistic sound he made, before he excused himself, and left. I cried every day after that for a year. I cried when I got home from the party I never should have been at. I cried when I realized I could never tell anyone what had happened to me, including my mother, because if I did, it would never be anybody's fault but mine. I cried when I missed my period. I cried when, after walking to the little family-owned pharmacy up the street one day after school, I got a positive test result in that same pharmacy bathroom stall. I cried when I sat in my room and crafted the story I'd told my mom and everyone else, which was that I had met a guy at a party and had sex with him, because it was easier to tell people that I'd made the choice to do it than it would have been to tell people that something so precious was taken away from me.

HUNTER GARRETT

"So first you go like this. And then you pull this around here like that. And then you push this end in there like so." I'm standing in the mirror next to Artie and Emerson, trying to teach them how to tie a tie through demonstration. Artie is standing next to me, barefoot on the tile floor, chin pinned to his chest, trying to guide the bottom end of the tie through the loop at the top. I can tell by the way his tiny fingers twist the material that today won't be the day he learns how to put a real tie on by himself.

"Like this Dad?" Artie asks, his tongue hanging out of his mouth as he focuses intently on the knotted-up tie hanging around his neck.

"Hmm. That's pretty close, bud," I lie. Emerson looks at me like I'm insane. He's got his own tie on correctly, and is old enough to know that his brother looks ridiculous with that twisted up tie hanging off his neck.

"Artie," he says, crinkling his nose to push his glasses back up, hands free, "you have to do it like this." He unties his tie, then instructs Artie with a demonstration.

A soft chuckle comes from behind me. It's Leah. I turn to see her enter the bedroom. She looks absolutely stunning in a long light gray dress, her hair dancing at her shoulders. "Wow," she says, reaching out to ruffle Artie's hair, "three handsome

138

men." She leans forward, and kisses one of the bruises on my face.

"Mommy look!" Artie screams, standing tall and pointing at the knotted tie around his neck. "I did it myself!" Emerson rolls his eyes.

"Wow," she says in that motherly voice she always uses with them, "I see that." She laughs again.

"We're still going to the aquarium today, right?" Emerson asks, annoyed.

"Of course, we are Em, why wouldn't we? Now let your Daddy fix your tie, Artie," she says, laughing and leaving for the closet.

"Alright, come here." I say, dropping to my knees and gesturing for Artie to come towards me. After decades of tying ties, I get the job done in seconds, and I'm just standing back up to take care of my own tie when I hear, "Daddy, can you help me?" It's Artie, looking up at me, with big round eyes, two tiny black dress shoes in tow. Those laces are hanging down on the sides, their ends frayed from being dragged across the ground. He's waiting for me.

"Ummm. I…" Through the corner of my eye, I catch a glimpse of Leah pausing on her way back downstairs, seemingly intrigued by my apparent hesitation at our son's innocent request. But I can't do it. I can't because I keep imagining those things tied around my throat, strangling me, as if to avenge the dead. Leah's eyes are drilling holes into my back and Artie's still standing there holding those shoes out in front of me. But I can't do it, so I say, "Daddy's gotta finish up something. Why don't you ask your Mom to do it for you?" Artie doesn't think twice about it. He just turns away, skips over to Leah and says, "Mommy, can you put these on?" I can feel her eyes on me, but I return to the mirror to finish getting dressed.

"Oh Artie," she says, you're a big boy. How old are you now?"

"Five!" Artie shouts.

"Five? At five, you're starting to get old, she coos. "I know you can put your shoes on by yourself."

"Okay," he reluctantly agrees. I just need help tying them."

"Yes, you do," Leah laughs. "Your shoes are always untied!"

SAMUEL NOBLE

That kid just doesn't know when to give it a rest does he? I mean after what happened when he invited Amanda over? After I told him, *that's Gregory's girl, Carter, you know that's Gregory girl.* After I told him off and stormed out of his fucking house he still had the nerve to make a joke about us at the party in front of dozens of people? I should have done a lot worse than just punch him. It's Sunday. Mom and Dad are at church, but I decided not to go. It's just too difficult to go sit there in the pews like everything's okay. Fake hugs and fake love from the congregation won't do anything to make anything better

I'm lying on my bed in silence, watching that ceiling fan go round and round trying to figure out what the hell is wrong with me. It's odd, how I'm feeling right now. There's no sadness inside of me anymore which seems weird since Gregory just died on Thursday. I never would have guessed I would have gotten over it so quick. Based on how I bawled my eyes out at the police station, I would have thought I'd still be crying 10 years from now. But what's inside my heart today is the same thing that was there last night in the car at the protests. It's anger. It's hot and it's red and it's dangerous, and worst of all, it's growing and expanding by the second. I can't stop thinking about how nothing ever *does* anything. Like the protest. What does it do? Does it take any pain away? No. What does forced sympathy from people at church do? Does it bring Gregory back? What does all the people saying I'm sorry for your loss do? Is anyone punished? Is anyone held accountable?

I'm wishing there was some way for me to just talk to everyone at once, when I realize there is a way. I shoot my Mom a text.

My phone buzzes on my nightstand.

Carter: Hey man

Me: Face OK?

Carter: All good

Me:

Carter: I'm really sorry. Should have kept my mouth shut...I guess I was just trynna make the situation less bad. Maybe make you laugh, or at least distract myself. I'm sorry for real.

Me: I shouldn't have punched you.

Carter: Are we cool? If not, I have an idea

Me: What?

Carter: You know water can really help you chill. Like my parents have all these miniature water fountains and waterfalls and shit all over the house and they're always telling me how the visuals and sounds that water creates is really soothing and shit

Me: Umm...okay?

Carter: So last night when I came home with a black eye, they didn't say anything, but when I woke up I saw that they had put this mini fountain on my nightstand. And at first, I was like wtf? Is that supposed to make my eye better? But the longer I was in there I kinda realized, like, that stuff really does help you chill

Me: True. So, what's your idea?

Carter: The aquarium

Me: WTF? Why would we go to the aquarium?

Carter: Water= Calm

Me: Carter, that's not a legitimate reason.

Carter: It is a legitimate reason, it's just not the only reason. The other reason is that my parents want me to take my brother there. They think it will be good for him. Plus, we get in cheap with student IDs.

I'm still really pissed at Carter, but I know it took a lot for him to actually bring himself to apologize to me, and honestly, I have nothing else to do today, so I say...

Me: Sure. What time?

Carter: Come by in an hour?

Me: Sure.

MONAY DAVIS

Numbness fills my body to the brim on my way to church. Though I was struck by the pervasiveness of the sparks we'd automatically and seamlessly created in each other's presence, being that close to someone always reminds me of what happened to me. It's like, in order for me to experience anyone else in an intimate way, I must also brave the side effect of being forced to relive my rape. For me, touch goes hand in hand with a replay of the first time a man ever touched me, and I become that 15-year-old girl again, suffocated by a monster, doomed to wallow in pain and resentment for an eternity. I swear those flashbacks are so real.

It's one of those gray days inside and out, as both my heart and the storm-colored skies are matching hues. There's no need for music; the soft patter of droplets hitting my window, accompanied by the alternating swipes of my windshield wipers across the glass does just enough to stave off the silence I work so hard to keep from consuming me.

Unfortunately, the make-shift tune created by the raindrops and wipers isn't enough to keep me from thinking. There are just too many things going on, and I'm pulling up and dusting off old memories and secrets I'd worked so hard to lock away in the furthest, most obsolete corners of my mind. I'd moved out of Alabama, given them away, graduated, graduated again, gotten the big job, the ritzy apartment, the flat screen TV that fills up the room with noise for me, so I don't have to be left at the mercy of my ever-churning mind, and still there is no escaping, no blocking it out, no running away from my past. The skeletons in my closet are standing up, and on the move and clawing at me from the deaths of my subconscious, beckoning me with bony fingers, to return to the dark place I vowed I'd never go back to.

But I can't help but drown in thoughts and memories of Gregory and Sam and how that monster of a man is the reason why I even had to make the decision to give them away. When I looked into their eyes, seconds after they were born, after I got past their curly hair, and tiny toes, and adorable 'O' shaped yawning mouths, I got flashes of him. Of that horrible tiger tattoo and that disgusting potato chip smell. And so, I knew that I had made the right choice in giving them away. There is no way I would have been able to take those boys home with me. They served only as reminders of what had been done to me, and of what had been taken away from me. There was no way I would ever be able to look at them and not see and feel all those things. And now here I am, 17, (almost 18) years later, one of them is dead, and the other one, I may never see again.

"I'd like... to take a moment, to discuss what it is that's been going on in our *community*." Pastor Wallis stands at the front of the church speaking slowly, in statements and phases separated by frequent pauses and exaggerated inflection, as he often does. "And do not be mistaken: by 'our community', I do not mean the Atlanta Metro Area. I'm talking, about what's going on in the *black community*, and particularly with our young black men and boys." He wears large black glasses with so-called 'hipster' frames, which is odd considering the man has to be in his seventies.

The place is full today, and rows and rows of stereotypical

church folks crowd the pews. There's something inexplicably comforting about being around a lot of other Black people. It's like for once, I don't have to be defensive or explain why my hair is springy and kinky, because we're all on the same page when it comes to cultural issues and politics. I mean, let's be real: Black Republicans are like unicorns, they're talked about but never seen. I bet White people feel the same way about other White people. I'm sitting about three rows from the back, subtly scanning the people around me. Occasionally, Jay shows up here, and I'm really hoping that today he does.

"As you all probably know, another young Black teenager has been shot and killed by a White man with a gun." Oh no. Pastor Wallis, please don't talk about this. I'd been avoiding the news at all costs, just so I didn't have to hear about it. "And just like we've seen previously, when events like these have taken place before, the shooter, a man named Hunter Garrett, has been released on 50,000-dollar bail."

I'm assuming Hunter Garrett is the name of the shooter. "And...what really hurts me," Wallis places his hand over his chest, "the reason why this man, this murderer was able to get out of jail is because thousands," he makes a mild gesture, "of Americans took the liberty of sitting down, logging onto the computer and giving money to support this man and bail him out of jail." What? The man who shot a kid--*my son*--in cold blood is out on the streets? I want to scream, and I'm about to until I remember I'm in church. "And like before," Pastor continues, "we're seeing *riots* break out all across the nation. "Black Americans who are angry, and frustrated, and fed up with this corrupt justice system are taking to the streets to fight for the prosecution of this man Hunter Garrett. But, my brothers and sisters, in the process they are destroying their own neighborhoods and looting their own stores. I would urge you all to protest in peace and without violence, the way our brother Martin Luther King Jr. taught us to, so many years ago." The multitudes of people erupt into decibels of clapping in support of the Pastor's words, while I sit in silence, unsure of what to do. At least it's over.

"And so now," he continues, "I'd like to welcome Sister Tamara Moore to speak briefly on the loss of her son Benjamin. Let's give her a hearty Amen this morning." 'Amens' come from all around the congregation as a short, dark, morbidly obese woman waddles her way to the front of the church.

"Good mornin," she says.

"Good morning," everyone else says.

"So as many of you already know," she begins, switching the microphone to her other hand, "my son Benjamin Michael Moore was shot and killed by a police officer last summer. He was 16 years old." I sit in silence while I come to grips with the fact that there's no sense in me feeling sorry for her, since she and I are essentially in the same shoes. "Ben was out one-night driving home alone from a party. He was not drunk, or under the influence of any substances, but he was driving too fast--just five miles per hour above the speed limit. A White police officer pulled Ben over, and asked to see his license. When he reached over to get his wallet, which had fallen to the floor of the passenger seat, the officer falsely assumed Ben was reaching for a gun."

The woman puts her hand over her mouth. She closes her eyes, and when she opens them again, a wet trail of tears shines against her brown skin. She moves her hand away in strength and continues on. "So, he pulled out his own gun, and fired six times. My Benjamin was hit twice in the chest." Though the woman is steadily crying now, I can tell even from here that she is clothed in strength. The congregation comforts her with verbal encouragement. "And the, the man… who ki- killed my son," her voice shakes, yet is loud enough and full enough not to be mistaken for weakness, "is still out there." She lowers the mic from her face and sighs, trying to and succeeding in maintaining her composure. "So… what I would like to say to all of ya'll is that you should just remember, throughout all of this, that this boy Gregory, who was killed, was a real human who was loved deeply by his mother and father and any siblings he had and that you just have to remember that and be respectful of it, and treat him like a person and not solely like a political issue, or as an excuse to destroy our own streets." After a brief silence, the congregation around me stands to their feet, and bursts into a supportive applause.

I stay seated, and the woman on my left grabs, my shoulder, startling me out of a trance. "Are you alright?" I'm looking up at her trying to figure out why she looks so concerned when I realize my cheeks are wet, for the first time since Gregory died. Only now am I experiencing just the slightest hint of the pain a mother feels at the loss of her child. I'm about to tell the woman I'm fine, and that the story just had an impact on me, when my phone vibrates in my purse. It's Robert. A wave of excitement flashes over my body as I look back up to smile and nod at the concerned woman, forgetting what it was she had asked. Side-stepping through the row of people in the pew, then turning out into the center aisle, I disappear quietly behind the church door of the sanctuary. When it shuts behind me and the clapping and talking is contained, I realize how heavy I'm breathing, and how hard my heart is thumping in my chest.

"Hello?" I answer, wiping the tears from my chin, caught simultaneously in a frenzy of darkness and unbridled hope and anticipation.

"Hiya, sorry to bother you Mo, I know you're probably in church right now."

"Hey Robert, no it's no problem. What's up?" I ask attempting to put forth a calm and collected tone.

"I got a call back from Sam's mother. She says he texted her out of the blue and changed his mind about the interview. He wants to come in tomorrow."

When those words make it from Robert's lips to my ear, my face smiles so wide, it's hard for me to move my mouth in the way I need to, in order to form a word.

"Wow, that's, that's great!"

"So, it's all good for you? You're set for it?"

"Yep. All set, Robert. Thanks."

"See you Monday. Enjoy your Sunday."

HUNTER GARRETT

Tiny, sticky fingers press against the back of my neck as Artie squirms and twists in my arms. There are tons of people crowding the spaces around the wall-size fish tanks. Within these crowds Artie feels the need to disappear constantly, so I've got no choice but to hold him, unless I want to see his face on the back of a milk carton. His hands are still partially coated in the yogurt he refused to let us wash off of his hands after lunch.

Leah and Emerson are a few paces behind, stopping to read the little information thingy at each tank, at Emerson's request. I'm feeling pretty OK right now. And even if I wasn't I'd have to fake it. Going to church honestly helped a lot. I wasn't alone there. Everyone supported me, and everyone understood. Nobody gave me dirty looks, but instead hugs, and firm handshakes, and promises that they'd be praying for me. They sided with me, which was refreshing after having heard people call me murderer.

Pastor MacGruber actually talked for a while before the sermon about how the south has become corrupted in many ways, both by Blacks who think we owe them something, and by the twisted liberal politicians who agree with them. Overall, it helped me to realize that I'm really not alone, and that assurance truly eased my mind to peace.

"Oohhh Daddy look!" Artie unapologetically screeches into my ear. "What is it?" he asks, his eyes wide. I turn towards the tank to see globs of jellyfish suspended in the water, drifting about as if in slow motion.

"Those are jellyfish buddy," I say, lowering him to the floor and watching him run over and press his face against the glass.

"Oohhh," he says in awe, "what are those stringy things?"

"They're called tentacles."

"Why do they need Tent-claws?"

A small voice from behind me goes, "C'mon Artie, they're called TENT-AC-LES, say it right." It's Emerson, who's just caught up to us. "And their tentacles help them move and capture prey."

All I can do is look up at my wife and smile. Our eyes meet and nonverbally we say to each other, "Can you believe our seven-year-old is that freaking smart?" Her expression changes, and her face crinkles up. She's not looking at me, but past me. She puts a hand over her mouth and takes steps backwards until she's practically pressed against the tank of jellyfish, eyes wide.

Before I can turn around, Emerson points in the same direction and says, "Look Daddy, it's Gregory." Chills rattle my spinal cord. Should I even turn around? I shouldn't turn around. I turn around and there he is. He's got the same skin color, same eyes, same build, same exact face, and he's looking me right in the eye. His shoelaces are untied. His body is stiff, his neck taught, his face unmoving, his hands twisted into fists at his sides. Blinking rapidly, I'm tempted to pinch myself. Maybe I'm dreaming. Artie grabs hold of my leg, gripping onto the bottom of my pants, obviously frightened. I can't breathe, I can't even breathe. Everyone's looking at me. My stomach lurches, and I know I'm gonna be sick.

SAMUEL NOBLE

"Nigga, I am telling you though, Donald freakin' Trump could actually be our next President." Like I said, the only thing worse than a guy that calls himself Daddy, is a non-Black guy who thinks it's ok to call people 'nigga', and apparently, Carter is both of these guys. We're at the aquarium just wandering around aimlessly between walls of people staring at floor to ceiling fish tanks.

Matthew is slightly ahead of us, moving excitedly from tank to tank, wide eyed and in awe through his innocent and simplistic fascination with fish. I can tell by the way he half skips from display to display, red sweatshirt hanging haphazardly off of his shoulder, that he is completely consumed. With every glimpse I get of the childish grin on his face, my mind is flooded with memories of when Gregory and I were that age.

Matthew, being seven years old and slightly autistic, is just so happy, so blissfully unaware of the pain and suffering in the world around him, and it's beautiful. Although it's been a little awkward hanging out with Carter and trying not to look at the black and blue mark I left on his face, being a part of making his little brother that happy, has made it all worth it. Every toothy grin of his reminds me that there is still good in the world, and a thought like that does way more for my mental peace than trickling water or whatever.

"So, how'd you explain that to your parents?" I ask,

gesturing towards his face.

"Oh, this little thing?" he laughs a fake laugh. "I told them I was at this party, and there was this guy starting to mess around with this girl who obviously didn't want to mess around, so I got up and went over to see what was up, because that's just the knight in shining armor I am." He's explaining this to me almost like he's recounting something that actually happened, rather than explaining some unlikely fantasy. "So, I went over and got between this real aggressive older guy, and this poor helpless girl," he continues, "and he just boom," he pounds his fist into his hand, to demonstrate, "hit me right across the face. And that fountain was there in the morning."

"And they bought that?" I ask, humored.

"Of course!" He throws his arms dramatically into the air before bringing his hands over his heart and saying, "They could never believe their perfect little Asian son Carter would do anything wrong." Carter turns his head to check on Matthew, making sure he hasn't gone off too far.

Following Carter's gaze, I see Matthew jumping up and down and clapping excitedly in front of a tank full of jellyfish. "Was that you're first time ever hitting someone like that?"

"Umm, yeah. I'm not really about that violent life you know?"

"No, yeah, I get it. I get it, you're about that pacifist life. Asalama lakum, my brother," he jokes, lowering his voice and over-enunciating his words. I laugh, amused partially by Carter's poor accent, and partly by his consistent ability to crack jokes and be funny regardless of the circumstances, friends dying, fist fights, or otherwise.

The aquarium is crowded and dimly lit. In the semi-darkness, the people look like shadows moving in waves from one tank and display to another. I can tell Matthew is just about worn out by the way he actually drags a bit behind us now. Whenever he gets too far away from us, he takes a few quick steps and grabs onto Carter's arm without him even having to say anything. The blue and green lights shining through the water in the tanks cast an eerie glow on the aisles and on the people passing by. In the tank on our left there are these little fish with massive lips. On the sign next to the fish says, 'Kissing gourami'. The little guys are only a few inches long, and every now and then two of them will pair up and do what actually looks like kissing. Carter laughs, and I'm expecting him to make some lewd joke, but he doesn't; probably because he remembers he has an exhausted seven-year-old in tow.

Now that I know I wouldn't really be cutting Matthew's fun short, I'm about to mention to Carter that we'll have to leave soon so I can get home and head to the airport, when he stops walking and I nearly run right into him. "Bro, what? -" I begin, before turning to look where he's looking. And when I look where he's looking, I see what he sees. He's thinner in real life than in the pictures I've seen on TV. But even so, his features are distinct enough that I can tell it's definitely him. Something catches Matthew's eye out of the corner and he immediately attempts to bolt in that direction, but Carter's arms are on his shoulders lighting fast, pulling him back and holding him close. But for a split second it's me he should be holding back. My face goes hot, and I realize both of my hands have instinctively formed themselves into fists, and every fiber in my body is telling me to rush him. I'm just staring at his side profile, and time slows down, and I easily have four or five inches and 30 plus pounds on him. And my left foot actually takes a half step towards him when I remember the way I felt in the car last night, and I'm thinking about how I'm a Black man in a sea of all these fucking White people, and how nothing I do here can end well for me. And my body relaxes.

"How is he out?" I ask Carter through gritted teeth.

Carter shrugs. "I mean... I knew there was a chance he could get out on bail, but I didn't actually think that...he actually would." My blood rushes in my ears.

A woman, his wife I presume, is standing beside him in a dress and two little kids, are standing at their feet. The younger one, who's got his face pressed against the glass, keeps turning around to face his father like he's asking him questions or something. The taller one keeps pushing his glasses up his nose like some sort of certified nerd. Then he points right at me and says something to his father. The mom has her hand on her face and looks like she'd be on the floor right now if it weren't for the tank behind her. Hunter Garrett turns around and looks at me. His eyes stay green as ever, but his face goes pale. He's panicking, and I'm thinking about how much my brother probably panicked when he looked at that face and realized it would probably be the last one he'd ever see. We stay that way for a while; me looking at him, him looking back at me. Then he turns away and immediately disappears into the shadows around us, his wife calling after him.

HUNTER GARRETT

Waves of people part like the Red Sea before me as I rush to the end of the earth- or at least as far away from that kid as I can get. I barrel into the door to the men's bathroom. Thank God nobody's in here. Sweat is soaking through my white dress shirt, yet my body feels cold. Shit, my hands are shaking. This has to be a dream. There's no way that kid could have been there. I know he's dead because I'm the guy who fucking killed him. It must have been a hallucination. It had to be.

But Emerson. Emerson's the one who pointed him out to me. So, he must've seen him too. I look into the bathroom mirror just as hot tears spring from my eyes. Another wave of nausea crests in my stomach, and I'm forced to lean forward and grip the edge of the sink to support my weight. Holy crap. Am I crazy? First the madman in the cell and now this? Still crying. How did this happen? Even my kid knows I'm a murder. He said it so matter -o-factly too. *Daddy look. It's the black boy you killed.* Why am I banging my hands against my head like this? There's not enough strength left in my body to keep me standing. I don't fight against the weight of my body crumpling to the floor. The tile feels cold against my back. I can't go back out there. My heart beats slow as I lay on the floor of the Aquarium bathroom.

I'm startled by a knock at the door, and by the soft, muffled voice that follows, "Hunter?" It's Leah.

I'm laying here crying on the dingy aquarium bathroom floor, but I say, "Yeah?" Like everything's OK. There's a pause, and then she says, "Are you alone in there?"

Oh shoot. Please don't come in here. "Um. Yeah," I say. I hear the door creak open, and a blonde head peeks in. She gasps, as I struggle to sit up, so my wife is staring at me on the floor, crying. Before I can actually sit up or say anything, she kneels onto the floor beside me and lifts my head into her lap.

I feel like such a pussy, but at the same time, her hand feels so good in my hair. "Did you see him?" I ask, looking up at her.

"I saw a Black kid," she whispers. "We both know it couldn't have been him. I mean it was dark in there, and, and so many people too..." She sounds so sure of herself, but when I close my eyes, I see that red sweatshirt and white lips, and I know for sure it was him.

"Where are the kids?" I ask, remembering Artie and Emerson.

"Oh, they um. There was this couple and their two kids, a boy and a girl, camped out in front of the sharks, and neither of the boys could look away from the tank next door; so, I asked the woman if she could just watch them for a short minute."

I'm looking at her like she's crazy for leaving our children with a stranger in the middle of a crowded aquarium, and I guess she picks up on it because she says, "They're literally right outside the door."

"H-how did Emerson know?" I ask.

He had stops stroking my hair for a half second, before she continues and speaks. "I don't know, I mean...I've really been trying to keep the TV off...But he could have heard something at school...or, maybe I left it on once accidentally."

I want to ask her how she could *accidentally* leave the TV on. A part of me genuinely wants to go off, and to say 'How could you let them see me like that? How could you let that happen?' But I don't. Instead, with what little strength I have left, I sigh, sit up and say, "Well we better go and get them then."

We stand up and she wraps her arms around me and kisses my cheek. She leans her head against my shoulder and we look in the mirror at ourselves. She looks beautiful as usual, blonde hair tumbling over her shoulders. I hate myself for being mad it her. It's not her fault. What was her mistake? Marrying me?

Although my thoughts are still running in circles and I'm not convinced, I say, "You're right."

"Hmm?" she asks, pulling her head away from my chest and looking up at me.

"The kid could have been anybody. It was dark, there were a lot of people, we were far away...you're right." Sure, that doesn't explain why he was looking at me like he wanted to tear me to bits. Or maybe it does. Maybe he saw my face on the news and recognized me as that White guy who killed that Black guy and anger was just his natural response. Leah smiles, and we walk through the bathroom door, arm in arm, and back out into the crowded aquarium. Leah was right- the boys are literally just outside the door, faces pressed against the fish tank.

The second he sees me, Artie runs towards me pointing and screaming, "Look Daddy, sharks! Sharks!" I reach down to pick him up, his fingers just as sticky as before.

"Oh, I see. Do you want me to go in and put you in the tank

with 'em for a while?" I joke.

"No! No! I'm scared Daddy, what if he breaks the tank and bites me?" There are genuine little tears welling up in his eyes when he throws his arms around me and buries his face into my shoulder.

"Aww they're not gonna bite you Artie, I promise. Daddy wouldn't ever hurt you," I assure him, stroking his back. Emerson catches my eye. He's still standing over by the tank, straight and tall and still, and looking right at me. His head is unmoving, his eyes trained directly on mine. I hear his voice echoing over and over in my head: *Daddy look, it's the Black boy you killed.*

SAMUEL NOBLE

"Sam, you ready to go?" Mom calls from downstairs. "The limo is out there, and we'll miss our flight if we don't leave now."

I can tell by her tone she's trying to be gentle with me. I'm sitting on the edge of my bed, feet flat on the floor, thinking about him. Not Gregory, but the man who killed him. How could he have looked like that? A husband, a father, and a good one from what I saw. How could someone like that have gone and murdered someone? "Samuel, we need to leave," she says, louder this time. He'll have to pay for what he did. He'll have to.

Sliding off the bed, I shove my feet into my shoes and yell down the stairs at her, "OK, I'm coming!" I drag my suitcase down the stairs, through the kitchen, out of the garage door and into the limo. Mom and Dad are already in the middle row as I slide into the back one.

"Ready to roll?" Dad says in a fake happy voice.

Mom says, "Yep, let's roll." And pats her hands on her legs, gazing out the window. The limo driver nods and backs out of the driveway.

I love the city at night. I love how the street lights and lights from tall buildings stand out and shine against the heavy darkness around them. When Gregory and I were kids, our parents would take us to the Moon View drive-in movie theater on some weekends. In retrospect it was really just an open field with a crappy old screen raised high up in the air in front of the woods, but we absolutely loved it. We'd park the minivan and spread out on different rows and take it all in; the evening summer breeze, the smell of buttery popcorn and most importantly, the movie. It was in that brown grassy field that I saw some of the greatest movies of my childhood like *Happy Feet*, *Cars*, and *Ice Age*. But the best movie I ever saw at the Moon view drive -in theater was *Up*. Great movie, I mean you got the talking dogs, that chocolate eating bird thing and a house floating around attached to a bundle of brightly colored balloons. And oh, my God when the old guy's wife died, I cried. We all did. On the way home, it was always super dark out and all the city lights were shining and blurred as we whizzed down the road between rows of skyscrapers, and Gregory always had his face pressed against the window, eyes wide, just watching them go by. I guess I'm saying that because the lights outside the car window right now remind me of those days.

"So, we um, missed you in church yesterday," Mom says in a cheery voice. What is it she wants from me?

"Oh. Yeah, I was just really tired so…" I trail off.

"Oh, don't worry honey, I understand. Pastor Sloane did a really good sermon, didn't he?" She says turning to Dad.

"What?" He was obviously zoned out and paying no attention.

"The sermon…you know, church on Sunday?

"Oh, the sermon. Pastor Sloane. Yeah, right, it was good. Talked about revenge."

"It was, yes," she coos, "and there was this one verse he kept repeating over and over. Say it with me honey," she says, looking at Dad again. "I don't remember it word for word."

And they say together in unison: "Never take your own revenge, but leave room for the wrath of God, for it is written, "Vengeance is mine, I will repay." The car is filled with silence for a moment.

And then Mom sniffles, and she says, "And I really love that because... especially now. I mean just to know, you know? Just to know that everything will be taken care of," she says, exhaling, and letting her shoulder fall. Not in defeat but in comfort, in peace. When I see her face in the rearview mirror so relaxed, I'm jealous. How can she be calm? How can she be relaxed? How can she have peace, when I can't? When my blood is running hot with rage and fury in my veins?

Then Dad goes, "It was very powerful. Very good advice."

Mom senses the awkward silence and tries to eliminate it by saying, "So how was the aquarium?"

"Fine," I grumble. I'm not selfish enough to steal her joy by mentioning what I saw.

"Well that's good," she says, nodding. "And how's Carter? Does he know where he's going next year?"

"Mom, Carter's not going to college," I say, shaking my head. She's acting like she's never met him.

"Hey, you should be expecting an acceptance letter in the mail any day now, right?" Dad pipes up.

I watch him lift his eyebrows in the rearview mirror. He's right about me receiving a letter: Gregory and I both applied to NYU a while back.

"Yeah. Probably sometime this week."

"So," Mom is *still* talking, "are you excited about tomorrow?" she asks in a weirdly cautious way.

"Excited? I mean, I guess so. I've never been on TV before. Are you guys gonna be on too?"

"I don't think so. It sounded like they mainly want to talk to you. We just came along for the free trip," she says, nudging Dad.

"That's a little weird, isn't it? Just me on the show, I mean." There's a weird silence that fills the car again, and this time, it lasts until we get to the airport. I don't know what's up with them. I look out the window and at the lights and think to myself how much Gregory would have loved being on TV.

MONAY DAVIS

Breathe Mo, breathe. It's Monday morning and I'm sitting at my desk in the studio, long golden sun rays shining in through the wall-size window. Why I decided to get here so early, I don't know. I'm just staring at the chair Sam is going to be sitting in just a few hours from now, twisting a pen back and forth between my fingers nervously. Maybe I shouldn't have done this. Maybe I shouldn't have invited him. What am I even going to say? What was I thinking asking that poor family to fly here just a couple days after losing their son? My son. Now I'm able to say it without a problem. Listening to that woman at church yesterday talk about losing her boy struck a chord in me. Gregory and Sam are my sons. I hadn't really thought of them that way, since the day they were born. It's the first time that I don't feel like caring for them would be a burden, but instead, I desire it.

That call came at the perfect time. Right when I needed it most, and just as I was truly beginning to understand my current condition.

"I knew you'd be here," a voice calls from the entrance to the studio. I turn to see Jay standing tall in gray suit pants and a lavender colored dress shirt that stretches around buffness.

"Why are you here?" I ask, reaching for my iPhone to check the time. "It's freaking 5:00 am."

"Because," he says, practically floating towards me, briefcase in hand, "I knew *you'd* be here." He smiles, and I can tell it's a real one by the twinge of goofiness that comes with it. Jay's pretend, on-camera smiles are unnervingly flawless, but his genuine ones are slightly crooked, yet somehow perfectly imperfect.

He's holding strong eye contact with me as he sits confidently in Samuel's chair (the one he will sit in soon at least), and leans back, folding his hands back behind his head, stretching and yawning.

"So, you ready?" he asks, knowingly, his brown skin and brown eyes sparkling under the bright studio lights.

"Yeah, I, I think so," I let out a massive sigh. "I don't know."

"You'll be fine," he cocks his head to the side. "Just play it cool. You're an amazing interviewer."

"Thanks," I say, knowing I'd be blushing if I were white, "but this is different Jay."

"True, but he doesn't know that." He leans towards me so far in the chair that he has to rest his hands on his knees to support his weight. "He doesn't know you're his mother, so in that way it isn't any different. You're amazing. He's going to love you. Stop worrying, Mo."

"I guess." I say softly.

He smiles gently, sighs and leans back against the seat again. I'm about to ask him what he's thinking when he says, "So I'm thinking about the other night. When you got that call, and I uh, hugged you." He scratches the back of his head. My body goes hot. I was hoping he wouldn't bring it up. I never wanted him to know I'd gotten pregnant as a teenager: Forget casually mentioning that when he touched me it gave me flashbacks of that time I got raped.

"Oh yeah," I say like the other night wasn't weird.

"I'm sorry if I um, overstepped. I don't want it to be weird between us." I hate that he's blaming himself. It wasn't him.

"It's not you, Jay, it's just..." What am I supposed to say now? *It's just that hugging you reminded me of that time I got raped in high school and was impregnated with the kid whose face is now plastered on TV screens across the nation.* Yeah, not gonna fly. Ugh, he's still looking at me with those big round eyes, like he thinks he violated me or something. I look around the studio, just to make sure we're alone. Yep, no one but us two. There's intimacy in simply being alone with somebody. His concerned expression, the way his eyebrows are furrowed slightly, the way he's facing me completely, all wordlessly promise me that I have his full attention, and it makes me want to tell him so badly.

"OK," I begin. "I was umm. When I was in high school I-. I have a history of um, assault. Sexual assault," I finally spit it out.

He looks at me and swallows, Adam's apple bobbing in his throat. "What are you saying Mo?" His eyes are unflinchingly focused on mine, but I wished they weren't so he wouldn't slowly fill them with tears. I blink them away before a single one can escape from the corner of my eye or creep down my cheek. I have had this conversation a million times before, but never with anyone else. Only in my thoughts have I imagined what it would be like to tell somebody what happened to me.

"I was raped," I whisper, so softly I can hardly hear myself say it. And he just looks at me, silently, and I'm thinking maybe he didn't hear me, until I watch his bottom lip quiver for a half second, before he catches himself and stops it, tightening his jaw and turning his head away from me so he's staring at nothing. And he puts his head in his hands. And he stays like that for a while. And when he looks up at me again, his eyes are red, and his cheeks are wet.

"I'm so sorry Mo," he says, softer than I had spoken seconds before. "I'm so sorry." I can see his heart hurting in his eyes, and wondering what he must see in me if I am able to see that in him.

"It was my fault," I blurt out.

"It wasn't your fault," he says it so immediately that he practically cuts me off.

"You don't know Jay...it was, it was. I shouldn't have been-."

It's not. Your fault," he tells me. And I believe him.

We lean forward at the same time, reaching out for each other, and he wraps his arms around me, and puts his hand on the back of my head, and pulls me into him and he holds me. We stay that way.

And I sigh, and when I do, streams of silent tears are expelled from my body, and all of the shame, all of the self-disgust just comes right out of me. I've felt this hurt forever, but I've never been able to just sit, and feel it with someone else, and it feels so good to finally be able to do that. I sigh into him, then inhale his smell.

When we finally pull away, I watch as he searches my eyes. Jay is just looking into my eyes and it's a really weird feeling because he's not just looking at me, he's like, looking inside me, like he is seeing me, the realest version of me that there is. I literally just spilled everything. We're staring at each other. The room is silent, save for the faint hum of the air conditioning in the background. And he reaches out to me and lifts my chin, he does it with such gentleness, and he closes his eyes, and he kisses me, and when he does we practically sink into each other.

HUNTER GARRETT

I can feel him staring at me from the back seat of the car. I'm relieved I'm not at the wheel because if I was, I honestly don't think I'd be able to handle it. Against my will, I'm forced to change positions every second, from resting my arm on the inside of the passenger door to, to holding onto the little handle thingy above it, to practically wringing my hands in my lap. My legs are crossed, then uncrossed, then crossed again; I can't sit still.

Emerson *knows*. He seemed totally fine when we were in the mirror tying ties this morning, but since the aquarium, when he saw him, he hasn't said not one word.

Artie, on the other hand, oblivious as usual, is sitting in his car-seat and swinging his little legs and kicking the back of Leah's seat, raving about the sharks and the jellyfish and the dolphins.

"Oh my goodness Daddy," he shrieks, "those sharks were giant *and* huge!

"Giant and huge mean the same thing Artie. You don't have to say both," Emerson interjects in a tone oddly somber for a seven-year-old.

Out of the corner of my eye, I watch as Leah turns towards me to give me some kind of amused look, but I'm honestly too distracted to return it. It's January, and our rusty old Ford sucks at actually warming up the car, but somehow it still feels damn hot in here. I shuffle my feet, knocking old soda cans away from my feet. The seatbelt feels like it's cutting into the side of my neck.

I make the mistake of glancing up into the rearview mirror and there Emerson is, just straight up drilling me, his hands resting on the seat on either side of him, his head tilted downward ever so slightly, so that his glasses have slipped to the end of his nose. Before I even have to tell it to, my head snaps away from him and I look out the window instead. It's far from warm outside, but I let the window down anyway. Cool air rushes in chilling my sweaty face. If Leah is wondering why I'm letting all this cold air into the car, she doesn't say anything. And that's good because I think that if it wasn't open I'd pass out.

"Daddy, I'm cold," Artie whines.

"We're just about home now, you'll be fine," I say. It comes out harsher than I'd expected. For once, the kid isn't oblivious, senses something's up and keeps quiet. We pull into the quiet street of our neighborhood and pass house after house and brown front yard after brown front yard, until we get to old Ms. Thompson's house, and finally, our own, and there those shoelaces are, flapping in the wind as if to greet me. There's no way I can stand seeing those things waving at me every time I drive up to my own freaking house.

"Give me the keys." It comes out as a yell as Leah stops the car in the driveway.

She drops them in the palm of my hand, eyes round and confused. I push the car door open and stomp up to the front door, my head spinning and pounding. Warm air rushes at my face as soon as it opens, and my body is even hotter. I enter the kitchen, pulling open and slamming drawers until I find a good knife. Those shoelaces are pissing me the hell off. My mind feels frenzied. I can't look at them without seeing the dead kid and his untied black Nikes, or that dream.

"Artie, get the mail for me OK?" Leah calls from inside the car. I'm back outside, looking up at those things flapping in the wind, knife in hand. Those wires really aren't even that high up. It may seem crazy, but I threw javelin in middle and high school. I am not good at much, but I do have good aim, and I'm sure I can easily snip those laces with a quick toss of my knife. I'm sure I can. OK. Breathe. You can do this. Alright. I'm standing at the edge of the driveway, trying to ignore the pounding behind my eyes, and keep my T-shirt from sticking against my sweaty body. When I bring the knife up in front of my face, I realize my hand is shaking. I got this though, I have this.

Forcing myself to glue my tired eyes to the laces above me, and squinting into the sky, and into a sun only partially muffled by the light clouds, I breathe deeply in attempt to dismiss my lightheadedness. Breathe. It comes out ragged. I bring the knife in front of me, eyes still trained to the laces in the sky, and in one smooth motion toss it into the air. It flies upward, spinning towards the laces, as I stand and watch.

"Hunter—What the fuck? No, Artie!" I look over to see Leah screaming and scrambling across the yard like a madwoman towards, oh my God. Artie! The kid's standing right under the freaking shoelaces pulling envelopes out of the mailbox. The knife just narrowly misses the shoelaces (it may have even grazed them) and is on its way down out of the air. I'm consciously aware of the hot flash and adrenaline rush overtaking my body as I sprint towards him, yelling.

"Move Artie!" My voice comes out like a desperate, shrill shriek. The kid is oblivious as usual, struggling to carry a pile of ads and bills in his tiny arms. Time moves in slow motion, and for whatever reason, I imagine all three of us, Leah, me and the knife moving towards Artie from a bird's eye view. The question is, who's going to get there first?

The wind only works against me. All I've got to do is get there and push him out of the way. I'm already mentally slapping myself for throwing the thing up there in the first place. How did I actually think that would work?

"Artie! Artie! Artie! Move baby!" Leah's just repeating herself over and over again as she heads towards him. The knife, indifferent to its likely course of action, flips and spins downwards, now only a foot away from Artie's blonde hair.

"Heeeyyy!! Noooo!" Leah screams, fighting towards him against the wind. I'm so close. Come on. Damn it. It's too late. The knife hits him right in the shoulder, deep enough that it stays there, sticking out of his body. He screams like I've never heard any human scream before. He's in my arms before his body can reach the grass below him. His body seems way too small to produce screams that loud. Tears are streaming from his eye as he grips my arm, digging his fingernails into my skin. The knife is in there pretty good and is still sticking up straight from just above his collarbone. Blood spreads from around the area, soaking his white dress shirt. Leah's next to me now, pulling him away from me. When she jerks him like that, the knife wobbles in the open wound and he shrieks and cries even louder. As she lifts him into the air, the knife falls to the ground with the clatter. He's got his head buried into her shoulder, muffling his screams as she sets him in the back seat of the car.

"You're trying to kill him too!" a voice yells from behind me. Suddenly, I'm on the ground and Emerson's pounding me with his tiny fists. Tears are splattered on the inside of his glasses which are sitting crooked on the bridge of his nose.

"Emerson! Emerson stop!" I've got each of his balled-up hands in mine, holding them away from my face. He's actually pretty strong for a seven-year-old.

"You're gonna kill him too! You're gonna kill him too!" I push him off of me, with more force than I'd intended, and he tumbles to the grass beside me.

"Hunter, drive!" Leah calls from the car. I struggle to my feet and back towards the car and Artie's screams. I pass by the back seat and see Leah sitting there, cradling Artie, his head in her lap. I swear, when he sees me, he screams even louder.

I'm in the front seat of the car, pulling the keys out of my pocket when I hear the back car door slam shut. I turn around as the car starts up, to see Emerson, white shirt stained with green grassy streaks, staring at me from the back seat.

SAMUEL NOBLE

I don't actually look that bad. Standing in front of the hotel mirror, the suit is nice. But no matter what I look at, I can't see anything but him. It's like his face is etched into my eyes. No matter who I look at, I see his face. When I look at me, I see him, and my heart throbs with a hatred I've never known. Seeing him real, and happy, and with his family is just making me insane. My brain is beating against the inside of my skull, trying to reject that reality. I can't believe that he's out, and that he's just out and going to aquariums and shit. My phone buzzes. It's Carter.

Carter: LOL dude, that nigga flipped when he saw you.

Carter just can't take anything seriously, can he? Everything is a joke. It's like he doesn't get it. I don't respond, but a few minutes later he texts again.

Carter: guy prob doesn't know you're twins

Me: He ran away like a little bitch lol. Even left his wife and kids

When I don't respond again, he changes the subject.

Carter: So yeah, that lady on that show is kinda hot. I've always wanted to be with an older woman.

Carter. Never. Stops. Thinking. About. Sex.

174

Carter: already got the TV on the right channel.

Me: Cool

Carter: Cool

"I just got a text, car's here," Mom calls from the bedroom. "You ready to go?" I take one last look in the mirror, flip off the light, try to force the anger out of my mental space, and head back into the bedroom where my parents are.

"Aww," Mom gushes, "you look so handsome." She reaches over to fix my tie the way Moms do. "You sure you're OK with this?"

"Yeah. There's some stuff I wanna say, you know?"

She nods, sniffles and smiles, then says, "Let's head out then."

"Dad, are you coming?" I ask. He's awkwardly sitting on the edge of his bed fiddling with his watch. They've both been acting real weird since we got here last night.

"Yep," he says standing to his feet.

And with that, the three of us (I am still getting used to it being just the three of us) step into the quiet hotel hallway. The car is one of those big black SUVs that celebrities and politicians ride around in. The three of us sit in the back seat, me in the middle. It's got tan colored leather seats on the inside with plenty of leg room. Looking out the window, I know the windows are so dark that nobody can see me sitting inside.

Whenever I'm in a small space that anger just builds up. It's like I'm giving it off all the time, but it's able to dissipate or something when I'm like outside or in a room. But when I'm in a small space like a car, it just builds and builds and builds. Like all my pissed-off thoughts just get trapped in there with me bouncing back and forth, in and out of my head. It's just too much. I'm still feeling guilty about everything that happened with Amanda at Carter's house and then at the party on Friday. I can't imagine what she probably thinks of me after I said that stuff about her, then punched Carter. I'd be lying if I said that there wasn't a tiny part about me that has thought about the taste of her lips every day since it happened.

I keep forcing myself to remember that am not here to be pissed off, and I am definitely not here to think about Amanda. I'm here because of what I saw that night in the car.

"It's a beautiful day out," Mom says, absent-mindedly staring out the window. And when I look out the window, I don't see it. The sky is very blue, but I haven't seen beauty in anything since Gregory died. I don't know how she does it.

The car pulls into a massive parking lot with fresh white paint in front of a tall glass and silver building that reaches high into the sky. I lean over to check myself out one last time in the rearview mirror before hopping out of the car and heading towards the glass double doors. I'm actually kind of psyched to be on TV. The lobby of the building looks like the family room of a rich person's house, only with a front desk. A large flat-screen TV covers a good part of one wall, and a rushing waterfall fills up the space on the other side of the room. High ceilings meet the shiny wood floors which cover every corner of the room. Mom and Dad are off talking to the guy in the fancy suit at the desk, but I can't keep my eyes off that TV.

This early in the morning, and they're already showing bird's eye view footage of people swarming the streets. Looking at the people and the signs and the officers out there now feels different since I've been there and can relate to the amount of raw energy all those people are feeling. I really feel like it's my responsibility to say something to somehow calm people down, or let them know that rioting and looting stores isn't going to bring Gregory back or save the next kid from the same fate

"Sam let's go," Mom calls, and we step into an elevator. The last time I was in an elevator I was coming back up from the depths of the earth after seeing Gregory.

MONAY DAVIS

We're just sitting here grinning at each other like a couple of idiot in-love teenagers. At first, we say everything with our eyes. And then we talk, and we laugh, and we just sit there together, and neither of us is worried about anything, and it's like time isn't passing. It's like we've both been waiting for this for years, and we're both sure that it wasn't just one of us that felt this way and time is just irrelevant. The only measure of time I have is the fact that Robert has been here for a while, and he doesn't get here until closer to when we air.

"Mo," he says, smiling that grand smile of his.

"Yes?"

"You know they'll be here soon right?"

He licks his lips, and in response, I secretly struggle not to fall out of my chair. Tapping the home button on my iPhone, I realize he's right. "Shit. Yeah, yeah. We should…get in position." Oh. Bad wording. "I mean we should uh, you know, get ready for um, to do our jobs, which is hosting our show…." I trail off to fade out the fact that I just rambled myself into extreme embarrassment. He laughs, says nothing, lifts his eyebrows, smiles and turns on his heels towards the coffee table. Watching him walk away, I've got the same butterflies in my stomach now that I did when I was in high school.

I'm sifting through my notes, for the interview, my heart

pounding hard in anticipation. Now that I've told Jay about what happened to me, I feel inexplicably free as I flip through the details of the shooting. It still hurts like hell. That part hasn't subsided in the least. But that hurt is no longer paired with the shame that was attached to it before.

The door at the far end of the studio opens, and I turn around to face the source of the 'Hi's' and 'Nice to meet you's', I see him. When I do, my eyes burn with tears for the third time in two days. My heart is exploding. That's my son, and he is beautiful. He's tall and handsome, with light brown skin, and curly hair. He smiles politely as he greets Robert and the rest of the crew with a firm handshake. Every fiber in my body is bursting, elated. Seeing the up-close portrait of Gregory on a TV screen is so different from seeing my son, here, now, standing there right in front of me. It's like, before he wasn't even real. I mean he was, of course. Of course he was. But he wasn't here, I couldn't reach out and touch him, I couldn't watch a smile break out on his face like I can now. I couldn't hear him laugh. I'm smiling so hard, that I can taste my own salty tears on my tongue, and no matter how many times I wipe my eyes, they just don't stop crying, and no matter how many times I try to force my mouth out of a smile, it keeps coming back. They're headed my way now. All three of them, unfortunately.

In a panic, I rush to turn away from them and wipe my face off one last time, biting the insides of my cheeks to keep from smiling. I take the briefest side-eye glance at myself in the mirror on my desk, and as they approach, my mind is screaming at me to tell him I'm his mother, but I don't say it. Instead, I reach out my hand all bubbly-like and say, "Welcome! I'm so glad ya'll made it alright."

Mike Noble smiles a fairly genuine smile, and our hands

meet in a firm handshake. "Good to see you again Monay." He didn't. He did not. Tell me this man didn't just say 'again.' The fact that his face is turning bright red confirms my fear.

"Dad, what do you mean again?" Sam asks, lifting an eyebrow and looking back and forth between his 'Mom' and 'Dad'.

Mike scrambles to cover his tracks. "Oh no, uh, by again I just mean like how I watch your show every morning so meeting you now, it almost feels like I've met you before. Which is why I said 'again'." Nervous laughs escape his lips as he struggles to make his personal panic session less obvious. Hope the kid buys it.

Sam tilts his head sideways, squints and says, "Um, Dad, you don't even watch this show. Like ever." Ouch! That actually hurts. But hey, if I were in his position, it'd be awkward for me to watch it too.

"No no no no, I've seen it, I've seen it," Mike says nodding and avoiding eye contact with his 'son, 'You just haven't seen me see it."

My boy is smart enough to know something's up, but by the same token, he's also got enough sense to know when to give it a rest, and so he shrugs and drops it. I've always been a proponent of nature over nurture. I'm purposely trying not to ever look at him for more than a few seconds at a time, unless I have an excuse, because Sarah is already passively aggressively drilling me with those over protective, territorial, 'Mommy eyes.' And she's smiling a smile so fake, she must want me to know it isn't real.

"She says, "Hi Monay!" in the way an ex-wife might speak to

her ex-husband's new wife. The tension is so thick I could cut it with a knife. We shake hands and I give her the most real-looking fake smile I'm capable of pulling out of my ass at the moment. I don't wait for her reaction, but instead direct a question to all three of them.

"How was the flight?"

"Fine," Sarah says.

"Great!" Mike says

"Cool," Sam says, all kind of at the same time.

"Well, I know I mentioned it when I spoke on the phone to you earlier Sarah, but I just really want to, again, offer my sincere condolences on the loss of your son." Sarah and I hold eye contact the whole time I talk. Her eyes say so much, and I'm sure mine do too. "And I greatly appreciate your being here so soon." She doesn't say anything, but Sam does.

"It's not about her," he cuts in, his voice dipped in impatience. "Gregory would have wanted me to be here." We make eye contact for the first time, and it's weird because part of me is in complete awe of him, while the other part is somehow taken aback by the hot rage in his eyes.

HUNTER GARRETT

In case any of you ever wanted to know, yes, it is damn difficult to focus on driving a car when your five-year-old is bleeding to death in the back seat because you accidentally and indirectly stabbed him in the chest. It is even harder to drive when you're understandably panic-stricken wife is also screaming in your ear because you just stabbed her son in the chest. I'm not even going to say anything about what it's like to have your seven-year-old drill holes into your back with eyes filled of what can only be described as murderous intent.

"DRIVE YOU FUCKING IDIOT! DO YOU WANT HIM TO DIE?!!"

"Honey?" I say in the calmest voice possible, over Artie's wails "our son is not going to die, and I am driving as fast as I can." My voice shakes, my vision is blurred slightly by tears, and my head pounds without ceasing.

She slams the back of my headrest with her fist *hard*. Then she reaches around the seat and starts like clawing at my arm or something. "DRIVE FASTER!" A panic I've never heard before laces her words.

"Honey I'm try- I am <u>trying</u> to drive faster. I do not want us to get into an accident." She's slapping and grabbing my arm, so much so, I nearly lose control of the car. When we jerk left, Artie cries even louder.

"LEAH!" I have no choice but to join her in screaming. "Look! The hospital is right there!" I say, pointing to the brightly-lit Garner-Scott Memorial sign. She loosens her grip on my arm and returns her attention back to Artie gently shushing and hushing him and telling him we're almost there. When I glance into the rear-view mirror, I see that the sleeve of my white dress shirt is stained by dark red blood.

We bust through the emergency room doors and into a massive room with white walls and white floors and lights that just feel way too bright to my sore, wet eyes. A whiff of bleach and ammonia rushes up my nostrils. I realize that Artie, who's still nestled in Leah's arms, has been quiet for the last minute or two. When I look over I see that the top section of his button down is soaked in blood. His body is limp, legs hanging at odd angles, and his eyes are closed, although his little fingers are still gripping Leah's arm, nails digging into her skin.

"Hey! Help!" her voice is cracking and desperate. A swarm of doctors and nurses is already heading towards us, white coats flying behind them, stethoscopes bouncing around their necks. One of them is Black. I know it's wrong, but I am not about to gamble my son's life by letting some ignorant, low IQ black woman kill him with a simple mistake. But before I can say anything at all, she and an older, bearded white man pull Artie out of Leah's arms and set him down gently on a gurney.

"What happened?" he asks calmly as the nurse fumbles with an oxygen mask.

Leah and I look at each other, then back at the doc. I think both of us are about to say something, (probably different things) when Emerson says, "He tried to kill him. He threw a knife at my brother." His glasses are sliding down his nose, though he makes no effort to return them so their place, but instead points squarely at me. He looks up at the doctor expectantly, and the doctor just looks back at him.

"It was an accident," I say. "I mean, he got hit. He got hit with a knife, accidentally." I look to Leah for support, but she deliberately avoids eye contact and doesn't speak.

The doctor, without taking his eyes off of mine mumbles, "Get him to Trauma 2 and call child services."

SAMUEL NOBLE

Man. What. Is. Up. With. This. Lady? I mean, she's just like staring at me all deep and creepy like from the other side of the desk. I don't know...it's like she's proud of me or something. She's forcing smiles off of her face, and avoids looking at me for a few minutes, whenever I catch her staring.

I have no words to describe the ridiculousness that went on a couple of minutes ago with Dad saying 'again' then panicking and backtracking, and Mom having suffered from what you could call Resting Bitch Face throughout the entire unfortunate verbal exchange. I'm thinking maybe she's like one of Dad's ex-girlfriends or something? And Mom definitely knows her. That would explain why they were acting so weird when they first asked me if I wanted to come here.

As hot lights bake my skin from above, a short round man (I think his name is Robert), comes up to the table I'm sitting at with Monay. "On in five," Robert says, before immediately turning back in the direction from which he came. One look at his unfortunately balding head makes me wish I wasn't just another guy who's going to get old and go bald one day.

"OK," Mom, who's been standing behind me, says. "We'll be back over there," she gestures, "waiting for you when you're done?" She says it like it's a question and is definitely avoiding all eye contact with Monay.

"Alright," I say.

"Alright?" She says like she's asking me. Then they leave.

A tall, buff, thirty-something year old Black guy in a suit walks across the studio, right up to me, throws out a hand and gives me a shake. *Wow, his teeth are white!*

"Hi Sam, I'm Jayden, the Jay part of Jay and Monay. You ready for today?"

"Uh yeah. I think so." His eyes move slightly to the left of mine and focus on something behind me." When I turn around I see Monay grinning wide at him, and he looks back at her knowingly. "This screen right here shows what the folks at home are seeing on their TV," Jay says pointing at what has to be an 80-inch plasma on the wall in front of us.

"Live in two!" Robert yells.

"You ready, Sam?" Monay asks. I nod. OK, let's do this.

I have so much more respect for people who have to be on TV all the time. It's not the lights themselves that are actually bad, but rather the heat that said lights are constantly producing. That and the nerves have me just about sweating through my suit. When we go live, and she starts talking, I don't know what to do myself, but I try to make it seem like I'm relaxed and comfortable. I don't know, should I force a smile? My heart pounds as I resort to fake fixing the cuffs of my jacket while she talks.

"On a more serious note, the violent protests, demonstrations and even riots that have broken out across the country over the past week stem from outrage over the fatal shooting of the unarmed teenager, Gregory Noble. Noble was shot and killed early Thursday morning by night watchmen and father of two, thirty-six-year-old Hunter Garrett." The screen is split between Gregory's ROTC picture and an unflattering mugshot of Hunter Garrett. I guess I don't really have to say the picture of Hunter Garrett is unflattering, considering few mugshots are. His thin lips are pursed in skinny, pale pink lines, and wispy red hair hangs from his chin and over his eyes.

"Last night, a particularly violent confrontation broke out between a man and an officer in downtown Chicago. Take a look." Jay nods as the screen plays a cell phone camera quality video of a college-aged Black guy chucking a rock at a wall of well armored police officers. The cop strikes back with a baton and knocks the man backward into the raging, screaming crowds behind him. The people erupt like a wave, mobbing the line of cops. It's so dark and the camera is jerking around so much I can hardly tell what's going on. The video freezes and the screen cuts back to showing the three of us sitting at the table. Wow, that was intense. When I look back at Monay I see something in her eyes. There's more there. It reminds me of when I walked into Michael's office the morning Gregory died and could tell something had happened. It's funny how we're made that way. We can just look at another human being, even one we just met, and tell something's up.

MONAY DAVIS

I feel like I just got busted. Like I mean caught red-handed, smoking gone busted. He's looking at me like he knows that yes, 'I did steal the cookies from the cookie jar'. He knows something. I can tell. Damn that video was hard to watch. I think it's crazy for people to scream and shout and fight over a guy they don't even know, but then, I think it's just as crazy for me to cry over the same kid, whom I don't know either. Pull it together. OK introduce him. Time to introduce. Jay's looking at me like he's worried I might pass out again, and even Robert is over in the corner eyeing up the three of us. Just start talking.

"And today, we're very privileged to have with us, the identical twin brother of the late Gregory Noble, Samuel Noble here with us." Jay takes the words right out of my mouth, saving the day as usual. He turns to Sam and says, "Welcome to the show, Sam. I think I speak for all of us when I say that I am truly sorry for the loss of your brother, and I am heartbroken every time another unarmed young person of color is shot and killed by those very people who are supposed to protect us. How are you dealing with injustice, which has hit so close to home for you in particular?"

"Well, uh, thanks for having me," he says, his nerves evident to everyone in the room. "And... I really can't even put it into words. Like at first, I was just, I couldn't believe it, you know? Like, my brother, he's all I've ever had for real. I couldn't deal with it. And then I started thinking about how this is far from the first time this has happened." His voice strengthens. "It may be the first time it happened to me, but it has happened so many times before, to so many people." There are a few seconds of silence. "And it just makes me so mad. Especially when the people killing us just keep on getting away with it." His last sentence comes from deep down, and is saturated in bitterness, his nerves from before are drowned out by anger.

Jay and I both nod, and I say, "Tell us about Gregory. I understand that he was very talented; a light in your High School and in your community as well."

"Well uh, Gregory… was… extremely conscious of everything going on around him. I mean, he was super aware of problems the world faced and always did what he could to help, whether that was encouraging people to recycle, eat healthy and exercise, feeding the homeless, tutoring young kids, or raising money for a good cause. If there was a problem, Gregory was not only aware of it, but actively tackling it."

If I weren't on live TV I would be crying again. My heart is heavy and falling inside of me. He sounds like he was so amazing. My body aches for him, and for his brother who he left alone.

"Many people," Jay begins, "have compared what happened to your brother to the shootings of other young Black men like Trayvon Martin and Michael Brown. Do you feel these comparisons are accurate?"

Sam thinks for a second before heading in. "Of course, I do." It comes out cold and angry. "I mean, what happened to Gregory… It's the same old story over and over again, you know? Another Black boy killed by another White cop. We've seen it before. We've seen it way too many times, and too often we see the same result. The cop says he was scared and walks. Same story, different people, so of course there are similarities."

"I completely agree with you on that," I say. "It is a story we've all heard too often and it's really, excuse my language, complete BS that a cop, or in this case a neighborhood watchman armed with a gun, can say the reason he shot and killed someone is because he was scared. We do need to make a fundamental change, as a nation in the way cops and or guards in this case, interact with citizens, especially those who are unarmed."

"That's right," Jay says. "Unfortunately, we don't have much more time, but I'd like to finish this segment with one final question. What do you want those who are obviously enraged and frustrated by what's happened and are taking their anger out through violent riots and protests?"

Good Question. "Well," he begins, "I guess I would want people to know that he's a real person. I mean, I know that sounds stupid to say. Of course, he's a real person. But I mean, like yeah, he was real. He had dreams and hobbies and aspirations, and opinions and people he loved and people who loved him." He sighs and swallows, and I can tell he's trying hard not to cry. When he keeps talking I feel like I have to tilt my head back slightly to keep tears from flowing out of my eyes. "And when people go out there, yelling and stealing and destroying stuff— it's like they're forgetting that. They forget that he was a person, in exchange for treating him like a political issue or debate. And I get that. Trust me, I get being mad, I get being angry, I get being pissed off, and broken, and fed up. But Gregory never would have wanted violence. He was a very peaceful person. So yeah, remember that. And don't tear up your own stuff, your own stores and streets." He's trying to act cool, but it's obvious he's in a lot of pain. I want to reach across the desk and put a hand on his arm, or hug him or comfort him in any way, but I don't. Jay, who's sitting beside Sam locks eyes with me, reads my mind then says, "Wow. I wish my brothers were more like you. What you just said is very powerful." He pats him on the back in a way that affirms and comforts, yet doesn't make him look weak. I'm regretting giving him up so badly right now, my whole body physically hurts.

HUNTER GARRETT

Something about hospital waiting rooms is inherently depressing. Maybe it's the bleachy smell or the eerie silence, or all of the super bright artificial lighting. Maybe it's just that a good chunk of the other people in the room are doing the same thing Leah and I are; waiting. Everyone in here is waiting for something. Perhaps to find out if their loved one will live or die. And if they will live, for how long? Will they walk again? Will their lives be changed forever? Each of us has a different story. Leah's sitting next to me leaning forward, running her hand anxiously back and forth from her hip to the top of her knee. I'm trying to avoid looking at her, so I don't have to see again, that her gray dress is stained in our son's blood. I want to touch her, to hold her, to tell her Artie will definitely be 100% fine. But I can't for two reasons: A: She's understandingly fucking pissed as hell at me and B: I can't promise her that he will be. Emerson is on my right, but two seats away. He said he didn't want to sit next to me. I don't look at him either, so I just sit there all stiff in the chair, facing forward, eyes focused on anything but either of their faces.

I'm hoping we'll just be able to sit here together in silence until a doctor comes out and tells us Artie's fine and that we can go home, when Leah turns to me and says far too loudly for the silent waiting room, "What the hell were you thinking? I mean like- what were you even trying to do, throwing a fucking knife in the air?" She gestures with her hands, imitating me throwing the knife.

What the hell am I supposed to say? *Well you see honey, remember that kid I shot last week? Yeah well, his shoes were untied which inevitably led to me killing him because if he hadn't tripped then I never would have caught up to him, let alone end up standing over him. And by the way I dreamt I was being strangled by a pair of living shoelaces and I just couldn't handle seeing the things hanging over our house waving at me like that. It sounds ridiculous. It makes me sound insane. It is ridiculous, and I am insane. But anyway, you see, I thought that because I threw javelin in high school I could just snip those laces in midair and make it all go away.* I look at her, sigh and say, "I don't know, I just, just got tired of seeing the things up there and so..." I trail off and stare into her eyes. She looks sad and hurt and confused. Her eyes move away from mine and focus on something behind me. I quickly recognize the signature sound of high heels clicking across a linoleum floor. My heart jumps at the thought of the news we could possibly receive. As I turn to see a woman walking towards us, I wonder why she's wearing a red suit and not a long white coat.

"Mr. and Mrs. Garrett?" Her voice is nasally, and she sounds like she has a Boston accent.

Leah jumps to her feat eagerly. "Yes, yes. How is he? He's OK, right?" She's wringing her hands, her eyes filled with desperation.

"Oh, Mrs. Garrett, I apologize, but I'm not your son's physician, I'm with child services. Cathy," she says extending her arm for a handshake. Leah weakly grasps her hand and Cathy basically shakes her limp hand for a couple of seconds. I wrack my brain trying to cope with the thought of being accused of murder and child abuse in the same week.

"Oh," she says.

"And I assume this is your husband Hunter, correct?"

"Yes."

Cathy doesn't attempt to interact with me at all. She's probably already assumed I'm some violent abusive husband and father. "And this must be your older son, Emerson." She says, smiling one of those fake smiles adults use with little kids. Emerson, who's probably offended by this plays along and waves and smiles back, swinging his legs.

"Yep," Leah says. "Can I uh, help you or something, Cathy?"

"Well, yes, I'd like to talk to you for a few minutes about any possible abuse in the home." She says 'abuse' like it's a cuss word.

"Oh um, there's no *abuse* but I'd be glad to talk to you." Leah's obviously nervous, but is trying not to let me or Cathy know.

"OK that'd be great. Your husband can stay here with your son, and I'll ask one of the nurses to stay here as well and just to keep an eye on your little one and then we'll be back, and I'll talk to him for a bit. Sound good?" She doesn't look at me at all, or address any questions towards me. It's like I'm not even in the room. As they walk away together, I'm not worried. Leah won't lie. I'm a good husband and a good father. I'd never try to hurt either of my kids.

SAMUEL NOBLE

It's Tuesday. Again. And I'm back in the whitewashed hallways of my high school, numb to everything but the anger throbbing in my chest. The interview helped. To be able to sit there, even only for a few minutes, with a captive audience, able to speak my mind. It definitely helped. Unfortunately, whatever little progress I made there is gone now. My eyes feel heavy and dead, and everything I see is somehow dark and tinged with gray. When I see people smile I think it must be an illusion, like every good thing in this world is a mirage. There's something forming inside of me, I'm afraid of it. I don't know what it is, but I know it's dangerous. Like if somebody is sad, they're just sad. They might cry, they might stop eating, they might drown in their own depression. And if someone is angry they might go around being angry and mean and nasty and curse people out. But if you mix numbness with that anger, that's when it's dangerous. An angry person may want to seek revenge, and a few of them may truly try, to a certain extent; but the fact that they aren't actually numb holds them back, it makes them human, and that's how I know what's inside of me is so dangerous.

Somehow, Carter's beside me. "Hey," he's already smiling about something. He's always smiling. It's like he's a machine, or a puppet, and he's not smiling by his own will, but someone is forcing him to. Who smiles that much?

"Wassup Carter?" I ask, not even trying to mask the

exhaustion and indifference in my voice.

"Nothing man. You did good. On TV, I mean."

When I turn to look at him, surprised by his tone, I see the truth on his face. His mouth is still grinning, but his eyes are still and somber.

"Thanks," I say. The questions I had about his smile all but faded away. 'Thanks,' is all there is to say to him. He nods and adjusts the straps of his backpack on his shoulders. "I also noticed something."

"What's that?"

He laughs. "That lady. Why was she like, staring at you like that?"

"She was staring? Didn't notice," I lie.

"Right. Whatever." Carter looks over his shoulder at a girl's yoga pant-covered ass, until it disappears into the masses of people crowding the hallway.

"Oh, that reminds me…" he says, grinning and licking his lips. I can only imagine what a girl's essentially bare ass reminded Carter of. I wait for him to continue. "Remember that date I was telling you about? That I had last weekend?"

"Yep."

"Wait- are you sure I mentioned that to you?"

"Um, yeah. You were humping a sink and calling yourself 'Daddy' when you did," I say, shaking my head in disgust.

"Ohhhh. Now I remember. I did do that. Yep. Well it went well. Very well. Let's just say she knew what she was doing. So, I asked her to come over this weekend, and I thought you could come over and some other people and we could just chill, ya know?" I could care less about Carter and this girl. I want to ask about Amanda, but I don't.

He can tell there's something on the tip of my tongue. "What Sam?"

"Oh, um, nothing. I mean I was just gonna ask if maybe you could invite… Amanda?"

He laughs, shrugs. "Course I can," he says, his previously mechanic smile now genuine and smug across his face.

I feel myself unconsciously rolling my eyes. "I'm not trying to like, hit on her, I just want to apologize, clear the air. I've totally dissed her twice now."

"OK, OK, whatever you say," he says, hands held up in surrender, backing away from me as the warning bell rings.

MONAY DAVIS

I can't stop thinking about him. About the pain I saw on his face and in his heart when he talked about his brother. I mean… damn. The kid is definitely hurting and I, his mother, am just sitting around in my house like nothing even happened. For the first time, I feel this overwhelming sense of *knowing* I need to be there. I just know it. Somehow, I'd fooled myself into thinking that if I met him, if I got to see him in real life, to hear his voice, to reach out and shake his hand that it would be better. Like if I could just see him one time I'd somehow feel like I'd fulfilled my duty as a mother because I was there, even if only for a few seconds. But it isn't working out that way. Instead it's like I was drowning before. I was drowning, and for a second, someone pulled me out of my shame and misery and guilt, and gave me a full breath of oxygen, and when they let me go and I became submerged again, my lungs burned even hotter than before.

"So whaddya wanna do?" Jay asks. It's Monday night and I'm at his place at the kitchen table. He's standing a few feet away, bent over in a pair of fitted suit pants rifling through his refrigerator.

To be honest, I don't really feel like doing much—I'm just happy being here with him. However, this statement is wildly cliché and would make me sound hella clingy so instead I just say, "Netflix and Chill?"

A bottle of ketchup clatters to the floor as he stands up abruptly nearly hitting his head on the refrigerator ceiling. "What?" he asks.

I'm trying to figure out why he freaked out like that, I mean everyone has Netflix. "You do have Netflix, don't you?"

"Sure, I have Netflix. Everyone has Netflix."

"OK, what's the big deal then? Wanna watch or nah?"

He nods like he's just figured something out. "You don't know what that means, do you?" he says smiling a smile I can't quite decode.

"Umm. What do you mean? It's like watching Netflix and relaxing right?"

He smiles again, purses his lips together before bursting into laughter. He's laughing so hard that he bends over forward clutching his middle accidentally kicking the ketchup bottle across the floor. "Oh man, you," (belting laughter), "you really don't know do you?"

"Know what?"

"Netflix and Chill. It's like slang for having sex."

My cheeks flash with heat. "No way! What? You're lying."

"I'm not lying. It's true! Look it up on Urban Dictionary."

Before he even says it, I'm already pulling my phone out of my purse to look it up. Behold, the ever-trustworthy Urban Dictionary definition:

It means that you are going to go over to your partner's house and fuck with Netflix in the background.

Oh shit, 'Netflix and Chill' even has a Wikipedia page. Well it's official. Jeez, what the heck do I say now? I mean, does he want to? Do I?

"Wow. Now I feel hella dumb. How did you even know that?" I say.

"I'm still young ya know," he says, pretending to be offended.

We smile at each other for a couple of seconds until he says, "Well we can watch Netflix, if you want."

"OK." I stand, and we head towards the family room. It's completely dark until he turns on the TV and that signature glow fills the room.

"Pick your poison," he says as we sit down together. I'm wonderfully aware of how close together our bodies are. "We've got *House of Cards, Orange is the New Black, Daredevil. Breaking Bad* is really good."

"What about *Friends?*"

"*Friends?*" He laughs again. When he smiles, his white teeth look so bright against the darkness around him. "I've never met a Black person who watches *Friends*. It's like, a white show."

I can't help but laugh as I say, "So are most of the shows on Netflix."

"True. Let's go with the pilot," he chuckles. "*Friends*. What a throwback." He punches the remote, and the first ever episode of *Friends* starts to play on the flat screen. Jay puts his arm around me and I lean into his shoulder. As I do, he sighs heavily, and pulls me towards him. My body feels warm, radiating heat, and my heart thumps steadily in my chest. The characters on the screen are saying something, I assume, considering their mouths are moving. But I can't hear them. All I can *feel* is him. I want to turn and look at his face and kiss him all over again, but what if he isn't looking back?

Time continues to pass us by in silence, and although my head is resting against his chest, and I'm staring at the TV, all I see is him. His white smile. His clear brown eyes staring intensely into my own. I turn my head slowly to the left, trying to be subtle so I can just turn back if he isn't looking. But he is. And he's biting his lip. And when he does, I can't help but imagine how long he's been looking for. He looks down at my lips, then back up to my eyes. I lean in and our lips meet. An amazingly warm feeling spreads through my entire body. And we don't stop. It's been a long time since I kissed someone so hard, that I felt like I had to stop and breathe. Our lips break, but only briefly; just enough time for him to adjust his position and angle his body so that he's squarely facing me, and when our lips meet again, our bodies are even closer than before, and his chest is pressed against mine. I pull my face away from his kind of abruptly and watch as he opens his eyes, which are filled with hot desire. Like he *has* to have me. I stand up off the couch, never breaking eye contact with him.

"You coming, or not?"

That was the only hint he needed. He stands up to his full height, and lifts me off the ground before I wrap my legs around his body, locking my ankles behind him. I can feel him pressing hard against me as he carries me down the hall and into his bedroom.

SAMUEL NOBLE

I'm not gonna have sex with her." We got out of school only a few hours ago and I'm already chilling out at Carter's house. Amanda should be here any minute. Presently I'm sitting at his desk chair trying to convince him I don't want to do anything with Amanda. And that's mostly true. But somewhere inside, a part of me knows that I'm trying to convince myself too.

"Fine man whatever!" he says, grinning and shrugging, baggy blue sweatshirt hanging off his shoulders. "I'm not saying you are tryna do something. I believe you."

A concerted effort is required for me to ignore Carter's blatantly smuggish grin and condescending tone.

"So, when you asked her about coming over was she like—I mean, did she sound mad?" I ask.

"Mad? Nah, she said you were probably just really stressed out and stuff, you know, considering…" *Considering your brother died.* Is what he thinks but doesn't say. "She wasn't mad though, no."

There are a few moments of silence until he says, "So when is it?"

"When's what?"

"The…you know, the funeral?" I figured he'd be asking that at some point. I mean after all, he was a friend of Gregory too, so I tell him the truth.

"I, I don't know. Whenever they're done, I don't know, investigating the body or whatever." I'm expecting my heart to drop, in awe of my own ability to refer to my brother as 'the body,' but it doesn't. Instead, hot anger flashes over my body at the thought of having to lower him into the ground.

Carter's shoulders drop like he's just involuntarily imagined Gregory's dead face in his head. Unfortunately, I can relate because that happens to me on the regular, only worse because unlike him, I actually saw Gregory's dead face.

The doorbell rings and I guess at this point Amanda is cool enough with the Ahu's that Carter doesn't even get up to answer the door, I hear a muffled exchange of greetings, followed by footsteps thumping up the stairs.

The door creaks open and Amanda peeks her head inside cautiously, before stepping inside the room. I jump up immediately before Carter can say anything dumb. "Hey Amanda. Can I talk to you?" I can tell by the curious confusion on her face that she's taken aback by the way I jumped up off the floor so quickly.

And now I'm standing there all awkward in front of her, and this is one of those moments when I'm glad I'm Black, so no one can see how red my cheeks feel. I try not to look at Carter who's muffling his laughter with the sleeve of his sweatshirt from his bed.

"Umm OK," she says, brushing her long dark hair behind her ear. Her voice sounds confused yet anticipatory.

As we step out of the room together Carter says, "Have fun kids!" in this horribly fake high-pitched voice. It takes every last ounce of my inhibition not to turn around and knock him out again.

Amanda and I close the front door behind us and stand there in front of the house. It's a little chilly, but not quite cold. Well, not to me anyway. She shivers and hugs herself, rubbing her hands over her bare arms. I wish I had a jacket to offer her, but I don't.

Swallowing hard, I start to talk. Just to get it off my chest- to make things right. I clear my throat, shifting my feet on the concrete below. "So, I just want to like, say I'm sorry for, you know, treating you like that at the party the other night. I was totally 100% out of line." She doesn't say anything, just sways back and forth slightly, head tilted to the side, arms wrapped snugly across her chest.

When a few seconds pass and she still hasn't said anything, I continue. "And also, about the other day, when I saw that video. I... I was messed up. Like seeing that really messed me up, and you were there. I shouldn't have turned around and talked bad about you like that. I had no right." She sighs and looks me in the eyes like she's actually contemplating going off on me.

Then she starts talking real slow, and stepping closer to me as she does. "Yeah, I guess... it's OK." She's right in front of me, close enough that I'm really looking down to make eye contact with her. "Only because I know this is," she reaches up and lightly touches her hand against my cheek. Sparks fly through my body, "Hard for you."

"So, we're cool?" I ask, realizing that she's now slid her hand away from my face and is resting it against my chest.

"We're cool."

I take a step closer. Why did I take a step closer? She does too. We're face to face. Her eyes are closed. So are mine. We're kissing. Again. Only this time it's much better because neither of us is crying. When I pull away, the thought of her and Gregory creeps into my mind, but one flutter of her eyelash against my cheek sweeps all of those thoughts of him away.

HUNTER GARRETT

Still no news. I've been sitting here in silence avoiding eye contact with Emerson for a solid 15 minutes. Every time someone comes through double doors I basically jump out of my seat, thinking it's a doctor here to tell me how Artie's doing. Time after time, the long white coat that emerges from the doors is there to share news with someone else. I haven't looked at the nurse either, though she still sits dozing off on the other side of Emerson where the woman left her.

"Hey Dad?" he says in a small voice. My heart shivers.

When I turn to look at him, he looks like a normal scared seven-year-old boy. Not like the animal that burned holes into my body with his eyes and tackled me to the ground. He looks like a blonde haired, green eyed kid worried about his little brother.

Trying my best to comfort him, I say, "Emerson I know you're worried about your brother, but you shouldn't be. Don't worry. I promise you, Artie will be completely fine. He's a fighter, you know."

He stares at me unblinking. "That's not what I was going to say."

"What were you going to say?"

"I was going to say...I learned about how punishments and

stuff work."

"Punishments...What do you mean? You're in first grade."

"Not in school. I was watching The History Channel."

I can't help but laugh at that. "You're seven. No SpongeBob? No Scooby-doo? You're seven and you casually watch The History Channel in your free time?" He's just staring at me with a completely straight face. I guess it isn't funny to him. "What'd you learn?"

"An eye for an eye. Hammurabi's code." He stops swinging his legs and looks on, unblinking. "Daddy, you killed someone didn't you?" The room feels like it's closing in on me. What do I say? What do I do? He obviously already knows the answer to the question considering he pointed out that similar looking kid at the Aquarium. But still, am I just supposed to be like, *yeah, Daddy killed a kid?*

Before I can think of what to say, those double doors swing wide open all over again, for what seems like the millionth time in the past hour, and when I look up from my son, I see Leah and the child services lady, whose name I can't remember, walking towards us.

I stand and try to make eye contact with Leah, but as they approach, she looks down and always away from me, avoiding eye contact completely. Please tell me Artie is...

"Did you hear anything?" I ask, reaching out for her.

She steps back slightly and doesn't answer, head still angled downward.

"About your son? No." The woman snaps. What is up with this lady? I haven't done anything to her. "But you can go ahead and come with me."

"You got Emerson?" I ask Leah. Again, she ignores me, but sits in the seat beside him, and she is hugging him close to her body, so the lady and I turn to leave.

We're in some small office-like room. "You can sit right here Mr. Garrett," she says, gesturing to the seat on one side of the desk as she plops down in the one across from it.

"What's your name again?"

"Cathy," she says like she's already annoyed. Then she gets right to the point. "So, tell me about how Artie was injured?"

This bitch knows the answer to this crap already. I try to explain what happened in a way that doesn't make me sound like I'm mentally ill "Um. I was trying to uh, get rid of these shoelaces that were dangling from these telephone wires in front of our house, so I threw the knife in the air to try to cut them and apparently it hit Artie on the way down.

"Apparently?" she asks, lifting her eyebrows.

"Yeah. What is it?"

"Nothing. Apparently is just an odd word choice under these circumstances. Anyway, can you tell me why you suddenly felt the need to take down those shoelaces right at that moment?"

Again, with the difficult questions. How do I answer this one? "Um, I just got like, annoyed by them. They'd been there for a long time and I just thought they should come down." My words trail off and my brain stumbles. "I...I don't know...I guess I was feeling kinda sick at the time? Kinda stressed?"

She's looking at me with an absolute poker face, lips pursed tightly as she pens neat notes on the pad in front of her. "And you thought *throwing a knife* into the air was the best way to do this?" She asks as if it's a regular, valid question, as if my actions weren't rooted in insanity.

"I guess so, yeah," I shrug in defeat.

"Hmm," she says, like she's genuinely considering what I'm saying, "and you are aware of the fact that you're currently being accused of a crime." Shit, she knows that? Of course she knows that.

"Yes. I am aware."

She looks at me, pursing her lips like she was expecting a more dramatic reaction. I make it a point not to give her one. "Well, I just wanted to inform you that your wife expressed concern regarding the safety of your two sons, Artie and Emerson."

A sudden ache flashes over my whole body. "What?! She wouldn't- she didn't say that, I'd never hurt our kids!" I catch myself. "At least not on purpose…. Never."

"Yes Mr. Garrett. She did." She's emotionless, her chalky, thin white skin is taunt on her face. And because you are currently being accused of a serious and violent crime, and caused significant physical harm to your son, I have come to the conclusion that your children are in fact at significant risk of further harm if they are to remain in your care. My mouth can't form any words. "So, you will be restricted from having contact with your children for the time being."

"What? WHAT!?" I stand up, my body knocking the desk a little as I do. "You can't take my son!"

"Your wife has already taken him."

209

SAMUEL NOBLE

As we step back into Carter's house and climb the stairs to his room, our fingers are shamelessly interlaced. I'm not sure why...after we'd kissed and fallen into step side by side, it happened organically, and neither of us pulled away. When I push open his bedroom door, Carter takes one look at our hands, smiles smugly, nods, and goes back to whatever he was doing on his phone.

The two of us sit side by side on the floor, our backs against Carter's bed. She leans her head into my shoulder like she knows her hair smells freaking amazing and wants me to know it too.

"Damn," he says, shaking his head at the TV. Hunter Garrett's pale face is plastered on the screen. "You know that man really does live just down the street from us." Carter looks at Amanda and nods towards his bedroom window.

Amanda startles, lifting her head, green-gray eyes focused on Carter. "What?" You mean... that guy, Hunter Garrett? He lives in your fucking neighborhood?"

"Yeah," Carter says, dropping his phone against the carpet, standing up and heading over to his window in socked feet. He lives right there in the house with the shoelaces." Amanda joins him and leans over beside him, but I stay put as he points a finger against the glass.

"You knew? she asks, nodding in my direction. I shrug and

nod back. "We should go there," she says.

"What?" Amanda just blurts it out, and when she does, I jump up and join them without really thinking. "Why the hell would we do that?" I ask from behind Amanda, as I look over her head and out the window.

"Yeah, why would we do that?" Carter repeats.

"I don't know; I mean that guy like killed your brother. We should just like, I don't know..."

The three of us are crowded in front of the window, and as I stand behind her, Amanda's dark hair comes up to about my chin.

"I got spray-paint. And there's like, rocks outside, so..." Carter breaks the silence then trails off, always prepared for the opportunity to get into something.

I turn to face him, "You guys cannot be serious!" You wanna break into the guy's house?" I say it louder than intended.

"Shh dude! You know my parents are home."

"You can't be serious," I say, directing the question towards Amanda.

"I, I mean," she stumbles with her words. "The guy's a murderer. Nothing we do can ever be as bad as what he did. He killed your brother." Her last sentence is marked with a deliberate, even tone.

I can't believe what I'm hearing. "Your girl is smart." Carter adds.

I skillfully ignore the fact that he just called Amanda 'my girl' as my mind revs into thought. And when silence takes over the room again, that numb anger returns, and there's something new. It's a need for revenge, and it's gnawing at my bones.

I remain in that numb, anger, revenge-twinged state for a minute, holding my tongue. I let the silence fill the room even more.

And eventually, slowly, and intentionally, I say, "You know what? He did murder Gregory. He did. And nothing we do could be as bad as what he's done already." The silence that follows is perfect, because it gives me the chance to make peace with my decision, and I do.

They nod in unison, egging me on. I feel my body grow hot as my fists clench up unconsciously. I keep going. "And the justice system. You could say the justice system will take care of it, but come on—the justice system is corrupt and racist as fuck, and can't accomplish anything. I, I mean look at what happened with Trayvon and Mike Brown, and Alton Sterling." I shake my head. "And everyone else." And I feel bad, because in those two words, 'everyone else,' there are thousands of people.

"No justice," Carter says.

"You're right," Amanda agrees in a whisper, arms crossed over her chest as she stares blankly out the window.

"Yeah," I say. "Yeah. No justice. We could go there…"

"We should," Carter says quickly.

"Cause he'll probably get away with it," Amanda nods, deep in thought.

"We'll wait till it's dark."

MONAY DAVIS

When I open my eyes, I see him. His face. He looks adorable when he's sleeping. I'd be OK if his face was the first thing I saw when I woke up every day for the rest of my life. Our matching, chocolate brown skin perfectly contrasts against the crisp white sheets surrounding us. His well-muscled chest rises and falls as he sleeps peacefully, as golden rays of sunlight pour in through the window behind him. Wait, sun? That is WAY too much sun for five something in the morning. Shit. What time is it? It's Tuesday so we're live at 8:00 am. My phone buzzes from the kitchen table. The clock on the nightstand next to me reads 7:48. One second, I'm basking in the sun in bed with a beautiful man, the next I'm leaping out of the bed and tripping over blankets and clothes on the floor in my underwear hightailing it down the hall to the kitchen.

The last tab open on my iPhone is the Wikipedia page for 'Netflix and Chill.' So yeah, now I know what that means. Jeez, last night seems like ages ago. Eight missed calls and six text messages. All from Robert. They consist of several "Where the heck are you's?" occasionally mixed with a little profanity. I bet he blew up Jay's phone too. I turn to head back to the bedroom to wake him in the sexiest way possible, but I'm startled by him standing there shirtless in a pair of gray sweats, leaning against the kitchen entrance.

"Stop looking at my ass," I tease, turning so he gets an eyeful of it.

"I don't think I can," he smiles and bites his bottom lip. "Round two?"

"What?!" I act annoyed, "Jay, do you know what time it is?"

He furrows his eyebrows at me, then leans over to check the clock on the oven. He gasps. "It's freaking 8:00! Whatarewegonnado?"

"You're adorable when you're flustered," I say, unable to hold it back. It's true.

He looks at me confused, shoulders sagging forward in defeat. "You're not mad?"

I laugh. "I got like six texts from Robert. The last one says they're just gonna air a rerun. He's pissed though for sure."

"Huh," he says relieved. His face cracks into a smile. "Should we just go straight to Starbucks then?"

I tilt my head to the side and look him up and down. "Round two, then Starbucks."

HUNTER GARRETT

"YOU LET HER TAKE MY KIDS? What the HELL? Don't you need like permission or something to do that?" Cathy just sits and stares like she's enjoying the dramatic reaction I'm finally giving her, and it makes my head pound even harder.

"As a child protective services worker, it is my responsibility to determine whether children are at significant risk of further harm. At this point, I have determined that your children are in fact at risk of further harm. However, there will be a court hearing."

"A court hearing?"

"Yes. Your wife has decided not to press charges, but a court hearing will be necessary to determine at what time it will be appropriate for you to be reunited with your children. Until then, you are to have no contact with either of your sons." Suddenly I feel as though I'm underwater. The words coming out of her mouth seem so muffled I can't even hear what she's saying, and it's like there isn't enough breathable oxygen in the room. I feel myself start sweating through my T- shirt. I can handle being accused of murder. I can handle being hated by the world. I can handle my son being afraid of me, but I cannot handle my kids being taken away from me. I just can't. When I blink, tears spring from my eyes, and I don't even try to wipe them away. I watch the woman's thin lips flash a sadistic, quick half-second smirk at my pain.

She sits up straighter and says, "As I said before, my colleague has already left with your wife and children." The room spins as I turn away and burst through the door and stumble into the hospital hallway, my vision blurred by tears. My body feels heavy and my head spins on my shoulders as I enter the waiting room. The chairs we were sitting in earlier are empty now.

"Leah. LEAH! What the- why?!" I'm holding my head and screaming in the quiet waiting room. Everyone looks at me like I'm some kind of hysterical homeless guy. I don't care. Maybe they haven't left yet. Maybe they'll still hear me. "EMERSON! EMERSON, LEAH!" I'm standing in the center of the room hopelessly optimistic that Emerson will coming running to me from somewhere and fall into my arms, and I'll pick him up and tell him I love him and we'll all leave together with Artie like nothing ever even happened. But no. Two buff security guards stomp towards me, grab me by the arms, and drag me through the hospital exit.

"You need to leave Mr. Garrett."

"You're causing a disturbance."

I just let them drag me away, my body limp with defeat, calling out for Leah and Emerson until I'm back in the parking lot. Maybe they're still home. Maybe they didn't really leave... I race down the slick road away from the hospital, driving faster now than I did on the way there. Fuck. I'm gonna miss this light; it's yellow. It turns red. Fuck it. I go anyway, narrowly beating oncoming traffic from my right. I burn rubber cutting a hard left as I ignore the stop sign and turn onto our street. There's the house. Are there cars in the driveway? No. Shoes are still up there though. Maybe her 'colleague' just dropped them off and they're inside. I hustle to the door, taking quick steps across the icy slick surface of the driveway, and push it open. Don't tell me my kid is gone. "Leah! Emerson! EMERSON!" Nothing. Nothing at all. Just silence. Leaning against the closed front door, I lower my body to the floor. Emerson is gone and Artie…Artie…shit! I just left him there.

I pull my phone out of my pocket to call Leah. It rings…rings…rings…someone answers. There's just breathing on the other end. Part of me expects to hear Creepy Cathy's sadistic voice on the other end teasing me and cackling because she knows how bad she just screwed up my life.

But instead I hear a small voice say, "Daddy?" It's Emerson.

Don't mess this up Hunter. "Hey bud. Where's your mom?" Still breathing. No Answer. I try another route. "Where are you guys?" Still nothing. Now for the killer question, "Have you heard anything about your bro-."

"Don't call us anymore." His shaky little voice is laced with fear. "If you do… I'll, I'll kill you." He says it almost like he's asking a question, then hangs up, and silence presses against my ears again. My phone nearly slips out of my fingers. Did my kid just…threaten to kill me? I get a flashback of that old guy I saw in the jail cell, or at least the guy I thought I saw, or dreamt I saw, or whatever. I let my head fall back hard against the door.

SAMUEL NOBLE

"Ya'll ready?" Carter asks from his bed. I look up over Amanda's head to the window. It's finally dark out.

She jumps to her feet. "Let's do dis!" She seems excited. Second thoughts flood my brain, but I shove them right back out. This is the dude that killed my brother. He's a freaking murderer, a murderer who will probably get away with murder. We're not going to hurt him. We won't touch his kids. We'll just have a little fun. Exhale. I haven't done that in a long time. Amanda and Carter are looking at me expectantly. "Ready," I say, before I realize that, for whatever reason, I'm smiling when I say it.

"My man!" Carter slaps me hard on my back. "Whoo! I'll get the stuff!" Carter's brimming with excitement as he rushes out of the door and thumps down the stairs. He's already having way too much fun. Amanda and I are alone again. She turns to face me, looks at me, looks deep into my eyes. She's worried. "You OK with this Sam?"

"What? Me? Of course, are you kidding? It's not like were gonna kill him, and c'mon, you know he'll get away with what he did.

She sighs, nods, "You're right."

"Are you OK with it?"

She hits my shoulder kind of hard and looks at me like I'm crazy. "Are you kidding?" She laughs. "I've done worse than this before Sam."

"You've done worse than break into and trash a guy's house?" I ask. She smiles and nods. "Hmm. I thought you were... I don't know, a goodie-two-shoes or whatever."

"You thought wrong." She leans away just as Carter pushes the door open. His eyes are wide and excited and he's grinning like a maniac. In his right fist he's got a couple of black ski masks and under his left arm is a can of black spray paint.

"Alright, alright, ALRIGHT!" He tosses two ski masks onto the carpet in front of us. "Let's do this my niggas! Whoo!"

Amanda giggles a little then pulls one of the masks over her head.

I laugh. "I don't know if your face is too small or what, but your eyes just aren't matching up with the holes." There's no opening for the mouth, but I can still see the outline of her smile.

"You try," she says. Her voice sounds all muffled.

I pull a mask over my head too. It smells horrible. "UGHHH! Bro! This thing stinks!" Carter howls and cackles then falls to the floor shaking and laughing hysterically.

"DUUUDE! This isn't funny. It smells like you used it to wipe your friggin ass!"

Carter is snorting and laughing and struggling to catch his breath. "Naw man. I didn't wipe my ass with it. I think I just ate some Mexican food before I wore it last though."

"Does yours smell?" I nod towards Amanda. She shrugs and gives a small head shake.

"Lucky. Can I have yours man?" I basically beg Carter.

"Naw man, this one's mine."

"Why's that?"

"He pushes it against his nose, inhales deeply, closes his eyes and says, "Cause it just came out of the wash." He pulls it over his head too, and without looking in the mirror, I know the three of us look crazy.

"We should take a selfie." Amanda says.

"That'd give us away." I say, shaking my head.

"How?" Carter asks dumbly, his mask still twisted around his face.

"C'mon," I explain, "the three of us post a ski mask selfie on Instagram the same night and from the same neighborhood in which a like, break-in takes place, and that doesn't raise eyebrows?"

"True."

"You're right."

"OK. Let's go," I say, standing up. I reach out to help Amanda to her feet too. The three of us stand there in the middle of the room in ski masks looking stupid for a few seconds. I think all of us are having a burst of second thoughts when Carter says, "I think we should take two cars just in case, you know, one of them gets apprehended."

"Apprehended?" Amanda squints, "What does that even

mean?"

"It doesn't matter. Two cars are fine. Let's get outta here," I say, not wanting to lose the slight rush that's currently moving through my veins.

We file down the stairs, Amanda and I with bats, Carter with a rattling bottle of spray paint.

"Mom, we're gone. Be back in a few," Carter calls as we step outside.

"Um...Oh, okay. Isn't it kinda late for a Tuesday ni-" The door slams shut before Mrs. Zhu can finish her sentence. It's colder out now than it was when Amanda and I were out here earlier, and at just after 8:00, darkness is hanging heavy over the neighborhood.

All three of our cars are parked either in the driveway or on the street. "I'll drive with Amanda and you can take your car," I say. "In case one gets, you know, 'apprehended'. Carter eyes us through his mask like he thinks the two of us are about to try and sneak off to a hotel room or something afterwards.

"Cool." He tosses his keys into the air and catches them in his palm as he heads to his Ford Fusion in the driveway.

I open the passenger side door for Amanda and she smiles at me and climbs inside. I race around the car and get in on my side. Oh crap. There's bottles and wrappers and stuff everywhere.

"Sorry for the mess."

"I've seen worse," she shrugs, and reaches for her buckle. My phone buzzes in my pocket. It's Carter.

Carter: Come to my car real quick

Me: Why

Carter: Just do it

Me: K

Carter: Is it really that hard to type the O in front of the K???

"Be right back," I say to Amanda, before pushing my door open and climbing back out into the darkness. She looks indifferent.

Carter's headlights shining against the darkness make my eyes burn and water. I squint as I approach his car and tap on the window. He rolls it down halfway, reaches out a hand and dumps a handful of condoms into my palm.

"What are these for?" I ask dumbly.

"Dude," Carter laughs, "didn't you take 7th grade health class? Safe sex, ya know?" I try not to act embarrassed, but doing so is never worth it when you're around people who know you well.

"I'm not gonna need 'em."

"I don't know man," he shakes his head. "I think for you, tonight might be the night. That's why I said we should take two cars," he nods at the condoms, "just in case." I shake my head and turn away. As I make my way across the dark front yard, I hear him howling and cackling hysterically. I shove the condoms VERY deep down into the pocket of my jeans and attempt to get back into the car with Amanda like none of that happened when I realize from 7th grade sex-ed that you aren't supposed to keep condoms in your pockets.

"What was that about?" she asks.

"Nothing," I say, pulling off the ski mask so I can actually see as I start the engine. She shrugs like she doesn't care, and I can't tell if she's faking not caring or if she really just doesn't.

MONAY DAVIS

I've always secretly envied that obnoxiously in love couple that sits next to each other in the booth at the restaurant. Like really? Who does that? Jay and I do apparently. It's late Tuesday morning and it's actually a little early for us to be at Starbucks since we didn't host the show this morning. We're sitting so close together, our shoulders are touching. It's quiet and smells good in here, as usual. Sun shines through the big window in front of us.

Jay nudges me. "ISB 3 o'clock." He's grinning and pretending to be super focused on his drink so the old lady sitting at 3 o'clock doesn't know we're talking about her.

I look up to see a mega old-timer gawking at me from across the café. I laugh. "You're right," I whisper. "She looks like she was born in the 1800s."

"Do you think she heard about the emancipation proclamation?" Jay asks, looking serious.

"I don't know," I'm trying not to laugh. "What do you think it is?"

"Whaddya mean?" he asks.

"I mean, what do you think it is about me that makes it hard for her to believe I'm Black?" Jay looks me over-- over all of me, grinning. I feel so vulnerable and aware of his eyes and his smile.

"I don't know. It could be your ring or your necklace. Or your purse. Or the fact that we're at Starbucks. Starbucks isn't really a Black people place, you know."

"Jay!" I laugh, "What are you, a racist?" I joke. "So Black people can't name their kids what they want, watch *Friends* or eat at Starbucks in your world?"

"Calm down Mo, they're just stereotypes."

"I don't know, I mean, think about what you said last week." He looks at me dumbly. "About how White women like, grab their purses or whatever when they're walk past you. It's a stereotype that Black men are all violent and dangerous, and that stereotype obviously isn't true. But when women clutch their purses it perpetuates that stereotype and divides us, Blacks and Whites, even further." I can tell I've got his attention now. "And likewise, when you say stuff like 'Black people don't watch *Friends* or go to Starbucks,' it seems minor and innocent and funny and insignificant, but really, it's still a stereotype, and it still perpetuates that divide."

"You are soooo right Oprah," he jokes. "Oh shit. She's coming."

Sure enough, the mega old timer has struggled to her pale, bony legs, and is making her way around tables towards us.

"Probably wants us to go pick some cotton for her or something," Jay whispers out of the corner of his mouth. She's so close I think she might have heard him. I kick him hard under the table.

"Ouch! What was that for? She's too old to hear that well."

She's standing in front of us now. I have no clue what to

expect. Jay and I are sitting there grinning like two kindergarten kids pretending to be good in front of their teacher.

"Ma'am can I help you?" Jay asks politely, pretending to be on his best behavior.

"Are ya'll... the two colored folks from that TV show?" she asks in a raspy southern drawl.

Jay and I look at each other, then, back at her. I'm one hundred percent sure we're thinking the exact same thing: Did this woman just call us 'colored folks'? In 2016? Really? Some things never change.

Jay is busy biting his lip, so he doesn't laugh, so I take over. "Yes ma'am. We are. *Yesterday with Jay and Monay.*"

"Ahh, yes! That is, it ain't it? I just wanted to say that, well, when I was sitting over there looking at ya'll like that, I just wanted to tell you I really loved that segment ya'll did with that young boy yesterday. The Noble kid. Such an articulate young man. It was very powerful."

My heart sinks. I just realized I haven't even thought about Sam since the show yesterday since I've been so caught up with...

Jay cuts in. He knows I'm drowning. "Yes. Well thank you. It was an absolute pleasure to talk to him."

"Yeah, yeah. And I could just tell he was in so much pain." The lady won't quit. "He was definitely suffering. I remember watching the news once and they said those boys was adopted. It's really too bad. I bet he feels so alone not knowing any of his real family members. The only one he ever knew gone. At a time like this, a boy needs his mother. His real mother."

Jay and I sit there in stunned silence. Without even looking at him, I know he knows I'm fighting back tears. Come on. Keep it together. I let out a breath, but it comes out shaky. I know I can't talk.

Jay rescues me again. "You're probably right ma'am. Thanks so much for your compliments on the show."

"Of course. Ya'll have a great day."

"You as well," Jay says. Finally, she turns and limps back to where she came from.

There's silence for a second, and then his hand is covering mine. "Are you OK?" He sounds concerned. I want to tell him *no, I'm not OK, my son is dead and I'm the worst mother that ever lived and I'm too worried about tarnishing my own reputation to let people know, that yes, I was raped, and yes, I was a teen mom, and no, I'm not the flawless, blemish free black professional I pretend to be. I'm human, and I make mistakes, and right now, the biggest mistake I'm making is not being with my son.* But I don't say any of that. I can't because my mind is still calculating the implications of something he said. He said, 'You're right.' When the woman said Sam needs his real mother, he said, 'You're right.'

He's still looking at me, eyes filled with worry.

"So, you think…I should be there with him?" I sniff.

"Wha- what are you talking about?" He really doesn't know.

"When she said Sam needs his real mother you said she was right. Which means I should be there. With him. Somehow…. Right? So, this whole time you've been thinking that, and you never said anything?"

He's frozen. Has no clue what to say to me. It's obvious.

He's thinking carefully about what he says next. "I think that... I mean... Yeah. I guess if it were my kid. And their brother, my son, had died, I'd probably want to be with them. Yeah. Regardless of what some court said about it, even if I was ashamed of...the circumstances. I'd be there with my kid."

I'm briefly distracted by the fact that the words coming out of his mouth are showing me how amazing of a father he'd be...Focus. He's right.

"You're right. I need to go there. Today. Now."

"What?" he sits up straight beside me, "you're gonna just hop on a plane and fly to Alabama? You don't know where he is or anything."

"True. But Robert does." I know that Robert had to have their address in order to send the limo that took them to the airport. All I have to do is book a flight and give him a call. "I'm leaving." I start to stand up to go when Jay grabs my arm.

"Wait." He looks stressed.

"What? If I leave now, I can make it before dark."

"I, I know I just. I had plans for later."

"Plans? What plans?"

"Like I had umm, gotten us tickets to see-" he laughs like he's embarrassed. "To see *To Kill a Mockingbird*. The play."

I can't help but laugh a little and sit back down next to him. "But you hate *To Kill a Mockingbird*."

"I know," he says. "But you love it. And I love you." He looks surprised by the words that just came out of his mouth.

My heart just about jumps out of my chest. I'm stunned. Did he just say that? He couldn't have. The look of sheer pleasesayitback, pleasesayitback, pleasesayitback on his face tells me he did.

I put my hand against his cheek. Our lips meet, and we melt into each other. I pull away and say, "I love you too. And I'd love to see To Kill a Mockingbird with you, but tonight, I've gotta see my son."

He smiles and looks at me, drunk with infatuation. "OK," he whispers, "another time."

"Another time," I repeat, before standing up and walking out of the café.

HUNTER GARRETT

The pain in my neck is the first thing I notice when I open my eyes. The next thing I notice is the pain in my ass. Somehow, I managed to fall asleep on the floor against the front door. I click on my phone. Battery is 5% and apparently, it's Monday now. Jeez. My knees crack and pop as I stand up to hunt for an outlet. It stinks in here.

"Sawyer!" I whistle sharply. Whining and the sound of scratching paws comes from behind the guest room door. I plug in my phone, so I can make my calls and head over there. As soon as I open the door, Sawyer leaps out of the room nearly knocking me over. With him through the door comes a rancid, yet instantly recognizable odor. Dog shit. A pile of the stuff is resting in the center of the room. It looks so fresh, for a second, I feel like I can see little clouds of hot steam rising up from it. I don't have time for this now. I've got to check on Artie. I slam the bedroom door shut and stuff some clothes under the crack at the bottom to try and seal the smell in the room, then let Sawyer outside to take care of his business.

I dial Leah again. No answer. When I call the hospital, a cheery young voice answers immediately. "Garner-Scott memorial Hospital, this is Christie, how can I help you?"

"Hi, umm. I was calling about Artie Garrett?"

There's a pause, and then she says, "Oh, ummmm. I uh, are

you Mr...Garrett? Hunter Garrett?"

This can't be good. OK. Think fast. "No, it' not. This is his uncle Connor Garrett. Hunter's my brother." The lie comes to me that quick.

She buys it just as quickly. "Oh OK. Did you want the room number then?" So damn gullible.

"That'd be great Christie." I try not to sound artificial.

"OK. Give me one second. Let's see. Artie Garrett is room 307."

"307?" Great thanks.

"No problem."

"Take care now."

"Bye."

It only takes me four and a half minutes to get to the hospital and probably another 40 seconds tops to get from the car to right in front of room 307. I actually take the time to try and smooth the wrinkles out of my shirt and make sure there isn't anything on my face. I don't know if I'm going to see Artie only, or Artie, Emerson, and Leah, but I don't want to look bad for any of them. After taking a minute to catch my breath, I gently turn the door knob and it opens without a creak.

First, I notice a man standing with his back to me in a long white coat, head low, holding on to his wrist behind his back. I'm expecting him to turn around and escort me out of the room, but I guess the door opened so quietly, he doesn't know I'm there. Struggling to suppress my ragged breathing, I shift my eyes away from the doctor. Leah and Emerson's backs are to me and their leaning over the bed, blocking my view of Artie, though I can see the shape of his little feet halfway down the bed. They're both bent way over and Leah's whispering. I can hear her clearly from the doorway:

All powerful and merciful God, we commend to you your servant,

And I'm thinking, wait a second…

In your mercy and love, blot out the sins he had committed in human weakness,

No.

In this world where he has died

NO.

Let him live with you forever, through Christ our Lord

This isn't real.

Amen.

Shit. There's no way, there's no way, there's no way. Leah leans forward like she's kissing his forehead. I walk, shuffle slowly and silently, turning my head to see the doctor facing downward, his eyes closed completely, as I sidestep around to the foot of the bed until I see him. He's unmoving, his eyes are closed, his skin pale. He looks peaceful. Too peaceful. He looks dead. Neither of them has seen me. Their eyes are glued to Artie. It takes me a second to realize that the wetness on his face is from Leah's tears. It takes me another couple seconds to realize that my cheeks are wet too. He's dead. How did this happen?

And then I hear, "HEEYY!!!" It's like a crazed shriek that comes out of nowhere. It's Emerson. His head is angled sharply towards me, his cheeks red, messy blonde hair awry. Leah looks up too, from beside him, and I hear dress shoes click against linoleum as the doctor walks towards me.

"Hunter?" Leah asks. "What are you? How did you get-." Before she can finish her sentence, the doctor's firm grip is locked around my arm. I don't look away from Leah's red, wet eyes when she puts up a hand and motions for the doctor to stop. When she does, he immediately released my arm from his grip. Her lips open slightly, and I just stand there in silence, tears flowing down my face, legs weak as I wait for her to speak. And I'm standing there so ashamed and so broken, that I don't even notice that Emerson has stood up his full height, or that his fists are balled at his sides, until he's lunging towards me, sneakers squeaking against the shiny floor as he runs. At this point I'm just so weak and so in shock that when he makes contact, even the small amount of force carried by his little body just knocks me to the floor, and he climbs on top of me, banging my face with his tiny balled up fists. His glasses fall completely of his face, but he doesn't even seem to notice. Through his fists pounding my checks, mouth and eyes, I watch the doctors standing above me, frozen and astonished.

Leah's voice breaks through in between his screams, as he shouts, "YOU KILLED HIM, YOU KILLED HIM, YOU KILLED HIM!" I'm finally able to get both of his fists under control and push him off me, just as Leah rushes in, grabs him by his arms and drags him away from me as he struggles back against her. Once I stand shakily to my feet, my body shivering and sticky with sweat, she lets go, and he runs into me again and again, arms extended in front of him, pushing me closer and closer to the door. "GET OUT! GET OUUTT!!" Leah and the doctor stand by. It's like they're somehow subdued by the death hanging over the room. Finally, it's too much for me. I never wanted to hurt Emerson, but it's just too much.

"Get OFF of me!" I shove him hard backwards so hard that his head slams against the linoleum floor. He lays flat for a moment just staring at the ceiling before pushing himself up into a sitting position. He just looks at me, his mouth hanging open. And then he starts to cry. Emerson never cries. I stand there in the doorway just looking as Leah scoops him into her arms, holding him close so that his cries are muffled by her body. The doctor reappears to grab me again by the arm and lead me outside of the room, I look over my shoulder to see tears covering Leah's red, blotchy face as she cradles our son in her arms. And Artie- well- he's dead. He's dead. Just like Gregory. I killed him. I'm standing back in the hallway. As the door closes slowly, the last thing I get a glimpse of is the outline of Artie's still form clothed in white sheets.

SAMUEL NOBLE

"Nope. I don't see *anyone* in there," Amanda whispers for the 5th time.

"Are you *sure?*" Carter asks for the 5th time.

"YES! I'm sure, there's no one home. The house is empty. There's no cars in the driveway either, remember?"

"That's funny considering that dude's supposed to be here to guard our neighborhood or whatever," Carter says. "OK though, you can let her down man."

Finally. I'm standing in the dark round the side of Hunter Garrett's house with Amanda sitting on my shoulders, so she can see in through the side window.

I crouch a little lower so she can get down and hear her feet hit the ground with a quiet thump. Then she leans over and whispers in my ear, "You're really strong."

"Oh, thanks," I say shrugging like I'm not blushing on the inside. "Well, you're pretty light so you know." It's so dark, all I see is Amanda's glowing white teeth suddenly visible against the darkness surrounding her.

I'm pretty sure Carter's rolling his eyes when he says, "So are we going in or nah?"

"*Relax* man, you jealous or something?" I joke. "Yeah we're go-" I'm cut off by the unmistakable sound of shattering glass. Instinctively, I duck all the way down near the cold, wet grass and cover my face. Amanda just laughs.

I uncover my eyes and look up to see that the glass window I was just holding her up to is now broken and lined in jagged edges. "C'mon guys," she says like it's no big deal that she just threw a rock through some guy's window.

She jumps, grabs onto the little ledge in front of the window, and pulls her body up until she's got a knee up there too, then effortlessly pulls her body through the hole in the window with a graceful strength only a girl could ever have, and pretty much just steps inside. Damn.

"You comin' or what?"

Carter and I look at each other, then he tosses his spray paint up through the open window (Amanda catches it easily) and does the same, jumping up for the ledge and climbing into the house. Once he's in he says, "Hand me my bat," so I stand on my tippy-toes to pass him the bat.

She leans over the ledge and looks down at me. Her boobs are practically falling out of her bra and she has to know it. "Your turn," she says. So, I reach up like they did, hang from the ledge for a second before pulling myself up and pretty much just falling into the house, narrowly missing the jagged pieces of broken glass as I hit the floor, my knees and elbows banging against the hardwood floor

Carter snorts a laugh, but is still willing to reach out a hand to help me up. Amanda just giggles softly.

As I stand to my feet, I notice how good the warmth of the house feels in comparison to the night-time chill we just escaped from. I reach up to feel that my cheeks are still frozen and stinging from the cold. "Wait. My mask!"

Carter smugly pulls his freshly washed ski mask out of his pocket; as Amanda holds hers up I realize I never put mine back on.

"So what?" Amanda shrugs coolly. Her calmness radiates towards me, and when I exhale, all of my anxiety is expelled.

I'm actually kind of excited. My blood is rushing with adrenaline. I'm unsure of what exactly is going to happen, but still really pumped and alert. As I look around the house, I realize how quickly my eyes have adjusted. I pick up a bat from the floor and slam it into the jungle green vase on the kitchen table. It shatters into a trillion pieces. The three of us stand there in silence. I see four eyes all stretched wide and round, looking at me through the cutouts in the masks. Then Carter takes a swig at the dusty little chandelier hanging over the table. It shatters too. And then I know we're all smiling, even though I can't see either of their teeth. The three of us bend down almost simultaneously from a bottle of spray paint, then dart off in three different directions.

I'm feeling some type of really powerful high right now. Not that I know what being high feels like, but I just feel so wild and alert and, I don't know, hyped up or something. Not a care in the world. I feel loose and free. Yelling and yipping and crashing and banging and shattering around the house as I fly through the family room area and race into what I assume is the master bedroom. As soon as I open the door, a wall of stink hits me like a bus. I'm stumbling through the thickness of the odor trying to figure out what substance could give off a smell like that when my shoe lands on something mushy. I dare to look down and see that my shoe is several inches deep in (it can't be) ... dog shit. It is. Damn, these people are nasty! Who leaves a pile of dog shit in the middle of their carpeted bedroom floor? There's a dog there too, the likely suspect, just lounging in the corner of the room. When he looks up, I feel my body tense, but I relax again as he lowers his head back to the floor.

From behind me Carter laughs, "Shit. Literally." Then he smashes his shoe into the mound of poop and smears it deep into the carpet. For some reason, the fact that these people will have a permanent poop stain in the middle of their bedroom carpet doesn't bother me one bit.

I take a good whack at the lamp on the nightstand and the glass bulb shatters to the floor, and it's just so inexplicably satisfying. Carter thumps and whacks and bangs and shouts and drags the end of the bat along the wall as he races into the next room.

"Woo hooo!" he calls from across the house. He sounds out of breath. "Where do you think these people are though?" Carter laughs. It's a school night isn't it? And doesn't he have kids?"

"Who gives a shit, as long as they're not here," I say, yanking on the edge of a bookcase and knocking it over. Books and magazines and jewelry and a bunch of other random stuff falls out onto the carpet.

"True," he says. "Now you're getting the idea. Hey where's your girl though?"

I shrug even though Carter can't see me. Stepping into the bathroom, I see that there's a flowerpot sitting peacefully on the window ledge. Why not knock it to the floor?

"Where's Amanda?" Carter asks again.

Stepping over the shattered flower pot I mutter, "In here somewhere I guess."

Then I catch a glimpse of myself in the mirror. Me. Holding a bat and a can of spray paint. My eyes are wild. For a half second, doubt starts seeping back into my mind. For a half-second, I'm thinking, *what am I doing here? Why am I here? Who's getting anything out of this?* And then, looking in the mirror, I watch Amanda saunter into the bathroom, beanie hanging low on her head, wavy dark hair twisting about her shoulders. She stands behind me and to the left, resting her head on my shoulder and we look into the mirror at ourselves.

"You took your mask off?" I ask.

She shrugs coolly, "Wasn't my style." She wraps her arm around the back of my waist and leans into me. I lean into her too, and when I do, I'm conveniently reminded of the condoms in my pocket and briefly wonder if I'll need them. Still me, in the mirror. Me, holding a bat and a can of spray paint, with fucking Amanda Bentley leaning on my shoulder, my skin covered in a thin sheen of sweat. And I just feel broken. My brain, my body, my heart. Everything. Amanda, instinctively sensing my apprehension, stands on her tippy toes and presses her lips against my cheek. I watch in the mirror as she does.

"We're doing this for Gregory, remember?" I watch myself nod in the mirror as I say it. The words are strong, but somehow empty like it won't matter in the end. I'm unable to look away from the reflection of myself, but out of the corner of my eyes, I see her look down to the can in my hand.

"You used your spray paint yet?" she asks.

"No."

"Let's." She wraps her fingers around my fingers gripping the can. "Right here on the mirror. That's always how they do shit in movies." She leaves her hand on mine and brings the can up in front of us. My body is frozen as she holds down the nozzle and slowly moves our hands around. One line of paint, vertically drawn along midpoint of the mirror. A horizontal line across the first. I shift my eyes away from the paint and focus in on the reflection of her face. She looks focused, tongue poking out of the corner of her mouth a little as she holds the can steadily. When I look back at the paint I see letter '4.' Then on the second line, a small 'G' begins to form. Followed by an 'R.' Her fingers are still gripping mine, controlling my arm and forming an 'E,' a 'G,' an 'O,' and an 'R' horizontally across There's no room for the 'Y.' She stops moving our arms and releases the nozzle. After a pause, she presses down again, draws a dash after the 'R' and on the third line, finishes with the 'Y.' Finally, she lets go of my hand and our arms swing back to our sides. Our graffiti reads like:

4

GREGORY

I can't help but laugh and say, "For Gregor-why."

She shoves me gently. "I think he'll know." We're just standing there side by side, leaning into each other in silence, looking at my brother's name.

"For Gregor-why?" Carter's voice disrupts the silence.

I feel Amanda's shoulders droop forward. She turns away

from me and says, "Carter, you know what it's supposed to say!" like she's begging him to say he does.

He looks at the mirror again, eyes wide against the darkness. "Oooohhh." He slaps a hand against his forehead, "For Gregory." His tone becomes almost somber. "I get it," he whispers. "I get it." There's more silence. That happens so often now, since Gregory died. It's like we're all thinking the same stuff, feeling the same pain, and we all know that words can't describe it. What death feels like.

He sighs, sniffles, and then he's gone and it's just us again, standing in front of the mirror.

I turn so we're facing each other and wrap my arms around her body, staring into her piercing green eyes. She looks like she's waiting for me to say or do something.

"Hey," I say.

"Hey," she says.

She strokes my back and wraps her arms around me even tighter, and when she does, I can't help but lean into her because her body against mine makes me feel warmer than I have since Gregory died. Her green eyes shine into mine against the darkness. She tilts her head up slightly, and when she does, I reach my hand out and guide her chin upwards until our lips meet.

When I open my eyes, she's looking back at me, smiling shyly. "You know my…my parents aren't… home tonight," I say before I know why

She lifts an eyebrow. "No?"

"No." Her eyes search mine. "Do you wanna… come over?"

I ask, my heart thumping in my chest.

She pulls me closer until our faces are just inches apart. "Let's go," she says.

In seconds we're moving through the house, hands interlaced, jumping over the junk littered across the floor. Carter was right when he said the job was done. He got shit done while we were standing there wasting time painting the mirror. The TV in the family room is bashed in and the DVDs that probably used to be lined up neatly on the shelf below the screen are now sprawled and broken across the floor. The couch and carpet are soaked in wet lines of black paint. We step over shattered lamps and broken plates and glasses all the way to the kitchen. It takes me a second to realize that the brown footprints leading to the fist sized hole in one of the walls are from the poop he stepped in earlier. Amanda's just about to step on some when I say, "Careful, that's dog shit." She freezes and wobbles standing on one leg, and I grab her arm to keep her from falling into it face first. I feel crazy satisfaction, knowing we're leaving this place such a mess. I'd give anything to see that dude's face when he walks in here and sees what happens. Hopefully he understands why we did it. Why we *had* to do it.

We hop back out through the window and creep across the yard. The silence presses against my ears and my heart thumps in my chest. I'm scared someone's just going to jump out of nowhere and tell us to "FREEZE" or sirens are going to rise up from the distance and we'll promptly be shoved into the back of a cop car.

My body is filled with relief as we plop down into our respective seats of Dad's car.

"Whew!" she says, "that was close. It just *felt* like it was close.

I thought someone was chasing us."

"Same," I say, already looking over my shoulder and backing out of the driveway.

She giggles a little and knowingly says, "Why you in such a hurry Sam?"

MONAY DAVIS

I'm just stepping off the plane when my phone finally realizes it has cell service again, and I get the usual post-flight flood of text messages and emails. There are several from Robert asking for the 3rd, 4th, and 5th times, why I needed him to give me Sam's address earlier today, one asking me whether or not I'll be there for the show tomorrow and another two in all caps telling me I BETTER NOT BE STALKING THAT POOR KID, (too late for that), and of course, there's one from Jay.

Jay: U made it?

Me: Just landed. He only lives 10 mins away… kinda scared

Jay: Don't be. Do what u need to do

Me: What if he hates me

Jay: He might but ur his mom. Lots of teens hate their parents at some point lol

Me: True…thx

Jay: You got this Mo

It doesn't take me long to make it through the busy airport, down the escalator to the rotating luggage thingy and out into the breezy night air. It's warmer here than it is back in Atlanta, and the skies are clearer, stars shining against the darkness.

I climb into my rental car, a Nissan a couple of steps down from my BMW back home, and punch Sam's address. Driving down the road with the windows rolled low, The Weeknd's voice dripping like honey from the speakers, I take in the unfortunate condition of the city around me.

The light cast down from the streetlights reveals that graffitied-up worn-out buildings with broken windows line the streets, some of them sealed shut with black garbage bags. The illuminated area of grass under each lamp is brown and yellow and dead.

How is it that I'm living in a big condo in the city driving nice cars and my own son is here living with poor white trash. He's going to hate me. Maybe I should just turn around. Just go straight back to the airport and catch a flight home.

I'm strongly considering cutting this wheel and making a quick U-turn back to the airport when Google Maps tells me, "Your destination is on the left."

And there it is. A modest, white, two-story with light blue shutters. It's dark inside except for the light shining from the window on the 2nd floor. It's ten o'clock. What am I doing knocking on someone's door at ten o'clock on a Tuesday night? I feel like a major stalker standing there against the side of the car outside of someone's house in the dark like this. I think it'd be even creepier if I tried to slide back into the car and leave at this point, so I'm walking up the path to the front door, heart jumping, hands shaking. I'm three yards away when the door opens a crack. I freeze. The door is pushed open completely and Sam stands still in the doorway for a second, before bounding down the steps and the path in front of his house. His head is low, and his tall form moves so quickly through the darkness that he plows straight into me, nearly knocking me over.

"What the FUCK?" It sounds like a growl, his words obviously laced in anger and frustration. He takes a step back and looks up at me. "YOU? From that show?" Only one side of his face is illuminated by the light beside the front door. I'm unable to force any response from my lips.

"What the hell are you DOING HERE?!!" He's out of breath, his chest heaving, the whites of his eyes piercing through the darkness.

I stumble backwards in silence. What do I say to that? "I, I'm sorry to you know, intrude, but I just-."

"WHAT? Not now." He groans and puts his hands on his head in frustration. "Get the hell away from my house!" His voice cracks, and he turns away, footsteps pounding towards the waiting car in the driveway.

I realize this moment is about to come and go. If I don't do it now I might never get a second chance, so just as he's reaching out to open the driver side door, I spin around, and I say it. I say, "I'm your mom."

He freezes, temporarily knocked out of his fit of rage. "What?" He turns his head towards me, hand still resting on the door handle.

When he looks at me, and the lights once again cast an eerie glow on his cheeks, I see a hint of fear in his face.

"Yeah, I'm, I'm your mom." I say, shrugging like an idiot in the darkness.

He straightens up to his full height, stunned, and then he smirks, shakes his head and starts to laugh, laughs so loudly and hysterically I'm scared a neighbor's going to come out of the house next door and tell us to shut the hell up.

"You know what…" he shakes his head, cackling. "You're fucking with me, aren't you? You think this is FUNNY?!" He's pacing around by his car, running his hands over his face. "Showing up at my house at fuckin', what is it, like ten o'clock to tell me some bullshit like this? You're crazy. Get the fuck out."

"Sam!" I'm yelling and rushing the car, palms against the sealed window. He ignores me, shifting into gear and backing haphazardly out of the driveway and out into the street. The engine roars as he pulls away. With the glow of the headlights gone, the darkness returns.

HUNTER GARRETT

When I left the hospital, my heart in my knees, my vision so blurred I didn't think I could drive I kept cursing out that kid. I thought about it like this: If he hadn't been creeping around in a hood with his hands in his pockets in this part of town, tripping on his fucking shoelaces, I never would have caught up to him. If I'd never caught up with him, I never would have shot him. If I'd never shot him those laces never would have meant shit to me. If those laces never meant anything to me, then I never would have tried to get them down and if I'd never tried to get them down, then Artie would still be here.

But now I see it like this: If I hadn't assumed the worst. If I hadn't demonized him, if I hadn't been such a fucking racist, then NONE of this would have happened. It took me hours of resting my head against the rough pier and staring up at the sky trying to hold the tears inside my eyes to figure this out. One of the easiest things for a person to do is credit themselves with good things; with things that go right, but hardest to take responsibility and call yourself out when it's you who'd done wrong.

I sit up and hang my feet over the edge, jeans rolled up from the bottom, toes just tickling the water's surface. The sun is just about gone from the sky and the faint purple glow reflects across the water. Now, not one, but two dead faces are ingrained in my mind. Thinking back, their faces had one thing in common:

248

peace. They both looked peaceful, no longer burdened by the lows and the struggles and the pain and uncertainty of this world. I guess we can find peace in the certainty of anything, including death.

And that's how I feel right now. I feel certain. Certain of what it is I have to do next. There's an evil force in this world that killed two people in one week. All I have to do is remove it. I have to remove myself. Out of the equation, for Emerson and for Leah. If I don't do it myself I'm sure he'll do it himself. I haven't forgotten what that homeless psychotic bum told me in that jail cell. At the time, it seemed so ridiculous, I'd hardly thought about it twice, but now, I don't blame him. If the roles were reversed, I'd do the same. A man has got to avenge his brother.

When I stand up, there's more peace, it feels good, like I'm floating because I know what has to happen and I know it's almost over. It's almost over.

In my car, windows down headlights piercing through the darkness ahead of me, it's surreal to think that the key to my release has been right there in front of me all this time in a shoebox under the bed. I sigh relief and my heart, for the first time in a long time, beats slowly, basking in the comfort of certainty. The stars are shining bright for me tonight like they're telling me goodbye, or maybe that's for Artie and it's their way of welcoming him. Who cares? It's beautiful, I don't question it.

I'm in the driveway. I'm on the porch. The only thing that could change my mind at this point would be for Artie, and Leah, and Emerson to be inside the house right now, running towards me. But the universe must not want me here, because when I push open the front door, I see nothing like that. Broken glass, records spilled across the floor, trails of paint leading from the door.

The chandelier that usually hangs above the kitchen table has been reduced to glass shards spread all across the hardwood floor. The walls have been bashed in to the yellow fluffy stuff behind it and the vase Leah and I got on our anniversary lay fractured and broken in the corner. I'm bracing myself for a wave of hot anger and rage so intense I'm punching the walls myself, but it never comes. I wait some more, standing in the middle of the family room breathing heavily. Nothing. I feel-how do I say it? – Subdued. The silence in the house, which would usually suffocate me, now calms me. The wave doesn't come because none of this matters. None of this matters, because it's over. All I have to do is find the key. I'm in the bedroom. The dog poop is now smeared deep into the carpet. My shoulders shrug before I'm even able to process the fact that this stain will probably be here forever. So what? I won't be here to see it. Or smell it, sheesh.

In a pushup position beside the bed I reach into the dust cave under the mattress for the shoebox. I slide my hand across the carpet, fingers running over dust bunnies and knocking against used solo cups. I reach all the way up near the head of the bed frame then back down to the foot. No box. I flick on the flashlight on my phone and shine it around. No box.

Oh. Shit. It finally sinks in. He must've taken it. Emerson. Damn. Everything that bum said is going to come true. I knock the back of my skull against the bottom edge of the bed frame, struggling to stand as a wave of nausea hits me. At some point he must've come and gotten it.

On the floor in the bathroom, I am gripping the cool edges

of the toilet, worshipping the porcelain throne for the 2nd time this week. Stumbling to my feet, I'm in front of the mirror again, there's vomit running down my chin and resting on my T-shirt. On the glass is the message:

4

GREGORY

For Gregor -why? No. For Gregory. Gregory. That was his name. My heart just about drops out of my ass. It wasn't Leah or Emerson who did this. This was some type of revenge for what I did to that kid. For what I did to Gregory. I back away from the mirror. My gun is gone, but who took it? Emerson or the people who did this? And who's going to kill me first? I slide down against the wall until I'm on the floor. I pull out my phone and Google, "How to kill yourself." The first result is a number for a suicide hotline.

I scroll past it and click on the first real link.

The list is as follows:

7. Carbon monoxide Inhalation

6. Sleeping pills

5. Anesthesia

4. Lethal injection

3. Drowning

2. Hanging

1. Shooting in the head or heart.

Hmm… decisions, decisions. I could get in the tub.

Drowning would be fairly quick, and it wouldn't fuck up my body the way a bullet hole in my face would, but all I can see is Leah reaching in and pulling my dead, wet body up out of the water. If we had a real garage I could get in the car and suffocate myself. No. Too dramatic. Easiest and least interesting way to go out is with pills.

Unsurprisingly there are none in the medicine cabinet. Leah had hidden them as soon as Emerson had started walking, out of fear that he'd get a bottle open somehow and kill himself. How ironic. It's no big deal though. The Walmart is only three minutes away. And I get another chance to see those stars.

SAMUEL NOBLE

"You know what?" Her voice is breathy and laced with relaxation.

I sigh softly into her strawberry scented hair, pulling her naked body closer to mine, "What?"

"I think everything happens for a reason."

"Whadda ya mean?" I ask, turning on the mattress so I can see her eyes.

She pauses for a second, then continues. "I mean like us right here right now together. I mean… what we just did."

I turn away, staring up through the darkness at the ceiling for a minute, before looking back at her and smiling "…Yeah…"

There's a beautiful silence radiating around the room. I don't feel anything. Not pain, not anger, not hurt, only the gentle touch of her hand stroking my chest.

She continues. "I know it sounds bad but, we never would have happened if Gregory hadn't died. Maybe it's all part of a pla-" I don't even let her finish.

"WHAT?" I'm pushing myself up from beside her, propping myself up and resting all my weight on my left arm. It's like my body was just jolted back to life with a thousand bolts of electricity.

She flips over on her back and looks up at me dreamily like she didn't just say what I think she said. She giggles and reaches up to touch my face. "Jeez baby, I'm just saying. If Gregory had been here to see you steal me away like this he would have been real, you know, hurt. He really liked me, I think."

I knock her hand away and sit facing away from her over on the edge of the bed, my feet are hanging down to the floor. "I mean, I knew you liked him because of the prom thing, but I didn't know that you...that you knew he liked you... You knew that and you still... You still had sex with me? After he was dead?"

She sits up too, her hair tumbling over her shoulders, looking at me like I've got two heads. She shrugs. "Of course I knew. Girls always know."

I stand up and the room spins around me. I can't believe what I'm hearing. And her word choice. Did she have to say I 'stole' her.

I run my hands over my face. "Stole? You think I *stole you* from him?"

"Sam. Just relax. Come here and lay back down with me. It's alright," she says rubbing circles in my spot on the bed next to her.

The girl can't be serious right now. "Alright? It's alright to you? Are you serious about what you said?" The room is shrinking around me as she sits in silence. "You think I stole you! From my DEAD brother! Couldn't you have told me before we..."

She's quiet for a minute, her eyes dart far left, then back to me again. She's choosing her words carefully. "Well I mean if

254

you knew he was into me… which it sounds like you did. And then like five days after he dies you go and sleep with me, then, you know, it's kind of like yeah, like you stole me. I mean that's not the best choice of words since he's gone." She's rambling now. "I mean can't you steal something from a dead person, can you?"

My heart sinks lower and lower and lower with every word as I realize she's right. What the fuck did I just do? Man, I know it's kind of stupid to think about, but Gregory could be up there right now, watching me. Watching us. If he knew, if he saw, what would he say? My mind, body and soul are overwhelmed by a caliber of guilt I didn't know a human could experience. How could she say that to me? How could she say that I stole her? How could she blame *this*, blame *us* on *me*?

I look over at her sitting there in the bed looking at me, now holding her T-shirt up to cover her body. She looks so fucking stupid to me now. Not beautiful. Her round green eyes give her a look of ignorance, her upturned nose makes her look selfish. How could I do that? How did I fall for such a manipulative bitch?

"Dammit!" It comes out of my body like a legitimate scream. I bend over holding my body. How did I get here? Before I can think, I realize I just slapped my palm against my face. It stings which makes me even more upset. I grab a shoe and chuck it across the room. It smashes into the glass soldier on the dresser and knocks it to the floor with a crash. Amanda jumps up and runs over towards me, tripping over the sheets tied around her ankles. "Sam! STOP! She's next to me and I feel her warm hands grip my arm to get me to stop. I jerk away as soon as she touches me.

"Get AWAY!" She's too stubborn to listen and reaches out for me again, trying to touch my face.

"Sam, it's OK." She's lying. None of this is OK

She's still in my space, her hand on my back, breathing on me and shit. She looks me in the eye again and says, "Sam," but I don't let her finish. I just shove her backwards. I don't feel like I hit her that hard, but apparently, I did because her eyes get real wide as she stumbles backwards before falling, her momentum bringing her naked body to the floor and her head against the bedpost. For a second, she just sits there in shock looking at me. In stunned silence, I look back. Then her face contorts, and she looks like she's about to cry.

"Get OUT!" I yell, taking a step closer. She jumps off the ground and reaches for the pile of clothes I tore off her body only a few minutes ago. It feels like ages ago. As she scrambles to dress herself in the semi-dark room, I notice a tear running down her cheek, illuminated by the blue light from the TV. As she scoops up the clothes, something drops to the floor. She freezes, then bends over real quick to pick it up before I can tell what it is, then turns her back to me to block her view and hide it. I feel so exposed, like Gregory's watching me, and I know that if he is watching, he's crying, crying because of what I've done because of who I've become. What kind of terrible person does it take to make a dead man cry?

"What is that?" I ask.

She turns and looks at me innocently, her pale body glowing in the darkness and cocks her head to the side, long neck stretched and fully exposed before me.

"What?" she asks, facing me but holding the thing behind

her back. It reminds me of the PROM sign she hid from me in the hallway a lifetime ago. This bitch is still playing games with me. I stare at her from across the room trying to convey to her with my eyes the gravity of this situation. She doesn't get the hint and shrugs. I rush her without a second thought, knocking her back. When the things hits the floor between my feet, I see that it's a gun.

"Where the fuck did you get this?"

She's curled up in the corner now knees to her chest, ankles crossed. Her wet cheeks shine in the glow of the moonlight cast across her body. I feel powerful towering over her folded, shrunken form.

She stutters, she shakes, she's scared of me; fearless Amanda Bentley. I think she should be. "The guy's house," she whispers, "it was under the bed." She sniffles and lets out a shaky sigh.

I bend down to pick up the gun. The closest I'd ever gotten to touching a gun before was when Gregory and I played with the fake ones at the arcade. It's heavier than I thought it would be, yet fits perfectly and almost comfortably in my hand. As I straighten back up I hear a gasp. It's the type of gasp a person would make the first time they lay their eyes on hell itself. It's a gasp full of fear. Of course, it comes from Amanda. I stand in front of her, gun in hand and she starts wailing like a fucking baby.

"SamSamSam, stop, please please *please* don't hurt me." Her voice fades to an inaudible whisper, but her lips keeps moving and her head keeps shaking back and forth like she's still begging me not to kill her. "Please please *please* just let me go." I've never had such a profound effect on anyone's disposition. I've never made anyone this *afraid* before. Now she's sniffling and gasping and crying and I'm just standing here in front of her with this gun. How did I get here? Who the hell am I?

"Just go," I say, gesturing with the gun towards the bedroom door. She's out of the room in seconds, bare feet slapping against the hardwood hallway and down the stairs and out the front door. It closes with a slam that makes the whole house shake. I'm alone again and finally aware of how heavily I'm breathing and how hard my heart is beating in my chest. What the hell did I just do? How's Amanda, whose butt ass naked by the way, going to make it back to Carter's to get her car? Jeez. I pound down the stairs, hoping she's still there. I open the door. Nothing but a wall of darkness. Damnit. And it's only like 40 degrees out here too. She'll freeze to death. What am I? My stomach rumbles and flips as warmth rises up my throat. I barely make it to the toilet in time to empty the contents of my stomach. Why did I sleep with that girl? I mean, what the hell kind of brother am I? I'm looking at myself in the mirror, still shirtless, chest heaving, body covered in sweat, vomit dripping off my chin. I pointed a fucking gun at her. Like I was going to kill her or something. The guilt I'm feeling now is unlike anything I've experienced before. It's like world on my shoulders, a rock in my stomach and the sensation of being watched all at once. I'm seriously considering calling 911 to tell them there's a petrified naked girl running around in nearly freezing weather when I notice I've still got the thing in my hand. The gun. I pace around the house with it wrapped safely inside my fingers. Upstairs, back downstairs, to the kitchen, my eyes glued to it, mesmerized by its power. The power to end a life. My life. I feel naked and exposed and ashamed. How can I, in good conscience, stand over Gregory's grave in a few days across from Amanda (who will probably be there) and act like I didn't betray him?

Then I walk into the den where the TV is still on, and in the dark room, I realize whose life it is I need to end. The face on the screen. The red hair, scruffy beard, green eyes. He caused it all anyway, didn't he? Gregory's death, us trashing the house, me and Amanda: I wouldn't have had to do any of the things I just did if it weren't for him. Maybe he's home now. Chances are he's not since we were just there, but there's a chance, right? There's a chance all of this can end tonight. There's a chance that racist son of a bitch will meet his maker, and I can see Gregory again, all before the night ends.

I step outside, only one thing on my mind: sending that bastard back home to hell. It's the only way, right? The only way to set things right.

I walk straight into something but it's so dark out here compared to inside that I have to blink and wait a few seconds to let my eyes adjust so I can see. It's a person, I realize, right as I plow into them.

"Amanda?"

My eyes finally adjust enough that I can see it is her; that morning TV show host standing on my front porch in the dark. That's weird right? That's creepy. I can't explain or rationalize my level of frustration here. I feel so guilty so dirty, so hurt and I finally had the answer, right? I had the answer and now the same God that killed my brother and made me fuck Amanda just decided to drop a TV show host on my front porch right in my way. "What the FUCK?" My mouth says. "YOU? From that show? What the hell are you DOING HERE?!! "

She stumbles backwards like I just scared her half to death, face looking just like Amanda's a couple of minutes ago.

But she doesn't even answer my freaking question. Just stares at me like an idiot, mouth gaping open in disbelief, still standing in the middle of the path between me and the car. I shake my head. "Not now." I brush right past her.

Then, just as I get a grip on the handle, I hear, "I'm your mom."

My heart goes cold, and so does the blood in veins. It has to be a joke, right? "What?" I look at her again. She's still standing there all stiff in the middle of the walkway, her round white eyes standing out starkly against her brown skin and the darkness around us.

"Yeah, I'm, I'm your mom."

Either this is a joke, I'm hallucinating, or the universe somehow managed to be even more fucked up than I thought it was.

"You know what..." I'm shaking my head and laughing so hard I don't know what to do with myself. I can hardly breathe. "You're fucking with me, aren't you? You think this is FUNNY?!" I'm trying to figure out how a woman comes to my house telling me she's my mother at the exact same time I'm executing my plan to kill a man. "Showing up at my house at fuckin', what is it, like nine o'clock at night to tell me some bullshit like this? You're crazy. Get the fuck out." I've never hallucinated before, so I guess the universe is just fucked up. I open the car door and climb in before slamming it shut.

I hear the muffled sound of her calling my name and nearly jump out of my skin when her palms slam against my side window.

MONAY DAVIS

I'm left in the dark, shaking. He seems like a completely different person now than the young, articulate man I'd met and admired on set last week. If what just happened was the only encounter, I'd ever had with this guy and he wasn't my son I'd leave him alone forever. But it's not and he is, so I jump in my rental and follow him to wherever he's going. It doesn't matter where he's going. He's my son and I'll follow him to the ends of the earth if I have to. The streets are way too dark for this kid to be flying through a residential area at 50 miles an hour, but I keep up. I don't even think he knows I'm following him; he's so focused on whatever it is he's doing. I get text from Jay.

> **Jay**: How's it going?
>
> **Me**: Not good
>
> **Jay**: What happened?
>
> **Me**: He told me to GTFO

There's a pause like he's figuring out how to respond, and then:

> **Jay**: Well he's a teenager. Lots of teenagers have probably said that to their parents.
>
> **Jay**: hang in there.
>
> **Me**: I will. Call u later.
>
> **Jay**: OK.

Sam brakes so suddenly I almost rear end the kid. We're pretty much stopped in the middle of the road and I'm legitimately scared some bum is going to pop out of nowhere and bang on my window asking for money or something. Sam cuts the engine, so I cut mine too. He just sits there, so I sit too. There's a house a way down from where we are and with the help of the streetlights, I can see that Sam is leaning forward craning his neck awkwardly to get a good look at the house. I'm just about to bite the bullet and step out of my car to try this shit again when a man steps out of the house, dressed in black, walking tall and confident. He gets in his car and seconds later pulls out of his driveway. As if on cue, Sam starts up his car and follows him. I don't know if this is some type of gang initiation shit or what, but I follow him anyway. The three of us slide down the dark street in a single file line, Sam a way back from the man in front and me a couple of car lengths behind him. Sam makes a hard left, following the man into a Walmart parking lot.

I sit in the silent car for a few seconds convincing myself that I'm in the right place and that I cannot and will not leave Alabama without making sure my son knows who his mother is. Gregory died without ever knowing the woman who gave birth to him, without ever knowing me. What kind of dark cloud must a mystery like that leave hanging over your head? If you don't know where you came from, how can you know who you are?

OK let's do this. I've just got to go up to him. Have a conversation. Tell him I'm sorry I left him and I'm sorry about Gregory and I'm sorry *he* didn't get to know me and that you never knew me either, but I'm here now. As I step out the car, Sam's door pops open and he hustles across the dark lot towards the man in black entering through the automatic double doors.

HUNTER GARRETT

It's weird walking though Walmart without two kids pulling me by hand in two different directions towards the toy sections while whining and begging for each and every appealing piece of plastic on the shelves. It's even weirder knowing that the whole reason why you're here is to buy sleeping pills with which you plan to kill yourself. I drift down the aisles. The place is empty. I guess people don't usually hang out at Walmart at ten o'clock on a Tuesday night. It's peaceful and it's quiet and soft music is playing from the speakers above and a few other people push faintly squeaky carts down the aisles stopping occasionally to pick up a roll of toilet paper or a stick of deodorant.

On the wall before me, there is a surplus of bottles of different shapes and sizes housing pills of different colors and strengths. That list didn't say anything about which type of pill is best. I grab the most expensive ones and head over to checkout.

SAMUEL NOBLE

I'm keeping my eye on him from a few steps behind. The dude looks so calm, just walking down aisles like everything's OK. He has no idea what he's caused or how filthy he's made me feel. His head is high, shoulders relaxed. He looks comfortable and that just pisses me off even more. The gun is still under my jacket, concealed from the world and from the ignorant people here for paper towels and cough medicine. I don't know how it is I'm going to do this but at some point, this guy's going to have to go back outside, right? Leaning over and down the aisle in which he's standing, I watch as he stands there in front of a wall of pills. He shrugs, grabs one off the shelf and heads to the front counter. As I pass through the aisle behind him, I realize the one he picked is the most expensive one there. Spoiled motherfucker.

I'm standing there behind him as he checks out. I don't have anything to buy so there's no need for me to be up by the front of the store. Should I wait for him outside? I nervously reach under my jacket to make sure the gun is still there.

"HEY!" The sound of his voice makes me jump and I almost let the gun clatter to the floor. Looking up, I see that it's the guy checking out Hunter Garrett who's got his eyes glued to me like a freaking Rottweiler. I freeze. Did he see the gun?

"Boy, you stealing something?" Whew. I'm actually relieved all he thinks I have under my jacket is some crappy Walmart merchandise. The cashier steps from behind the counter and makes his way towards me, pot belly jiggling over his belt as he does. He steps right around Hunter Garrett who's standing there looking at me stunned.

Hunter Garrett stumbles backwards, knocking over a stand of DVDs and boxes of candy. The store is silent save for the clattering of plastic, glass and paper boxes hitting the floor. I can see the panic in his eyes. Then he turns and runs, arms flailing, coat flying behind him with the same look he had on his face when I saw him at the aquarium. Before the potbellied cashier can get his hands on me, I leap over the fallen stand, avoiding the boxes of candy scattered on the floor and rush through the double doors after him.

MONAY DAVIS

You know how sometimes you can just get a certain energy from someone? Like you see them, right? And something about them, like the way they're standing or their facial expressions or whatever just give you a bad vibe and you get a feeling in your stomach like shit's about to go down? That's the type of feeling I'm getting right now, standing behind Sam. Something about how his feet are pointed outwards and how one of his hands is balled up in a tight fist at his side and the other, across his chest, hand hidden under his jacket, and the way his back and neck looks so stiff like he can hardly breathe. He kind of looks like he's waiting in line behind the guy he followed here, but all I can see is the back of his head from where I'm standing. Should I tap him on the shoulder? I feel like if I did that he'd spin around and knock me out with an elbow to the face, considering his reaction to me back at his house. But I've got to do something right? I can't go back to Atlanta knowing that was the last interaction I had with my son.

"HEY!" The voice pierces the relative silence in the store and a round guy steps around the counter in front of Sam.

"Boy, you stealing something?" Wow that racial profiling is real subtle. Just because he's Black and has his hand in his jacket he must be stealing right? That's Alabama for you. When the guy we stalked here turns around to see what the commotion is about, his face contorts, and I almost feel like I'm actually watching his heart freeze up in his chest. He trips over his feet, eyes wide and knocks over a stand full of movies and candy. When I see him facing me, I notice two things:

1. He's Hunter Garrett, the guy who killed Gregory

2. When he extends his arm to grab the container of pills on the counter, his sleeve rides up just enough that I see the briefest flash of a tattoo on his wrist. It looks like a tattoo of a tiger's open mouth.

There's no time for me to digest what it is I'm seeing. That's the guy who killed Gregory. And that's the guy who... It can't be. And Sam's about to... the two of them race out of the store and to the parking lot.

HUNTER GARRETT

Is this real-life right now? The kid's chasing me. I can't blame him, can I? If I could kill the guy who killed Artie, I would. I will. My legs are moving faster than I thought they could, feet slapping across the wet pavement, heart pounding in my chest. I can't run as fast as I used to, but I can still run. Not faster than him though. In a foot race, he'll always win. There's no point to this. He'll always win. Maybe I should stop. I'm almost out of breath. I've got a side stitch. Maybe I should tell him I'm sorry. Sorrier than he'll ever know. It's crazy what had to happen for me to realize how wrong I was. But I get it now, I get it. So, I stop running, and I let it happen.

SAMUEL NOBLE

Sure the guy's fast, but not as fast as me. The bottoms of my Nikes slide against the wet pavement with each step. I'm gaining on him, only an arm's length away. If I wanted to, I could reach out and grab the hood of his sweatshirt. Then he stops, without warning I slam right into his back knocking him to the ground. As I stand over him, watching as he struggles to his feet, the knee part of his jeans soaked through from the wet ground, I realize he doesn't look worried. I pull out the gun and he stands in front of me, face wet, hands held up in surrender. Funny how some people only surrender when they've got no other option. His eyes are red, and he looks like he was crying recently, as I place the barrel right between his red eyes. Snot is dripping out of his nose too. It's weird how mucous always comes with tears. As the stuff approaches his top lip, he scrunches up his face and sniffs the stuff straight back up into his nasal cavity. It makes a surprisingly loud and disgusting snort sound that seems to fill the quiet parking lot. Damn, I almost feel like a guy's got to practice every day to learn how to make a sound that loud and gross on cue. He's nodding his head, eyes crossed as he looks straight down the barrel of the gun. I wonder if he knows that this is how Gregory felt when he shot and killed him. I cock the gun.

He inhales and sighs hard, swallowing. If it weren't for him Gregory would be here and they'd be going to prom together in a few weeks and then the two of us would have left for New

York together in August. My finger is on the trigger. It's twitching already. Then there are hands on my body, grabbing and pulling on my arm and a voice from behind me saying "NO NO NO. Sam, DON'T." But I'm oblivious to her words and too strong for her arms to move me much.

I make eye contact with Hunter Garrett and just as he says, "I'm sorr-" my finger twitches just a little too much, a bang pierces the silence, and he drops. Part of me expects to hear silence wailing immediately, but instead I hear a woman doing the wailing. It's Monay, on the ground next to me, hands over her face, and she's shaking and crying. She looks up at me and says, "That was your father."

ABOUT THE AUTHOR

Niara Savage is a Fisk University student and freelance journalist. She is passionate about Black issues and hopes to obtain a Ph.D. in Africana Studies.

@niaratheauthor

www.themodernabolitionist.com

www.ingramcontent.com/pod-product-compliance
Lightning Source LLC
Chambersburg PA
CBHW020737250626
47155CB00003B/803